Derek bb ng off the grour fo ed u up again p r ay. Another walk vo escape routes, both blocked. Derek glanced up at the play set, but we were against a solid wall of plastic, a crow's nest ten feet overhead. There was a fireman's pole ten feet away, but that wouldn't take us anywhere useful.

The men looked like they were in their twenties. One was tall and lean with blond hair to his collar. He wore a plaid jacket and boots, and looked like he hadn't bothered with a razor in days. His companion was shorter and beefier, swarthy with dark hair. He wore a leather jacket and sneakers.

Neither looked like the kind of guy you'd expect to hang out in a park, hassling kids for cigarettes and pocket money. Hanging out at the monster truck races, maybe, hassling girls for their names and phone numbers.

They didn't seem drunk either. They were walking straight and their eyes looked clear, glittering in the dark like . . .

I shrank back.

Derek's hands tightened on my shoulders and he leaned down, whispering, "Werewolves."

KELLEY ARMSTRONG

THE DARKEST POWERS TRILOGY

The Summoning
The Awakening
The Reckoning

THE DARKNESS RISING SERIES

The Gathering

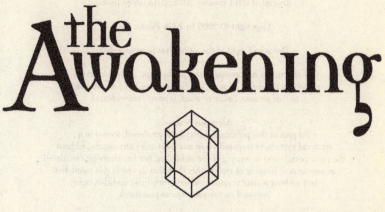

the Awakening

KELLEY ARMSTRONG

www.atombooks.net

ATOM

First published in Great Britain in 2009 by Orbit
This paperback edition published in 2011 by Atom
Reprinted 2011 (twice), 2012, 2013 (three times)

A CIP catalogue record for this book
is available from the British Library.

ISBN 978-1-907410-07-9

Typeset in Bodoni Book by Palimpsest Book Production Limited,
Falkirk, Stirlingshire
Printed and bound in Great Britain by
Clays Ltd, St Ives plc

Papers used by Atom are from well-managed forests
and other responsible sources.

MIX
Paper from
responsible sources
FSC® C104740

Atom
An imprint of
Little, Brown Book Group
100 Victoria Embankment
London EC4Y 0DY

An Hachette UK Company
www.hachette.co.uk

www.atombooks.net

For Julia

one

WHEN THE DOOR TO my cell clicked open, the first thought that flitted through my doped-up brain was that Liz had changed her mind and come back. But ghosts don't open doors. They will, on occasion, ask me to open one, so I can raise and interrogate the zombies of supernaturals killed by a mad scientist, but they never need one opened for themselves.

I sat up in bed and rubbed my bleary eyes, blinking away the lingering fog of the sedative. For a moment, the door stayed open only a crack. I slid from the bed, tiptoeing across the thick carpet of my fake hotel room, praying the person on the other side had been called away and I could escape before these people started whatever experiments they'd brought me here to—

"Hello, Chloe." Dr. Davidoff beamed his best kindly-old-man smile as he pushed the door wide. He wasn't that old—maybe fifty—but in a movie, I'd cast him as the doddering absentminded scientist. It was an act I'm sure he'd worked on until he got it just right.

The woman behind him had chic blond hair and a New York suit. I'd cast her as the mother of the nastiest girl in class. Which was cheating, because that's exactly who she was. Mother of Victoria—Tori—Enright, the one housemate we'd left out of our plans when we'd escaped from Lyle House, and for good cause, considering she was one of the reasons I'd needed to escape.

Tori's mom carried a Macy's bag, like she'd just been out shopping and popped in to conduct a few horrific experiments before heading to lunch.

"I know you have a lot of questions, Chloe," Dr. Davidoff said as I sat on the edge of the bed. "We're here to answer them for you. We just need a little help from you first."

"Simon and Derek," Mrs. Enright said. "Where are they?"

I looked from her to Dr. Davidoff, who smiled and nodded encouragingly, like he fully expected me to turn in my friends.

I'd never been an angry kid. I'd never run away from home. Never stamped my feet and screamed that life was unfair and I wished I'd never been born. Whenever my dad told me we were moving again and I needed to transfer schools, I'd swallowed a whiny "but I just made new friends," nod, and tell him I understood.

Accept your lot. Count your blessings. Be a big girl.

Now, looking back at a life of doing what I was told, I realized I'd bought into the game. When adults patted me on the head and told me I was so grown-up, what they really meant was that they were glad I wasn't grown-up enough yet to question, to fight back.

Looking at Dr. Davidoff and Mrs. Enright, I thought of what they'd done to me—lying to me, locking me up—and I *wanted* to stamp my feet. Wanted to scream. But I wasn't going to give them that satisfaction.

I widened my eyes as I met Mrs. Enright's gaze. "You mean you haven't found them yet?"

I think she would have slapped me if Dr. Davidoff hadn't lifted his hand.

"No, Chloe, we haven't found the boys," he said. "We're very concerned for Simon's safety."

"Because you think Derek might hurt him?"

"Not intentionally, of course. I know Derek's fond of Simon."

Fond? What a strange word to use. Derek and Simon were foster brothers, tighter than any blood brothers I knew. Sure, Derek was a werewolf, but that wolf part of him was what would *stop* him from ever hurting Simon. He'd protect him at all costs—I'd already seen that.

My skepticism must have shown on my face, because Dr. Davidoff shook his head, as if disappointed in me. "All right, Chloe. If you can't spare any concern for Simon's safety, maybe you can for his health."

"W-what ab-bou—" My stutter cropped up most when I was nervous, and I couldn't let them know they'd struck a nerve. So I tried again, slower now. "What about his health?"

"His condition."

Apparently I wasn't the only one who watched too many movies. Now they would tell me that Simon had some rare medical condition and if he didn't get his medicine within twelve hours, he'd spontaneously combust.

"What condition?"

"He has diabetes," Dr. Davidoff said. "His blood sugar levels need to be monitored and regulated."

"With one of those blood testing things?" I said slowly, thinking back. Simon had always disappeared into the bathroom before meals. I'd thought he just liked to wash up. I'd bumped into him once coming out as he'd been shoving a small black case into his pocket.

"That's right," Dr. Davidoff said. "With proper care, diabetes is easily managed. You weren't aware of it because you didn't need to be. Simon leads a normal life."

"Except for one thing," Tori's mom said.

She reached into the Macy's bag and took out a backpack.

It looked like Simon's, but I wasn't falling for that—they'd probably bought a matching one. Sure, she pulled out a hoodie I recognized as Simon's, but he'd left behind a whole closet of clothing at Lyle House. Easy enough to grab stuff from there.

Next came a pad of paper and pouch of colored pencils. Simon's room was filled with his comic book sketches. Again, easy enough to—

Mrs. Enright flipped through the sketch pad, holding up pages. Simon's work in progress. He'd never have left that behind.

Finally, she laid a flashlight on the table. The flashlight from Lyle House—the one I'd watched him put into his bag.

"Simon slipped going over the fence," she said. "He had his backpack over one shoulder. It fell. Our people were right behind him so he had to leave it. There's something in here that Simon needs much more than clothing and art supplies."

She opened a navy nylon pouch. Inside were two pen-like vials, one filled with cloudy liquid, the other clear. "The insulin to replace what Simon's body can't produce. He injects himself with these three times a day."

"What happens if he doesn't?"

Dr. Davidoff took over. "We aren't going to scare you and say that if Simon skips a single shot, he'll die. He's already missed his morning one, and I'm sure he only feels a bit out of sorts. But by tomorrow, he'll be vomiting. In about three days, he'll lapse into a diabetic coma." He took the pouch from Tori's mom and set it in front of me. "We need to get this to Simon. To do that, you need to tell us where he is."

I agreed to try.

TWO

IN A GOOD DRAMA, the protagonist never takes the straight line to the prize. She must set out, hit an obstacle, detour around it, hit another, take a longer detour, another obstacle, another detour. . . . Only when she has built up the strength of character to *deserve* the prize does she finally succeed.

My story was already fitting the time-honored pattern. Fitting, I guess, for a film student. Or, I should say, former film student. Chloe Saunders, fifteen-year-old Steven Spielberg wannabe, her dreams of writing and directing Hollywood blockbusters shattered on the day she got her first period and started living the kind of life she'd once imagined putting on the screen.

That's when I started seeing ghosts. After freaking out at school, I was taken away by the men in the white jackets and shipped off to a group home for mentally disturbed teens. Problem is, I really *did* see ghosts. And I wasn't the only kid at Lyle House with supernatural powers.

Simon could cast spells. Rae could burn people with her bare fingers. Derek had superhuman strength and senses and, apparently, soon would be able to change into a wolf. Tori . . . well, I didn't know what Tori was—maybe just a screwed-up kid put in Lyle House because her mom helped run it.

Simon, Derek, Rae, and I realized it was no coincidence we were in the same place, and we escaped. Rae and I got separated from the guys and, after running to my aunt Lauren—the person I had trusted most in the world—I ended up here, in some kind of laboratory run by the same people who owned Lyle House.

Now they expected me to help them bring in Simon and Derek?

Well, it was time to introduce a few obstacles of my own. So, in the spirit of proper storytelling, I told Dr. Davidoff where to find Simon and Derek.

Step one: establish the goal. "Rae and I were supposed to hide while the guys stayed behind to distract you with Simon's magic," I told Dr. Davidoff. "Rae ran on ahead so she didn't hear, but at the last second Simon pulled me back and said, if we got separated, we'd meet at the rendezvous point."

Step two: introduce the obstacle. "Where is the rendezvous point? That's the problem. I don't *know* where it is. We talked about needing one, but everything was so crazy that day. We'd only just decided to escape, and then Derek was saying it had to be that night. The guys must have picked a rendezvous point, and forgot they never told me where it was."

Step three: map out the detour. "But I do have some ideas—places we talked about. One of them must be the rendezvous point. I could help you find it. They'll be looking for me, so they might hide until they see me."

Rather than escape this place, I'd let them take me out by using me as bait. I'd list places I'd never discussed with Simon or Derek, and there would be no chance they'd get captured. A brilliant plan.

The response?

"We'll keep that in mind, Chloe. But for now, just tell us the locations. We have ways to find the boys once we get there."

Obstacles. An essential part of the storytelling process. But in real life? They suck.

After Dr. Davidoff and Tori's mom had gotten my list of fake rendezvous points, they left, giving me nothing in return—no answers, no clues about why I was here or what would happen to me.

I sat cross-legged on my bed, staring down at the necklace in my hands as if it were a crystal ball that could provide all those answers. My mom had given it to me back when I was seeing "bogeymen"—ghosts, as I now knew. She said the necklace would stop them from coming, and it did. I'd always figured, like my dad said, that it was psychological. I believed in it, so it worked. Now, I wasn't so sure.

Had my mom known I was a necromancer? She must have, if the blood ran in her family. Was the necklace supposed to ward off ghosts? If so, its power must have faded. It even looked faded—I swore the bright red jewel had gone a purplish color. One thing it didn't do, though, was answer my questions. That I had to do for myself.

I put the necklace back on. Whatever Dr. Davidoff and the others wanted from me, it wasn't good. You don't lock up kids you want to help.

I certainly wasn't going to tell them how to find Simon. If he needed insulin, Derek would get it, even if it meant breaking into a drugstore.

I had to concentrate on getting Rae and me out. But this wasn't Lyle House, where the only thing standing between us and freedom was an alarm system. This room might look like it belonged in a nice hotel—with a double bed, a carpeted floor, an armchair, desk, and private bathroom—but there were no windows and no knob on the inside of the door.

I'd hoped to get Liz's help escaping. My roommate at Lyle House, Liz hadn't made it out alive, so when I first got here, I'd summoned her ghost, hoping she could help me find a way out. Only problem? Liz didn't realize she was dead. As gently as I could, I'd broken the news. She'd flipped out, accusing me of lying, and disappeared.

Maybe she'd had enough time to cool off. I doubted it, but I couldn't wait. I had to try summoning her again.

Three

I PREPARED FOR A séance. As set pieces went, this one was so lame I'd never put it in a movie. No sputtering candles to cast eerie shadows on the walls, no moldy skulls forming a ritual circle, no chalices filled with what the audience would suppose was red wine but secretly hope was blood.

Did experienced necromancers use stuff like candles and incense? From the little I'd learned about the supernatural world, I knew some of what we see in movies is true. Maybe, way back in history, people had known about necromancers and witches and werewolves, and those stories are based, if very loosely, on old truths.

My method—if I can call it a method since I've only used it twice—came from trial and error and a few grudging tips from Derek. As a guy who was taking college-level courses at sixteen, being confident of his facts is important to Derek.

If he isn't sure, he'd rather keep his mouth shut. But when I'd pushed him, he'd told me that he'd heard that necromancers summoned ghosts either by being at a graveside or by using a personal effect, like Liz's hoodie, so I was sitting cross-legged on the carpet, clutching it.

I pictured Liz and imagined myself pulling her out of limbo. At first, I didn't try very hard. The last time I'd focused all my power into summoning a ghost, I'd summoned two right back into their buried corpses. I wasn't near a grave this time, but that didn't mean there weren't bodies around somewhere. So I kept the voltage low at first, gradually ramping it up, focusing harder and harder until . . .

"What the—? Hey, who are you?"

My eyes flew open. There stood a dark-haired boy about my age with the build, looks, and arrogant chin tilt of a star quarterback. Finding the ghost of another teenager in this place wasn't a coincidence. A name popped into my head—that of another Lyle House resident who'd been taken away before I arrived, supposedly transferred to a mental hospital, like Liz.

"Brady?" I said tentatively.

"Yeah, but I don't know you. Or this place."

He pivoted, scanning the room, then rubbed the back of his neck. I stopped myself before asking if he was okay. Of course he wasn't okay. He was dead. Like Liz. I swallowed.

"What happened to you?" I asked softly.

He jumped, as if startled by my voice.

"Is someone else here?" I asked, hoping he sensed Liz, beyond the pale where I couldn't see her.

"I thought I heard . . ." He studied me, frowning. "You brought me here?"

"I—I didn't mean to. But . . . since you *are* here, can you tell me—?"

"Nothing. I can't tell you anything." He squared his shoulders. "Whatever you want to talk about, I'm not interested."

He looked away, *determined* not to be interested. When he started to fade, I was ready to let him go. Rest in peace. Then I thought about Rae and Simon and Derek. If I didn't get some answers, we might all join Brady in the afterlife.

"My name's Chloe," I said quickly. "I'm a friend of Rae's. From Lyle House. I was there with her, after you—"

He kept fading.

"Wait!" I said. "I c-can prove it. Back at Lyle House. You tried getting into a fight with Derek, and Simon shoved you away. Only he didn't touch you. He used magic."

"Magic?"

"It was a spell that knocks people back. Simon's a sorcerer. All the kids in Lyle House—"

"I knew it. I *knew* it." He swore under his breath as he rematerialized. "All that time, they kept trying to shove their diagnosis down my throat, and I told them where else they could shove it, but I couldn't prove anything."

"You told the nurses what happened with Simon, didn't you?"

"Nurses?" He snorted. "Glorified security guards. I wanted to speak to the real boss: Davidoff. They took me to see him at this other place, looked like a warehouse."

I described what I'd seen of this building when we'd arrived.

"Yeah, that's it. They took me inside and . . ." His face screwed up in thought. "A woman came to talk to me. A blonde. Said she was a doctor. Bellows? Fellows?"

Aunt Lauren. My heart battered my rib cage. "So this woman, Dr. Fellows . . ."

"She wanted me to say Derek started the fight. That he threatened me, punched me, shoved me, whatever. I considered it. A little payback for all the attitude I had to put up with from that jerk. I'd just been goofing around with him when Simon got all up in my face and smacked me with that spell."

In the version I'd heard, Brady had been the one getting in Derek's face. Simon had a good reason for interfering, too—the last time Derek took a swing, he'd broken a kid's back.

"So Dr. Fellows wanted you to say Derek started the fight. . . ."

"I wouldn't. I'd have to deal with the fallout when I went back to Lyle House and I didn't need that grief. That's when Davidoff came in. He hauled her out of the room, but I could

15 ◆

still hear him chewing her out in the hall. She kept saying Derek was a menace and the only reason Davidoff kept him was because he couldn't admit he made a mistake by including Derek's type."

"Type?"

"In the experiment."

A chill settled in my gut. "Ex-experiment?"

Brady shrugged. "That's all she said. Davidoff told her to shove off. He said he made a mistake with the others, but Derek was different."

Others? Did he mean other werewolves? Or other subjects in this experiment? Was I a subject in this experiment?

"Did they say any—?" I began.

His head whipped to the side, as if seeing something out of the corner of his eye.

"What is it?" I asked.

"Don't you hear that?"

I listened. "What is it?"

"Whispering."

"It could be Liz. She—"

Brady went rigid. His eyes rolled. Then his head flew back, the tendons in his neck popping out, bones crackling. His throat convulsed and he gurgled. Instinctively I reached out to help. My hands passed through him, but I could feel the heat of his body, a scorching heat that made me fall back in surprise.

As I recovered, Brady went still again. His chin lowered

and he rolled his shoulders, as if working out the kinks. Then he looked down at me. His dark eyes were now a glowing yellowish-orange. The chill in my gut slunk up my spine.

"Frightened, child?" The voice coming out of Brady's mouth was a woman's, so high and light it was almost girlish. "Your instincts are excellent, but you have nothing to fear from me."

"W-where's Brady?"

She looked down at the body she was possessing. "Do you like him? He *is* pretty, isn't he? All of dear Dr. Lyle's creations are so very pretty. Perfect balls of perfect energy, waiting to explode."

In a blink, "Brady" was in front of me, his face coming down to mine, bathing me in scorching hot breath that smelled strangely sweet. Those orange eyes met mine, the pupils slitted like a cat's.

"The boy can't help you, child. But I can. You just need to—"

Her eyes rolled back, darkening to Brady's brown, then back to orange as she snarled.

"They're pulling him back to the other side. Call me, child. Quickly."

"C-call—"

"Call me forth. I can—"

Her eyes rolled again, her snarl deepening into something inhuman, a sound that made the chill in my veins harden to ice. I stepped back and smacked into the wall.

"Call me forth," she said, voice going ragged, deepening into Brady's. "I can answer all your questions. Call me——"

Brady's image wavered, then popped, like a TV screen after the power cord is pulled. One flash of white light and he was gone. I thought I heard a knock at the door but couldn't move, just stared at the spot where Brady had been.

The door opened, and Dr. Davidoff stepped in to find me plastered to the wall.

"Chloe?"

I staggered forward, rubbing my arms.

"Chloe?"

"S-spider," I said, pointing to the bed. "It r-ran under there."

Dr. Davidoff struggled against a smile. "Don't worry. I'll get someone to take care of it, while we're gone. We're going to go for a walk. It's time you got a proper tour and a proper explanation."

FOUR

S I FOLLOWED DR. Davidoff down the hall, I tried to shake off thoughts of whatever had been in my room. I was a necromancer: ghosts were my one and only specialty. So it had to be a ghost, no matter how strongly every instinct in me insisted it wasn't. All I knew for sure was that I was in no hurry to go back in there.

"Now, Chloe—" Dr. Davidoff stopped, noticing me rubbing the lingering goose bumps on my arms. "Cold? I'll have them turn up the heat in your room. Your comfort is important to us."

We started walking again.

"But comfort isn't just physical, is it?" he continued. "Equally important, perhaps even more, is mental comfort. A sense of security. I know you're upset and confused, and it didn't help when we refused to answer your questions. We were eager to start checking those places you listed."

He hadn't been gone long enough to visit spots miles away. I knew what he'd really been checking: whether Rae corroborated my story. She would. She didn't know the real rendezvous point, only that I'd said the guys would meet up with us.

Dr. Davidoff opened a door at the end of the hall. It was a security station, the wall lined with flat-screen monitors. Inside, a young man spun in his chair, like he'd been caught surfing porn sites.

"Why don't you go grab a coffee, Rob," Dr. Davidoff said. "We'll take over."

He turned to me as the guard left. "You'll be seeing more of the building later. For now"—he waved at the screens—"consider this the one-stop tour."

Did he think I was stupid? I knew what he was really doing: showing me how well guarded this place was, in case I was planning another escape. But he was also giving me a chance to study what I was up against.

"As you can see, there's no camera in your room," he said, "nor in any of the bedrooms. Just in the hallway."

Two hall cameras, one at each end. I scanned the other screens. Some flipped between cameras, giving multiple angles of halls and entryways. Two showed laboratories, both empty, the lights dim, probably because it was Sunday.

An older model monitor was propped on the desk, cords

every which way, like it had been quickly set up. The tiny picture screen was black-and-white and showed what looked like a storage room, all the boxes shoved along the walls. I could see the back of a girl in a beanbag chair.

She was slumped, sneakers stretched next to a game console, long curls spilling over the beanbag, the controller held between dark hands. It looked like Rae. Or maybe it was an impostor set up to convince me that she was okay, playing games, not locked up, screaming for—

The girl in the chair reached for her Diet 7UP and I saw her face. Rae.

"Yes, as Rae has informed us, that GameCube is terribly outdated. But once we promised to replace it with the latest model, she resigned herself to playing it."

As he spoke, his eyes never left the screen. The expression on his face was . . . fond. Weirdly, the very word he'd used earlier for Derek seemed to fit here.

When he turned to me, his expression rearranged itself, as if to say *I like you well enough, Chloe, but you're no Rachelle.* And I felt . . . bewildered. Maybe even a little hurt, like there was still part of me that wanted to please.

He waved at the screen. "As you can see, we weren't prepared to have you kids with us here, but we're adjusting. While it will never be as cozy as Lyle House, the five of you will be comfortable here, perhaps more so, with all those unfortunate misrepresentations corrected."

Five of us? That must mean he didn't plan to put Derek "down like a rabid dog," as Aunt Lauren wanted. I breathed a soft sigh of relief.

"I won't apologize, Chloe," Dr. Davidoff continued. "Perhaps I should, but we thought setting up Lyle House was the best way to handle the situation."

He waved me to a chair. There were two, the one the security guard had vacated and a second, pushed against the wall. As I stepped toward the second one, it rolled from the shadows and stopped right in front of me.

"No, that's not a ghost," Dr. Davidoff said. "They can't move objects in our world—unless they happen to be a very specific kind, namely the ghost of an Agito."

"A what?"

"Agito. It's Latin roughly translating to 'put into motion.' Half-demons come in many types, as you'll discover. An Agito's power, as the name might suggest, is telekinesis."

"Moving things with the mind."

"Very good. And it is an Agito who moved that chair, though one who is still very much alive."

"You?"

He smiled and, for a second, the mask of the doddering old fool cracked, and I caught a glimpse of the real man beneath. What I saw was pride and arrogance, like a classmate flashing his A+ paper as if to say *top that*.

"Yes, I'm a supernatural, as is almost everyone who works

here. I know what you must have been thinking—that we're humans who've discovered your powers and wish to destroy what we don't understand, like in those comic books."

"The *X-Men*."

I don't know what was more shocking, that Dr. David-off and his colleagues were supernaturals or the image of this stooped, awkward man reading *X-Men*. Had he pored over them as a boy, imagining himself in Xavier's School for Gifted Youngsters?

Did that mean Aunt Lauren was a necromancer? That she saw ghosts, too?

He continued before I could ask anything. "The Edison Group was founded by supernaturals eighty years ago. And as much as it has grown since those early days, it's still an institution run by supernaturals and for supernaturals, dedicated to bettering the lives of our kind."

"Edison Group?"

"Named after Thomas Edison."

"The guy who invented the lightbulb?"

"That's what he's best known for. He also invented the movie projector, which I'm sure *you're* grateful for. Yet you, Chloe, have accomplished something he dreamed of but never succeeded in doing." A dramatic pause. "Contacting the dead."

"Thomas Edison wanted to talk to the dead?"

"He believed in an afterlife and wanted to communicate

with it not through séances and spiritualism but through science. When he died, it's thought he was working on just such a device—a telephone to the afterlife. No plans for it were ever found." Dr. Davidoff smiled conspiratorially. "Or, at least, not officially. We adopted the name because, like Edison, we take a scientific approach to matters of the paranormal."

Improving supernatural lives through science. Where had I heard something like that? It took me a moment to remember, and when I did, I shivered.

The ghosts I'd raised in the Lyle House basement had been subjects of experiments by a sorcerer named Samuel Lyle. Willing subjects, at first, they'd said, because they'd been promised a better life. Instead, they'd ended up lab rats sacrificed to the vision of a madman, as one ghost had put it. And that thing in my room had called Brady—and me, I think—Samuel Lyle's "creations."

"Chloe?"

"S-sorry. I'm just—"

"Tired, I imagine, after being up all night. Would you like a rest?"

"No, I-I'm fine. It's just— So how do we fit in? And Lyle House? It's part of an experiment, isn't it?"

His chin lifted, not much, just enough of a reaction to tell me I'd caught him off guard and that he didn't like it. A pleasant smile erased the look and he eased back in his chair.

"It *is* an experiment, Chloe. I know how that must sound,

but I assure you, it's a noninvasive study, using only benign psychological therapy."

Benign? There was nothing benign about what had happened to Liz and Brady.

"Okay, so we're part of this experiment. . . ." I said.

"Being a supernatural is both a blessing and curse. Adolescence is the most difficult time for us, as our powers begin to manifest. One of the Edison Group's theories is that it might be easier if our children don't know of their future."

"Don't know they're supernatural?"

"Yes, instead allowing them to grow up as human, assimilating into human society without anxiety over the upcoming transition. You and the others are part of that study. For most, it has worked. But for others, such as you, your powers came too quickly. We needed to ease you into the truth and ensure you didn't harm yourselves or anyone else in the meantime."

So they put us into a group home and told us we were crazy? Drugged us? That made no sense. What about Simon and Derek, who'd already known what they were? How could they be part of this study? But Derek clearly was, if what Brady said was right.

What about that thing calling us Dr. Lyle's creations? What about Brady and Liz, permanently removed from this *study*? Murdered. You don't kill a subject when he doesn't respond well to your "benign psychological therapy."

They'd lied all along—did I really think they'd fess up now? If I wanted the truth, I needed to do what I'd been doing.

Search for my own answers.

So I let Dr. Davidoff blather on, telling me about their study, about the other kids, about how we'd be "fixed" and out of here in no time. And I smiled and nodded and started making my own plans.

five

WHEN DR. DAVIDOFF WAS done with the propaganda, he took me to see Rae, who was still in that make-shift game room playing Zelda. He opened the door and waved me in, then closed it, leaving us alone.

"Game time over?" Rae said, turning slowly. "Just let me finish—"

Seeing me, she leaped up, controller clattering to the floor. She hugged me, then pulled back.

"Your arm," she said. "Did I hurt—?"

"No, it's all bandaged up. It needed some stitches."

"Ouch." Rae took a long look at me. "You need some sleep, girl. You look like death."

"That's just the necromancer genes kicking in."

She laughed and gave me another hug before plunking

back down in her beanbag chair. Despite our long night on the run, Rae looked fine. But then Rae was one of those girls who always looked fine—perfect clear copper skin; copper eyes; and long curls that, if they caught the light right, glinted with copper, too.

"Pull up a box. I'd offer you a chair, but decorators these days?" She rolled her eyes. "So slow. When the renovations are done, though, you won't recognize the place. Stereo system, DVD player, computer . . . chairs. And, as of tomorrow, we're getting a Wii."

"Really?"

"Yep. I said, 'People, if I'm helping you with this study of yours, I need a little love in return. And a GameCube ain't gonna cut it.'"

"Did you ask for a bigger TV, too?"

"I should have. After the whole Lyle House screwup, they're tripping over themselves to make us happy. We are going to be so spoiled here. Of course, we deserve it."

"We do."

She grinned, her face glowing. "Did you hear? I'm a half-demon. An Exhaust—Exustio. That's the highest kind of fire demon you can be. Cool, huh?"

Being a half-demon *was* cool. But being a half-demon lab rat, teetering on the brink of extermination? Definitely not cool. As much as I longed to tell her the truth, though, I couldn't. Not yet.

Just last night, Rae had been lying on her bed at Lyle House, trying to light a match with her bare fingers, desperate for proof she had a supernatural ability. Now she'd discovered she was a special kind of half-demon. That was important to Rae in a way I couldn't understand—in a way that I just had to accept until I had more proof that this wasn't the best thing that ever happened to her.

"And you know what else?" she said. "They showed me pictures of my mom. My *real* mom. None of my dad, of course, being a demon. Kind of freaky when you think about it. Demons aren't exactly . . ." For the first time, worry clouded her eyes. She blinked it back. "But Dr. D. says that it doesn't make you evil or whatever. Anyway, my mom? Her name was Jacinda. Isn't that pretty?"

I opened my mouth to agree, but she kept rambling excitedly.

"She used to work here, like Simon's dad. They have pictures of her. She was gorgeous. Like a model. And Dr. D. said they might even know where to find her, and they're going to try. Just for me."

"What about your adoptive parents?"

The clouds descended again, lingering longer, and I felt bad, being the one to bring her down. First telling Liz she was dead, then making Brady relive his final evening, now reminding Rae of her parents . . . I was trying to get answers to help all of us. But it felt cruel.

After a moment, Rae said, "They aren't supernaturals."

"Oh?"

"Nope, just humans." She gave the word an ugly twist. "They said when my mom left here, she cut off all ties with the group. Somehow I got put up for adoption. Dr. D. says that must have been a mistake. Jacinda loved me. She'd never have given me up. He says that story my adoptive parents told me, about her not being able to keep me, was a lie, and if the Edison Group had known about the adoption, they'd have found me parents like us. By the time they tracked me down, though, it was too late, so all they could do was monitor me. When they found out I was having problems, they contacted my adoptive parents and offered me a free stay at Lyle House. I bet it'll probably be weeks before my folks even notice I'm not there anymore, and then they'll just breathe a big sigh of relief."

"I can't see—"

"I was at Lyle House for almost a month. Do you know how many times my parents came to visit? Called?" She held up her thumb and forefinger in an O.

"Maybe they weren't allowed to visit. Maybe they left messages that you never got."

Her nose scrunched. "Why wouldn't I get them?"

"Because your adoptive parents aren't supernaturals. Having them interfering would complicate things."

Her eyes grew distant as she considered this. A spark

flickered through them—hope that she'd been mistaken, that the only parents she'd ever known hadn't abandoned her.

She gave her head a sharp shake. "No, I was trouble, and Mom was glad to get rid of me." Her hands gripped the beanbag tight, then released it and patted out the creases. "It's better this way. *I'm* better this way."

Better a special half-demon embarking on a new life than a regular girl, sent back to her regular life with her regular parents. I reached over and took her game controller.

"How far have you gotten?" I asked.

"You set on beating me, girl?"

"Absolutely."

I had lunch with Rae. Pizza. Unlike Lyle House, here they seemed more concerned with keeping us happy than keeping us healthy.

Maybe because they aren't planning on keeping us alive?

Talking to Rae, hearing her excitement, I had enough distance from the pain and betrayal to face a very real, very disturbing possibility.

What if I was wrong? About everything?

I didn't have any evidence that the people here had actually killed Liz and Brady. Liz had "dreamed" of being in some kind of hospital room, restrained. For all I knew, she'd died in a car crash when they were bringing her here. Or she'd committed suicide that night. Or, in trying to restrain her, they'd accidentally killed her.

Liz and Brady just happened to both die accidentally after leaving Lyle House?

Okay, that was unlikely.

Rae's birth mom and Simon's dad both happened to have a falling-out with the Edison Group and fled, taking their study subject kids with them?

No, there was definitely something wrong here. I needed answers and I wasn't going to find them locked in my cell. Nor was I eager to meet that thing in my room again.

Just as I thought that, Dr. Davidoff arrived to take me back there. As I followed him down the hall, I scrambled for an excuse to go someplace else in the building, any way to add details to my mental map of the place.

I considered asking to speak to Aunt Lauren. I'd have to pretend I'd forgiven her for lying to me my entire life, betraying me, and tossing me to the mercy of the Edison Group. I wasn't that good an actor. And Aunt Lauren wasn't that stupid. There was a reason she hadn't tried to see me. She was biding her time, waiting until I got lonely for a familiar face, desperate for excuses. Until then, she'd stay away.

There was one other person I could ask to speak to. . . .

The thought made my skin crawl almost as much as the thought of seeing Aunt Lauren. But I needed answers.

"Dr. Davidoff?" I said as we approached my door.

"Yes, Chloe."

"Is Tori here?"

"She is."

"I was thinking . . . I'd like to see her, make sure she's all right."

six

D R. DAVIDOFF DECLARED THAT a "splendid idea," meaning he had no clue I'd figured out that Tori was the one who'd tipped them off to our escape. As for getting a better look at the place—that plan didn't work so well. Her cell turned out to be only a few doors from mine.

The doctor ushered me in, then locked the door. When the bolt slid home, I inched back, ready to scream at the first sign of trouble. At my last up-close-and-personal encounter with Victoria Enright, she'd knocked me out with a brick, tied me up, and left me alone in a pitch-black basement crawl space. So I could be forgiven if that locked door made me nervous.

The only light in the room came from the bedside clock. "Tori?"

A figure rose from the mattress, her short hair a halo of

spikes. "Huh. I guess if stern lectures don't work, they can always resort to torture. Tell them I surrender, as long as they take you away. Please."

"I came to—"

"Gloat?"

I stepped toward her. "Sure. I came to gloat. Get a good laugh at you, locked in a cell, just like I am down the hall."

"If you say 'we're in this together,' I'm going to hurl."

"Hey, we wouldn't be in this at all if it wasn't for you telling the nurses on us. Only you didn't count on getting locked away yourself. That's what we call dramatic irony."

A moment of silence. Then she gave a harsh laugh. "You think I ratted you out? If I'd known you were running away, I would have packed your bag."

"Not if I was leaving with Simon."

She swung her legs over the side of the bed. "So in a fit of jealous rage, I spill your plans, getting you and the guy who rejected me sent away to a mental hospital? What movie is that from?"

"The same one where the cheerleader knocks out the new girl with a brick and leaves her in a locked crawl space."

"I am not a cheerleader." She spat the word with such venom, you'd think I'd called her a slut. "I was going to let you out after dinner, but Prince Not-So-Charming got to you first." She slid from the bed. "I liked Simon, but no guy is worth humiliating myself over. You want someone to blame? Check the mirror. You're the one who stirred things up. You and your ghosts. You got Liz sent away, got Derek in trouble, got me in trouble."

"*You* got you in trouble. I didn't do anything."

"Of course you didn't."

She stepped closer. Her skin looked yellow, and purple underscored her brown eyes. "I've got a sister just like you, Chloe. *She's* the cheerleader, the cute little blonde, bats her eyelashes and everyone comes running. Just like you at Lyle House, with Simon tripping over himself to help you. Even Derek rushed to your rescue—"

"I didn't—"

"Do anything. That's the point. You can't do anything. You're a silly, useless Barbie, just like my sister. I'm smarter, tougher, more popular. But does that matter? No." She towered a head above me, staring down. "All anyone cares about is the helpless little blonde. But being helpless only works when there's someone around to save you."

She lifted her hands. Sparks leaped from her fingers. When I fell back, she grinned.

"Why don't you call Derek to help you now, Chloe? Or your little ghost friends?" Tori advanced, the sparks swirling into a ball of blue light between her raised hands. She whipped her hands down. I dove. The ball shot over my shoulder, hit the wall, and exploded into a shower of sparks that singed my cheek.

I got to my feet, backing toward the door. Tori raised her hands and swung them down, and an invisible force knocked me over again. The room shook, every piece of furniture rocking and chattering. Even Tori looked surprised.

"Y-you're a witch," I said.

"Am I?" She bore down on me, her eyes as wild as her hair. "Nice for someone to tell me. My mother insisted it was all in my head. She shipped me off to Lyle House, had me diagnosed as bipolar, and gave me a cartload of meds. And I gulped them because I didn't want to disappoint her."

She slammed down her hands. Lightning bolts flew from her fingertips, heading straight for me.

Tori's eyes went wide with shock, her lips parting in a silent *no!*

I tried to scramble out of the way, but I wasn't fast enough. As those crackling bolts came at me, a figure materialized— a girl in a nightgown. Liz. She shoved the dresser, and it shot from the wall and into the bolt's path. Wood splintered. The mirror glass shattered, raining shards down on me as I crouched, head down.

When I lifted my head, the room was silent and Liz was gone. The dresser lay on its side with a smoldering hole through it, and all I could think was: *That could have been me.*

Tori sat huddled on the floor, her knees pulled up, her face buried against them as she rocked. "I didn't mean it, I didn't mean it. I get so mad, so *mad*. And it just happens."

Like Liz, making things fly when she got angry. Like Rae, burning her mom in a fight. Like Derek, throwing a kid and breaking his back. What would happen if I got mad enough?

Uncontrollable powers. That wasn't normal for supernaturals. It couldn't be.

I took a slow step toward Tori. "Tori, I—"

The door whacked open, and Tori's mom barreled in. She stopped short when she saw the destruction.

"Victoria Enright!" The name came out in a snarl worthy of a werewolf. "What have you done?"

"I-it wasn't her," I said. "It was me. We argued and I—I . . ."

I stared at the hole blasted through the dresser and I couldn't finish the sentence.

"I know very well who's responsible for this, Miss Chloe." Tori's mom turned that snarl on me. "Though I don't doubt you played your role. You're quite the little instigator, aren't you?"

"Diane, that's enough," Dr. Davidoff snapped from the doorway. "Help your daughter clean up her mess. Chloe, come with me."

Instigator? Me? Two weeks ago, I would have laughed at the thought. But now . . . Tori said this all started with me, with the guys wanting to save the helpless little girl. I hated that idea. Yet she had a point.

Derek had wanted Simon to leave Lyle House and find their dad. Simon wouldn't leave Derek, who refused to go because he was afraid he'd hurt someone else. When Derek figured out I was a necromancer, he found his weapon to beat down Simon's defenses. One damsel in distress, to go.

I was the poor girl who didn't know anything about being a necromancer, who kept making mistakes, getting closer and closer to being shipped off to a mental hospital. *See her, Simon? She's in danger. She needs your help. Take her, find Dad, and he'll fix everything.*

I'd been furious with Derek, and I'd called him on it. But I hadn't refused to go along with the plan. We needed Simon's dad—all of us did. Even Derek, who'd eventually joined us when our escape had been uncovered and he had no choice.

If I'd known what was going to happen, would I have stopped searching for answers back at Lyle House? Would I have accepted the diagnosis, taken my meds, shut up, and gotten released?

No. Harsh truth was better than comfortable lies. It had to be.

Dr. Davidoff took me back to my room, and I told myself I was fine with that. I needed to be alone so I could try again to contact Liz, now that I knew she was still around.

I started slowly, gradually increasing my efforts until I heard a voice so soft it could have been a hiss from the vent. I looked around, hoping to see Liz in her Minnie Mouse night-shirt and giraffe socks. But there was only me.

"Liz?"

A soft, hesitant "Yes?"

"I'm sorry," I said, getting to my feet. "I know you're angry with me, but it didn't seem right not to tell you the truth."

She didn't answer.

"I'm going to find out who killed you. I promise."

The words flew to my lips like I was reading a script, but at least I'd had the sense to shut my mouth before promising to avenge her death. That was one of those things that made perfect sense on the screen, but in real life, you think *Great . . . and how exactly would I do that?* Liz stayed silent, like she was holding out for more.

"Can I see you?" I said. "Please?"

"I can't . . . come through. You need to try harder."

I sat back on the floor, hands wrapped in her hoodie and concentrated.

"Harder," she whispered.

I squeezed my eyes shut and imagined myself pulling Liz through. Just one huge yank and—

A familiar tinkling laugh sent me scrambling to my feet. Warm air slid along my unbandaged forearm.

I yanked my sleeve down. *"You.* I didn't call you."

"You didn't need to, child. When you summon, spirits must obey. You called to your friend and the shades of a thousand dead answered, winging their way back to their rotted shells." Her breath tickled my ear. "Shells buried in a cemetery two miles away. A thousand corpses ready to become a thousand zombies. A vast army of the dead for you to control."

"I—I didn't—"

"No, you didn't. Not yet. Your powers need time to mature. And then?" Her laugh filled the room. "Dear Dr. Lyle must be dancing in Hell today, his agonies borne away on the thrill of his triumph. Dearly departed, scarcely lamented, deeply demented Dr. Samuel Lyle. Creator of the prettiest, sweetest abomination I have ever seen."

"Wh-what?"

"A bit of this, a bit of that. A twist here, a tweak there. And look what we have."

I squeezed my eyes shut against the urge to ask what she meant. Whatever this thing was, I couldn't trust her, no more than I could trust Dr. Davidoff and the Edison Group.

"What do you want?" I asked.

"The same thing you do. Freedom from this place."

I settled onto the bed. As hard as I looked, though, I couldn't see any sign of her. There was only the voice and the warm breeze.

"You're trapped here?" I asked.

"Like a fairy under a bell jar, metaphorically speaking. Fairies are a product of the human imagination. Little people flitting about on wings? How positively quaint. A more fitting simile would be to say that I am trapped like a lightning bug in a bottle. For magical energy, nothing quite compares to a soul-bound demi-demon. Except, of course, a soul-bound *full* demon, but to summon one and attempt to harness its power would be suicide. Just ask Samuel Lyle."

"He died summoning a demon?"

"The summoning is usually a forgivable offense. It's soul binding that rather annoys them. Lyle should have been content with me, but humans are never satisfied, are they? Too arrogant to contemplate the possibility of failure, he neglected to pass along the true secret of his success: me."

"Your magic powers this place. And they don't even realize it?"

"Lyle guarded his secrets to the grave and beyond, though taking them into the afterlife was not his intention. I'm sure he meant to tell them about me . . . had he not died before he got around to it. Even a necromancer as powerful as you would have difficulty contacting a spirit in a hell dimension, so now I am bound here, my power enhancing the magics cast in this place. The others—this Edison Group—think it's built on the junction of ley lines or some such foolishness."

"So if I freed you . . . ?"

"The building would collapse into a pile of smoldering rubble, the evil souls within sucked into Hell, to be tormented by demons for eternity." She laughed. "A pleasant thought, but no, my departure would merely hamper their efforts. Significantly hamper, though—putting an end to their most ambitious projects."

Release the demon under promise that I'd be repaid handsomely, my enemies destroyed? Hmm, where had I seen this before? Oh, right. Every demon horror movie ever made. And the horror part started right after the releasing part.

"I don't think so," I said.

"Ah, yes. Set me free and I shall take my revenge on the world. Start wars and famines, hurl thunderbolts, raise the very dead from their graves . . . Perhaps you could help with that?"

The voice slid to my ear again. "You are still such a child, aren't you? Believing in bogeymen. Of all the wars and massacres in the last century, demons are responsible for perhaps a tenth; and that, some would say, gives us too much credit. Unlike humans, we are wise enough to know that destroying the world that sustains us is hardly in our best interests. Free me and, yes, I will have my fun, but I'm no more dangerous out there than I am in here."

I considered it . . . and imagined the audience screaming. "You stupid twit! It's a *demon*!"

"I don't think so."

Her sigh ruffled my shirt. "There is no sight sadder than a desperate demi-demon. After decades alone in this place, beating the bars of my cage, howling to deaf ears, I'm reduced to begging favors from a child. Ask me your questions, and I shall play schoolteacher, answering them at no cost. I *was* a schoolteacher once, you know, when a foolish witch summoned me and invited possession, which is never wise, even if you're trying to destroy the dreadful little Puritan village that accused you of—"

"I don't have any questions."

"None?"

"None."

Her voice snaked around me. "Speaking of witches, I could tell you a secret about the dark-haired one you visited. Her mother—too ambitious by far—heard of another witch bearing a sorcerer's child, so she had to do the same. Now she's paying the price. A mixed-blood spellcaster is always dangerous."

"Tori's dad is a sorcerer?" I said in spite of myself.

"The man she calls Daddy? No. Her real father? Yes."

"So that is why—" I stopped. "No, I don't want to know."

"Of course you do. How about the wolf boy? I heard them talking to you about him. I remember the pups. They lived here, you know."

"They?"

"Four pups, cute as could be. Perfect little predators, flashing fangs and claws even before they could change forms—all but the biggest of the litter. The lone wolf. The smart wolf. When his Pack brothers flashed those fangs and claws one time too many, those who'd opposed the inclusion of the beasties got their way."

"What happened?"

"What happens to pups that bite their owner's hand? They were killed, of course. All but the clever one who didn't play their wolfie games. He got to go away and be a real boy." Her voice tickled my ear again. "What else can I tell you . . . ?"

"Nothing. I want you to leave."

She laughed. "Which is why you're lapping up my every word like sweet mead."

Fighting my curiosity, I found my iPod, stuck in my ear-buds, and cranked up the volume.

seven

LATER THAT AFTERNOON, DR. Davidoff knocked at my door again. Time for a history lesson, apparently. He led me to his office and entered the code to a closet-sized vault lined with bookshelves.

"We have more reference books than this, naturally. The rest are in the library, which you'll visit soon. However, this"—he waved at the closet—"is what a public library would call its special collection, containing the rarest and most prized volumes."

He slid a red leather-bound one from the shelf. Silver letters spelled out *Nekromantia*.

"The early history of the necromancer race. This is an eighteenth-century reproduction. There are only three known copies, including this one."

He lowered it into my hands with all the ceremony of passing over the crown jewels. I didn't want to be impressed, but when I felt the worn leather, smelled the mustiness of time, a thrill rippled through me. I was every great fantasy hero raised in ignominy, then handed the magic book and told "this is who you really are." I couldn't help falling for it—the story was hardwired in my brain.

Dr. Davidoff opened a second door. Inside was a surprisingly cozy sitting room with leather chairs, a jungle of plants, and a skylight.

"My secret hiding spot," he said. "You can read your book in here while I work in my office."

After he left, I checked out the narrow skylight, but even if I could manage to climb twenty feet to get to it, I'd never fit through. So I settled into the chair with the book.

I'd just opened it when he returned.

"Chloe? I need to leave. Is that all right?"

Leave me alone in his office? I tried not to nod too enthusiastically.

"If you need anything, dial nine for front reception," he said. "This door will be locked."

Of course . . .

I waited until I heard the outer door close. I was sure he'd locked my door, as promised, but I had to check.

It was a rich girl lock, Rae would say—the kind that keep out only kids who've never had to share a bathroom and, occasionally, break in to grab a hairbrush while their sister hogs the shower.

A side table held a stack of paperbacks. I found one with a cover sturdy enough to do the job, then copied Rae by wriggling it in the door crack until the lock clicked.

Voilà, my first break-in. Or break*out*.

I stepped into Dr. Davidoff's office. What I needed was a file cabinet, stuffed with records on the study, but all I could see was a desktop computer.

At least it was a Mac—I was more familiar with those than PCs. I jiggled the mouse and the computer popped out of sleep mode. The user login screen appeared. There was only one user account—Davidoff, with an eight ball as the graphic. I clicked it and got the password box. Ignoring it, I clicked on "Forgot password." The hint appeared: *usual*. In other words, his usual password, I supposed. That really helped.

At the password prompt, I typed *Davidoff*. Then *Marcel*. *Uh, do you really think it could be that easy?*

I tried every variation on Lyle House and Edison Group, then, in what I considered a stroke of insight: Agito, with several possible spellings. After my third wrong guess, it had again prompted me with the hint: *usual*. A few more tries and it asked me to enter the master password so I could reset the user account password. Great. If I knew what the master password was . . .

I remembered reading that most people kept their password written near their computer. I checked under the keyboard, under the mouse pad, under the monitor. As I peered under the desk, a voice whispered, "It's Jacinda."

I jumped so fast I banged my head.

A tinkling laugh. "Careful, child." It was the demi-demon. Again.

"The password is Jacinda?" I said as I backed out from under the desk. "That's Rae's mom's name. Why would he—?" I stopped myself.

"What connection does Dr. Davidoff have with Rae and her mother? Another delicious secret. All these scientists, so proud and lofty, pretending they are above mere human frailties. Foolishness. They are prey to them all—greed, ambition, pride, lust. I'm particularly fond of lust. Very amusing."

As she prattled, I typed in *Jacinda*. The password box vanished and Dr. Davidoff's desktop began to load.

I opened a Finder window and searched on my name. The window began filling with hits. I tried clicking on one in a folder labeled "Genesis II subjects," but misjudged and instead opened a file called simply "Genesis II" in the root folder of the same name.

The first paragraph looked like something out of Aunt Lauren's medical journals—the summary of an experiment. I read:

The blessing of supernatural powers is tempered by two serious disadvantages: dangerous or unpleasant side effects and the constant struggle to assimilate into human society. This study attempts to reduce or eliminate these disadvantages through genetic modification.

Genetic modification? The hairs on my scalp prickled.

The DNA of five subjects from five of the major races was modified in vitro. This modification was primarily designed to reduce the side effects of supernatural powers. It was expected that reducing these effects would aid assimilation, but this was further tested by raising twenty of the children in ignorance of their heritage. The remaining five served as a control group and were raised as supernaturals. During the intervening years, the study experienced some subject attrition (Appendix A), though contact has been reestablished with most.

Attrition? They must mean kids they lost track of—like Rae, Simon, and Derek. Did that mean there were others like us out there, ones they hadn't found?

As the remaining subjects proceed through puberty, side effects have been drastically reduced in nine

(Appendix B). However, in those subjects who did not improve, the genetic modification itself has had serious and unexpected side effects (Appendix C).

Fingers shaking, I typed "Appendix C" into the Find box. The document scrolled down.

One problem noted in the nine successful subjects was a general reduction in powers, which may be an unavoidable consequence of reducing negative side effects. It appears, however, that with the unsuccessful subjects, the reverse occurred. Their powers were heightened, as were the negative side effects, particularly sudden onset of these powers and, more seriously, their uncontrollable nature, apparently emotion based.

Uncontrollable powers. Emotion based.

I remembered Tori sobbing that she couldn't help it, that when she got mad, things just happened. Like Liz. Like Derek. Like Rae. Like me?

I skimmed over the next page. It detailed how they'd handled these "unsuccessful" subjects—put them into a group home, tried to medicate their powers and convince them they were mentally ill. When that failed . . .

The powers of supernaturals increase through puberty, meaning the powers of these failed subjects will continue to grow. It can be reasonably hypothesized that their powers will become more volatile and uncontrollable, threatening the lives of the subjects; the lives of innocents around them; and, perhaps most important, posing an immense exposure risk to the entire supernatural world.

We undertook this experiment in hopes of bettering the lives of all supernaturals. We cannot, through our actions, endanger that same world. As responsible scientists, we must accept responsibility for our failures and deal with them decisively to minimize the damage. While the decision was not unanimous, it was agreed that if the predetermined rehabilitation process fails, the subject must, with deep regret, be terminated quickly and humanely.

At the bottom was a list of names. Beside each was their current status.

Peter Ricci—rehabilitated

Mila Andrews—rehabilitated

Amber Long—terminated

Brady Hirsch—terminated

Elizabeth Delany—terminated

Rachelle Rogers—rehabilitation progressing

Victoria Enright—rehabilitation progressing

And finally, at the bottom, two names.

Derek Souza—???
Chloe Saunders—???

I don't know how long I stared at that list—and those question marks—before something hit my skull. I spun as a stapler bounced onto the carpet.

"Café mocha," said Dr. Davidoff, right outside the door. "Decaf, nonfat."

As I logged off, my gaze flipped between the reading room door and the kneehole under the desk. The kneehole was closer, but then I'd be trapped. A spurt of courage sent me lunging for the door. I made it—*to* the door, not through it into the reading room—as the hall door clicked open. I wheeled and pressed myself against the wall, beside a tall bookcase. I was out of sight but just barely.

I reached for the reading room doorknob. If I opened it wide enough to get through, though, he'd notice.

Go to the desk, I pleaded. *Check your e-mail. Check your voice messages. Just please, please, please, don't check on me.*

His footsteps headed straight for me. I plastered myself to the wall and held my breath. His arm appeared. Then his knee. Then—

He stopped. The arm and knee turned toward the desk.

He bent and picked up the stapler.

Oh, God. He knew. I had to come clean. Make up a story and turn myself in before I was caught. I stepped forward. A chattering broke the silence. My teeth? No, the pen holder on his desk was shaking, pens and pencils rattling.

Dr. Davidoff stared at it, his head tilting as if to say, *Am I doing that?* He caught the pen holder. It stopped shaking. As he pulled back his hand, the mouse rolled across the pad.

"Well?" a voice said by my ear. "Are you just going to stand there?"

Liz stood at my shoulder. She jabbed her finger at the door.

"Go!"

I made sure Dr. Davidoff had his back to me, then eased through the door.

"Lock it!" she whispered.

I reached around and turned the lock. The pens chattered again, covering the click of the door latch.

Liz stepped through the wall and waved me to the chair like she was shooing a cat. I'd barely settled in with the book when the door opened.

Dr. Davidoff took a slow look around the room. I followed his gaze, frowning, like I was wondering what he was searching for. I forced myself to look past Liz perched on the side table.

"Dr. Davidoff?"

He said nothing, just looked around.

"Did you forget something?" I asked.

He murmured about checking on dinner, then left after pausing at the door for one last, slow look around.

"Thank you," I said to Liz after Dr. Davidoff had locked me in again. "I know you're mad at me, for saying you're dead—"

"Because I'm obviously not dead, am I? You said the reason I couldn't touch stuff or move it was because I was a ghost." She smiled smugly, pulling her knees up and hugging them. "So I worked really hard at moving stuff. If I concentrate, I can. That means I must be a shaman."

Earlier I'd tried to explain why I hadn't told her sooner that she was a ghost. I'd said I'd thought she might be a shaman, because Derek said they could astral-project—appear without their bodies.

"They've got me drugged up," she continued. "That's why I keep getting all confused. I can't wake up, so my spirit is moving around instead."

She dangled her legs again and made figure eights with her feet, watching the giraffes on her socks dance. She didn't believe what she was saying. She knew she was dead. But she wasn't ready to face it.

As for being able to move objects, Dr. Davidoff had said one kind of ghost could: a telekinetic half-demon. When Liz got mad, objects had attacked whoever she was angry at. Now, as a ghost, she'd finally learned to harness her power.

In life, Liz thought she had a poltergeist. In death, she was one. She just couldn't accept that yet. And I wasn't going to force her.

eight

WE HAD SPAGHETTI AND meatballs for dinner. Rae's favorite. I couldn't eat, only sipping at a glass of flat Coke, but she didn't notice my loss of appetite. She was like a kid on her first day back from camp, with so much to tell that it burbled out in one endless stream.

She'd had a training session, a demonology lecture, and a long talk with Dr. Davidoff, who told her all about her mother and their hopes of contacting her. And as she talked, all I could think was, *We've been genetically modified. We're Frankenstein monsters—failed Frankenstein monsters. And I have no idea how I'm going to break it to you.*

"I saw Brady today," I finally blurted.

Rae stopped, fork raised, dangling spaghetti strands swaying. "Brady? Seriously? He's here. Oh my God, that is so

57 ◆

cool." Her grin blazed. "And you know what the first words out of that boy's mouth are gonna be? 'I told you so.' He kept saying there was nothing wrong with him, that something weird was going on—"

"He's dead Rae. I contacted his ghost."

She blinked. One slow blink, and then it was like someone paralyzed every muscle in her face, and it went completely still, her eyes empty, expressionless.

"I-I'm sorry. I didn't mean to blurt it out like—"

"Why would you make up such a"—she seemed to chew over her words, searching for the best, before spitting out—"*vicious* lie."

"Lie? No! I'd never—"

"Why are you doing this, Chloe?"

"Because we're in danger. We've been genetically modified and it didn't work. The Edison Group killed Liz and Brady and—"

"And it's only a matter of time before they kill us all. *Mwah-ha-ha!* You really do watch too many movies, don't you? And now those boys have brainwashed you with their conspiracy theory crap."

"Conspiracy theory?"

"All their talk about Lyle House and the evil people Simon's dad worked for. Those guys have you so brainwashed, you need to make the Edison Group into the bad guys. So don't tell me stories about Liz and Brady being dead."

My voice went as cold as hers. "You don't believe me?

Fine. I'll summon Liz and you can ask her a question only she could answer."

"Don't bother."

I stood. "No, really. I insist. It'll only take a sec."

When I closed my eyes, her chair squealed. Fingers clamped around my forearm. I opened my eyes to see her face, inches away.

"Don't play games, Chloe. I'm sure you can make me think Liz is here."

I looked into her eyes and saw a glimmer of fear. Rae wouldn't let me summon Liz because she didn't want to know the truth.

"Just let me—" I began.

"No."

She gripped my arm tighter, her fingers scorching hot. I gasped and yanked back. She let go quickly and a stricken look crossed her face. She started to apologize, then stopped herself, marched across the room, called reception, and said we were done with dinner.

I was actually glad to get back to my cell. I needed to figure out how I could convince Rae that we needed to escape . . . and what I'd do if I couldn't.

I had to get out. Those question marks beside Derek's name meant they hadn't decided what to do with him, and I'd already known that. Now I'd seen the same marks beside my name.

I needed to come up with an escape plan fast. But the moment I stretched out on my bed to start thinking, I discovered that my Coke at dinner hadn't been just flat. It had been drugged.

I fell into a dreamless sleep and didn't wake until someone touched my shoulder. I opened my eyes to see Sue, the gray-haired woman who'd chased us at the factory yard. She stood there, smiling down at me like a kindly nurse. My stomach twisted and I had to glance away.

"Time to get up, honey," she said. "Dr. Davidoff let you sleep in today, but we have a full afternoon of lessons that I'm sure you don't want to miss."

"A-afternoon?" I said, sitting up. "What time is it?"

"Almost eleven thirty. Rachelle and Victoria are finishing up their morning lessons and they'll meet you in the dining room for lunch."

nine

LUNCH WAS VEGGIE WRAPS, salad, and bottled water. Tori's choice apparently. Rae said a polite hello to me, then not another word. At least she'd made eye contact, though, which was more than I could say for Tori.

We were finishing up when Dr. Davidoff came in.

"I apologize for the interruption, girls," he said, "but I need to speak to Chloe."

I rose. "Sure. Where——?"

"Here's fine."

He took his time settling into a chair. Sweat trickled down the back of my neck, like a kid singled out in front of the class.

"We appreciate the help you've given us to try finding Simon, Chloe. We're very worried, as you girls know."

"Sure," Rae said. "He needs that medicine. If I had any

idea where to find him, I'd tell—"

She stopped and looked at me. Tori did the same, and I understood why I wasn't getting this lecture in private.

"I gave you that list of places," I said quickly. "That's all I have."

"They weren't there, Chloe," Dr. Davidoff said. "So we've reconsidered your offer. We'd like to take you along on our search this afternoon."

That crash I heard? The collision of clichés. One: never look a gift horse in the mouth. Two: if it sounds too good to be true, it probably is. I'd been lied to and misled often enough in the last few days that I wasn't just questioning this horse's dental health—I was examining him from nose to tail.

"You want me to go with you . . ."

"Yes, and, with luck, the boys will see you and come out. There's just one problem."

Oh, I was sure there were *lots* of problems with this scenario.

"The places you've given us don't seem right," he said. "The boys are clever, and their dad taught them well. They'd either choose a private spot or a very public one, and the possibilities you've provided are neither. We think there might be one you forgot to mention." He paused, meeting my gaze. "If there isn't, then we don't see the point of taking you along."

That second crash? The sound of the other shoe dropping. Dr. Davidoff knew why I wanted to go with them, and he'd decided to play my game. Did I dare play along?

"Come on, Chloe," Rae whispered.

"You'd better not think you're protecting them by keeping your mouth shut," Tori said. "Simon's sick, Chloe. If he dies, I hope he haunts you until—"

"That's enough, Tori," Dr. Davidoff said.

"I . . . might have another idea," I said. Oh God, I'd *better* have another idea. As hard as I thought, though, I needed time to come up with something good, and I wasn't going to get that time. So I stumbled through a lame story about Derek and me running through that factory yard, until we found a hiding spot. Maybe that's where he meant for our rendezvous spot. Only it had been dark, and we'd run through so many buildings that I wasn't sure exactly which one we'd hidden in, but I'd recognize it when I saw it.

Dr. Davidoff smiled, and I braced for him to call me on it, but he just said, "Then it's a good thing you're coming, isn't it?"

"And me," Tori said. "I've barely been out of my room since we got here, and I haven't been *outside* since Chloe arrived at Lyle House. I want to go, too."

"It isn't a field trip," Rae muttered.

"Your help, while appreciated, won't be necessary," Dr. Davidoff said.

"You think I want to *help*? Sure, I'll look around, for Simon's sake. But I need to go shopping."

"Shopping?" Dr. Davidoff stared at her like he must have misheard. We all did.

"Do you know how long it's been since I got new stuff? It's spring, and everything I have is from last year."

"The *tragedy*. Someone call Amnesty International." Rae looked at Tori. "You'll survive. I'm sure it all still fits you."

"Which is more than we can say for your wardrobe. Like another wrap, Rachelle? You've only had two so far."

Rae lifted her hand, fingers splayed at Tori. "Like third-degree burns, Queen Victoria? You've only had first-degree so far."

"Girls, that's enough. Victoria—"

"And when my mom locked me away at Lyle House, she made me a deal. If I got better, she'd buy me a new laptop. Best on the market."

"Why?" Rae said. "So you can IM your friends faster?"

"No, so I can work on my entrance package for software design camp at MIT."

Rae laughed, and Tori glared. She was serious. Tori the computer geek? I tried to picture it, but even my imagination wasn't that good.

Tori turned to Dr. Davidoff. "Obviously I *can't* get better, and my mother knew it when she made that promise. So she owes me a laptop."

Dr. Davidoff frowned, as if trying to follow her logic. Then he shook his head. "All right, Victoria. We'll order you—"

"I know what I need and I'll pick it out myself."

Dr. Davidoff stood. "As you wish. Tomorrow we'll—"

"Today. And I want a spring wardrobe, too."

"Fine. I'll ask someone to take you—"

"You think I'm letting some middle-aged dweeb help me choose clothes? I'm going today so Chloe can give me a second opinion."

"You want Chloe to help you shop?" Rae said.

"Well, I sure don't want you, skater girl. Chloe may be a loser, but she's a loser with money, and someone has taught her some small degree of fashion sense."

"No, Victoria," Dr. Davidoff said. "You are not going—"

She walked over to him, rose onto her tiptoes, and whispered in his ear. A look passed over his face, one part shock, two parts sheer terror.

"I see," he said. "Yes, now that I think about it, perhaps you could help us find the boys."

"I thought so."

She sauntered back to her chair. Blackmail? Two weeks ago, I'd have been horrified. Today, I was impressed.

It's a classic movie moment. Our hero, trapped in a jungle prison, plots and schemes until finally he breaks free . . . to find himself miles from civilization with no idea how to get home. Likewise, my ploy to "help" find Simon and Derek had paid off, and I had only the faintest notion of how to use the opportunity.

And Dr. Davidoff didn't give me time to plot my next move. He called Sue and told the others to meet us at the front door. I asked for a pit stop at my room, to grab something warmer, but he said they'd do it for me. I had the foresight to specify which sweatshirt I wanted—Liz's green Gap hoodie.

As Tori and I waited up front with Sue, I felt a now-familiar warm current tickling across the back of my neck.

"Leaving without saying good-bye?" the demi-demon whispered in my ear. "And leaving me trapped here, after all I've done for you?"

There was no menace in her voice, just a teasing lilt.

"I'm sorry," I said automatically.

"An apology? My, my, such a polite child. No need to apologize. I didn't expect you to free me now. You'll be back when you're ready, and when you are, I'll be waiting."

"Girls?" Dr. Davidoff said, striding toward us. "Our car is here."

As we followed him out, that warm breeze ruffled my hair. "Good-bye, child. And do be careful, you and your little band of magic makers and monsters. Keep those lovely powers of yours in check. I'd hate for the apocalypse to start without me."

Ten

W E RODE IN A minivan with Dr. Davidoff, Tori's mom, and a driver I didn't recognize—a blond security guy. Behind us, in another car, was Sue, a balding driver, and the dark-haired man who'd had the gun the night we'd escaped Lyle House.

There was a fourth person in that car: Aunt Lauren. I hadn't seen her—I knew only because Dr. Davidoff said she would be. When he did, I'd scrambled into the van as fast as I could, so I wouldn't see her come out.

How was I going to face Aunt Lauren? Even thinking about it made my stomach ache. I'd spent the last twenty-four hours trying hard not to think about her, about what she'd done.

My mom died when I was five. Aunt Lauren was her younger sister. In all the years of moving around with my

67 ◆

dad, who was always away on business, leaving me with a succession of nannies and housekeepers, Aunt Lauren had been the one sure thing in my life. The person I could count on. So after I escaped, when I got hurt, and Rae and I were separated from the guys, we'd gone to her for help.

And Aunt Lauren took me back to Dr. Davidoff. If she'd thought she was sending her delusional niece back to the nice folks who could help her, then as angry and hurt as I'd have been, I'd have understood. But Aunt Lauren hadn't been tricked by these people. She was one of them.

She'd put me—or my mom, I guess—in their experiment. She'd let them kill Brady and Liz and the other girl, had maybe even helped them do it. And now, knowing all this, I had to face her and pretend it was okay.

The minivan had a middle seat that could turn around, and that's where Tori's mom sat. For the first part of the trip, she read her *Wall Street Journal*, gaze lifting now and then to be sure we hadn't vanished. Tori and I rode, staring out our respective side windows, as if they weren't too darkly tinted for us to see more than shapes outside.

There'd been no chance to grab my backpack. Even Tori hadn't been allowed to bring her purse, as much as she'd argued. At least I had money. I'd arrived at Lyle House with my wad of twenties and my bank card stuffed in my shoe, and they were still there. I wore jeans, a long-sleeved shirt, and sneakers. A change of underwear and socks would have been nice, but right now, my bigger concern was how thin my shirt was.

"Dr. Davidoff?" I leaned as far as my seat belt would allow. "Did you get that sweatshirt for me?"

"Oh, yes. And you'll need it. It's chilly out. Diane? Could you pass this to Chloe?"

When I saw the green hoodie coming over the seat, I let out a sigh of relief.

"Isn't that Liz's?" Tori said.

"I don't think so."

"No?" She snatched it from me and read the tag. "Since when do you wear a ladies' medium? I bet you aren't even out of the kid's department yet."

"Very funny. Yes, I usually wear a small—"

"*Extra*small."

"But I like my sweatshirts big, okay?"

"You think I'm stupid? This is the same hoodie I borrowed from Liz—the one you came into my room and asked about the other day."

Tori's mom lowered her newspaper.

"I—I thought Liz might want it back. Rae mentioned that you still had it so—"

"So you appointed yourself keeper of *my* friend's stuff?"

Tori's mom folded the paper onto her lap, her long red fingernails ironing the crease. "Is that Liz's sweatshirt, Chloe?"

"M-maybe. When we left Lyle House, I grabbed clothes in the dark. I have one that looks like it. I'll wear it today,

69 ◆

then give it to you, so you can get it to Liz."

"You better." Tori started handing it back to me.

Her mother plucked it from Tori's fingers and folded it onto her lap. "I'll see that Liz gets it."

"C-can I wear it today? Dr. Davidoff said it's c-cold—"

"You'll be fine."

Tori rolled her eyes. "It's no big deal, Mom. Just give it to her."

"I said, no. What part of that isn't clear, Victoria?"

Tori grumbled under her breath and turned back to her window.

Her mom looked at me, her expression unreadable. "I'm sure you'll be just fine without it."

When the driver dropped us off on the street behind the factory complex, my teeth were chattering, and not just from the cold. Tori's mom knew why I'd had that sweatshirt—and that I had realized Liz was dead. Why else would a necromancer make a point of getting a personal article from her?

First Dr. Davidoff, now Tori's mom. Did anyone *not* see through my schemes?

Maybe one person. The one who might still see me as sweet little Chloe. The one who thought I hadn't really meant to run away from Lyle House but just got caught up in the plots of those boys.

"Aunt Lauren?"

I walked over as she got out of the car with Sue. I felt like

I was looking at a stranger who'd taken my aunt's form.

"You're freezing." She rubbed my arms, being careful with the injured one. "Where's your coat?"

I saw Tori's mom watching. If I tattled to Aunt Lauren, she'd tell her why I wanted Liz's hoodie.

"I forgot it. It was warmer last week."

She looked around. "Does anyone have an extra—?"

The dark-haired man from Saturday night climbed from the front seat and held out a nylon jacket.

"Thanks, Mike," Aunt Lauren said, and helped me into it.

The sleeves dangled six inches past my fingertips. I rolled them up, hoping the extra folds would keep me warmer, but the jacket was so thin it didn't even seem to stop the wind.

"Do you have the insulin?" I asked.

"I do, hon. Don't worry."

As the group prepared for the search, I stayed close to Aunt Lauren. She liked that, and kept her arm around me, rubbing my shoulder, as if to keep me warm. I gritted my teeth and let her.

"Now, Chloe," Dr. Davidoff said when everyone was ready, "tell us where to look."

The real rendezvous point was the warehouse nearest the factory. So the goal was to keep them as far from that as possible, in case the guys decided now was a good time to check in.

"We started in the warehouse where you guys tracked us and I did this—" I lifted my injured arm.

"Climbing out the window," Dr. Davidoff said.

I nodded. "I didn't know I'd hurt myself, so we ran. Derek wanted to get us as far from that warehouse as possible. We seemed to run and run, going around all these storage buildings, trying to find a good hiding spot. I—I wasn't paying much attention. It was dark and I couldn't see. Derek could, so I followed him."

"A werewolf's enhanced night vision," Dr. Davidoff murmured.

"We finally found a spot that Derek said would make a good place to hide and we should stay there until you guys left. But then he smelled the blood—"

Aunt Lauren's hand tightened on my shoulder, as if imagining me seconds away from being devoured.

"So he *helped* me," I continued. "He bandaged it up. But he said it was bad and I needed stitches. Then he smelled Simon. That's why we left—because of my arm and Simon—but before we did, he said the spot would make a good hiding place, that we should remember it."

"And you didn't," Tori said. "Nice going."

"It was dark and I was confused. I figured he meant *he'd* remember it—"

"We understand, Chloe," Dr. Davidoff said. "And you're right. It certainly sounds more promising than your other suggestions. As for whether you'll know it when you see it, though . . ."

"We had to rip up my T-shirt to bandage my arm. The

rest of my shirt should still be there."

"All right, then. Chloe, you go with Mrs. Enright——"

Aunt Lauren's hands gripped my shoulders. "I'll take Chloe."

"No, you'll take Victoria."

"But——"

Tori's mom cut her off. "Do you have blur spells, Lauren?"

"No, but——"

"Do you have any powers at all?"

Aunt Lauren's grip on my shoulder tightened. "Yes, Diane. I have the power of medicine, which is why I should be the first on the scene when Simon is found——"

"You'll be nearby," Dr. Davidoff said. "I need Chloe to have an escort, but we can't let the boys *see* her escort. Diane will take care of that."

eleven

A BLUR SPELL TURNED out to be like something you see in sci-fi movies, where the villain all but disappears, camouflaged behind a magical force field. As an effect, it's easily done. Apparently, it's just as easy in real life, if you're a witch.

Tori's mom walked right beside me, nearly invisible. With no chance to take off, I had to play my role, searching for the rendezvous spot, which gave me the excuse to look for an escape opportunity. Maybe a hole in the wall too small for Tori's mom to follow me through or a precarious stack of boxes I could topple onto her head or an abandoned hammer I could brain her with.

I'd never "brained" anyone in my life, but with Tori's mom, I was willing to try.

From the front road, the place looked like a regular factory with a few outbuildings. Once you got back here, though, there were buildings everywhere, a lot of them not even being used. Prime real estate. Or it would be . . . without the smog-spouting factory to bring down the neighborhood.

Those spewing stacks were the only sign the factory was operational. Probably running well below capacity, barely hanging on, like a lot of industry in Buffalo. I had no idea what they made. Metal stuff, it looked like from the stock in the warehouses. Once, when we were darting between buildings, we had to duck behind some barrels as a trucker drove through the lot, but that was the only employee we saw.

The third building we checked was open, so Tori's mom didn't need to cast a spell to unlock it. As we stepped in, I thought, *This looks promising.* The last two had been filled with equipment and rolls of metal. This one seemed unused, and was scattered with crates. They weren't stacked precariously, but there was a whole warehouse to search.

As we moved in deeper, I saw what looked like an off-balance stack. Near it was a pile of small metal pipes, the perfect size for braining someone.

I headed toward the pipes, my gaze on the ground, as if searching for my torn shirt.

"I think we can stop this charade now, Chloe," Tori's mom said.

I turned slowly, taking a moment to plaster on my best wide-eyed look.

"There's no shirt here," she said, "or rendezvous point. Perhaps there is, somewhere in this complex, but not here."

"Let's try the next—"

She caught my arm as I walked past. "We all know you're trying to escape again. Marcel only hopes the real rendezvous point is nearby and that you're laying a trail right now, one that will entice Derek back to investigate once he thinks we're gone."

Laying a trail? Oh, no. Why hadn't I thought of that? I didn't need to be here to get Derek's attention. If he smelled that I'd been near the factory . . .

"I-I'm not trying to escape. I want to help Simon. We need to find—"

"The boys don't interest me. You do."

"Me?"

Her grip on my arm tightened. "All those kids had been at Lyle House for months, behaving themselves, working so hard to get better. Then you arrive and suddenly we have a full-scale mutiny on our hands. Within a week, four residents are on the run. Quite the little instigator, aren't you?"

I'd been the catalyst, not the instigator. But it wouldn't win me any brownie points to correct her.

She continued. "You took action while the rest swallowed our lies and prayed for rescue. My daughter didn't even have the guts to join you."

Umm, because you crushed any fight left in her? Because you made her think she had to play perfect patient to please you?

"The Fates played us a nasty twist, Chloe Saunders. They stuck you with dear Aunt Lauren, always fretting and wringing her hands. A perfect match for my spineless daughter. But where fate wrongs us, free will can make things right. I think you and I can reach an agreement that will benefit us both." She released my arm. "Dr. Gill tells me you contacted spirits from Lyle's early experiments."

I said nothing, my gaze steady.

"I know she confronted you," Tori's mom continued. "Something of a fanatic, our Dr. Gill, as I'm sure you noticed. She's obsessed with Lyle's secrets. Ambition is healthy. Obsession is not." She eyed me. "So what did these spirits tell you?"

"Nothing. I'd accidentally raised them from the dead, so they weren't too interested in chatting with me."

She laughed. "I suppose not. But for you, at your age, to raise the dead . . . ?" Her eyes glittered. "Remarkable."

Okay, that was dumb. I just confirmed I'd raised the dead. A lesson in playing it cool—don't.

"Could you contact them again?" she asked.

"I could try."

"Resourceful and reasonable. That's a combination that will take you far. Here's what we'll do, then. I'll tell Dr. Davidoff we found the spot here. The shirt was gone, likely taken by the boys. But they left this." She pulled a page from her pocket. It was from Simon's sketch pad, carefully torn out. On one side was a partial drawing, clearly Simon's work. On the other side, she'd written in block letters: BSC CAFE 2 PM.

"Meet at the Buffalo State cafeteria at two," I said. "The page is too clean, though. They'll know it wasn't left here."

I took it, walked over by the metal pipe, crouched, and brushed the note across the dirty floor. Then I paused, still hunched over, and looked up at her.

"What about the insulin?"

"I'm sure those boys have already found some."

"Can we leave it here, just in case?"

She hesitated. She didn't want to bother, but if it would win my trust . . .

"I'll get the vials from Lauren later and bring them back," she said. "Now, though, we need to report that note."

She turned to leave. I wrapped my fingers around a metal pipe, then sprang up, swinging it at the back of her head.

She spun, fingers flicking. I sailed backward into a stack of boxes, the pipe flying from my hands and clanging to the floor. I scrambled for it, but she was faster, snatching it up and brandishing it.

Her mouth opened, but before she could get out a word, a crate shot from the stack over my head. She sidestepped as it whizzed past. Behind it stood Liz.

I lunged for the pile of pipes, but Mrs. Enright hit me

with another spell. My feet sailed out, my outstretched hands hitting the floor, pain blasting through my injured arm. As I looked around, I caught a glimpse of Liz's nightshirt behind the stacks of crates.

"Elizabeth Delaney, I presume." Mrs. Enright moved back against a wall, her gaze flitting from side to side, ready for the next flying object. "So it seems, in death, you've finally mastered your powers. If only it had been sooner. Such a waste."

Liz froze between stacks, her face stricken as Mrs. Enright confirmed her death. Then she squared her shoulders and, eyes narrowing, fixed them on a stack of crates.

"Even in death, you can be useful, Elizabeth," Mrs. Enright said. "A poltergeist is a rare find, one that will help Dr. Davidoff overcome his disappointment at losing dear Simon and Derek."

The crates shuddered and cracked as Liz pushed, tendons popping with the strain. I frantically motioned for her to concentrate on just the top one. She nodded and pushed it . . . but Mrs. Enright simply stepped out of range.

"Enough of that, Elizabeth," she said calmly as the crates crashed behind her.

Liz grabbed a loose board and hurled it at her.

"I said, *enough*."

She hit me with another spell, this one a jolt of electricity that left me on the floor, gasping and shaking. Liz crouched over me. I whispered I was okay and pushed up until I was sitting. My whole body throbbed.

Mrs. Enright looked around, unable to see Liz unless she was moving something. "I can't hurt you, Elizabeth, but I can hurt Chloe. If so much as a scrap of wood flies, I'll hit her with another energy bolt. Is that clear?"

I struggled to my feet, then raced for the door. I made it five feet before I froze. Literally.

"It's called a binding spell," Mrs. Enright said. "Very useful. Now, Elizabeth, you are going to behave while Chloe and I—"

The spell broke. I stumbled, twisting to regain my balance, and looked up to see *her* frozen instead. A dark figure stepped from the shadows.

"A binding spell?" Tori strolled over. "Is that what you call it, Mom? You're right. It *is* useful."

She walked in front of her mother's still form. "So I'm a disappointment, am I? Chloe is the daughter you wish you'd had? You know, I'd be really hurt by that . . . if I thought you actually knew her. Or me." She stepped closer. "Shopping, Mom? I'm locked in a cell, my life is falling apart, and you really believed I wanted to go shopping? You don't know me any better than she does." She waved at me. "You—"

Tori staggered back with a gasp as her mother broke free and hit her with a spell.

"You've got a lot of learning to do, Victoria, if you think you can hurt me."

Tori met her mother's gaze. "You think I came here for revenge? This is called an escape."

"Escape? So you're going to run off and live on the streets? Daddy's princess sleeping in alleys?"

Tori's eyes flashed, but she only said calmly, "I'll be fine."

"With what? Did you bring money? A bank card?"

"And how would I get that, when you locked me up?"

"I bet Chloe has some. I bet she never left her room without it, just in case."

They both looked at me. I didn't say a word, but my answer must have shown on my face. Mrs. Enright laughed.

"Oh, I'm going to get money, Mom," Tori said. "I'll take it from you."

She slammed her arms down and a wave of energy smacked into her mother and me, tottering us backward. Tori waved her hands over her head. Sparks flew, caught in a gust of wind that wailed around us in a whirlwind of dirt and sawdust. I squeezed my eyes shut and covered my nose and mouth.

"You call that powerful magic, Victoria?" her mother shouted over the wind. "It's a temper tantrum. You haven't changed at all. Only now, you call on the forces of nature to howl and stomp for you."

"You think that's all I can do? Just watch——"

Tori froze in a binding spell. The wind stopped. The dust and sparks fluttered to the floor.

"I'm watching," Mrs. Enright said, "and all I see is a spoiled brat with a fancy new car, tearing around, not caring who gets hurt. As selfish and inconsiderate as ever."

Tori's eyes glistened with tears. As her mother advanced on her, I eased back toward the pile of metal pipes.

"Now, Victoria, if you're done throwing tantrums, I'm going to call Lauren to come and get you, and hopefully she can manage to *keep* you this time."

Liz was circling toward Mrs. Enright, her gaze on another pile of crates. I shook my head. The angle was wrong and she'd see it falling. I bent and lifted a bar.

"Lauren Fellows won't be the only person reprimanded for this little escapade," Mrs. Enright continued. "You've just earned yourself a week in your room, alone, no classes, no visitors, no MP3 player. Just a lot of time to think about—"

I swung the pipe. It hit the back of her head with an ugly *thwack.* The weapon flew from my hands. She teetered and I thought I hadn't hit her hard enough. I tripped over my feet to get to the pipe, now rolling away.

Then she fell.

Tori broke from the spell and raced to her mother, dropping beside her. I did the same and checked her pulse.

"I think she's okay," I said.

Tori just knelt there, staring down at her mother.

I touched her arm. "If we want to go, we have—"

She shook me off. I leaped to my feet, ready to leave her. Then I realized what she was doing—checking her mother's pockets.

"Nothing," she said through her teeth. "Not even a credit card."

"I've got money. Come on."

One last look at her mother, and she followed.

twelve

ORI AND I HUDDLED under the tarp covering a trailer bed. There wasn't a cab attached, so we were in no danger of our hiding place rolling away. I thought that made it the perfect spot. Tori disagreed.

"We're sitting ducks here," she hissed, crouching. "All they have to do is lift this cover and they'll see us."

"If they get close, we'll run."

"And how will we know that? We can't *see* anything."

"Liz is scouting." I uncrossed my legs. "About Liz—"

"She's dead." Her voice was a harsh rasp. "I heard my mother. She killed Liz, didn't she? Her and those people."

"I-I'll explain later. We need to be quiet. Someone could hear—"

"No one's around, remember? Because Liz—my *friend* Liz—is a ghost and she's standing watch. Apparently, she's been helping you for God knows how long, and you didn't even bother to tell me she was dead, that they *murdered* her."

"I told Rae——"

"Of course. Rachelle. How's that working out for you?" Tori met my gaze. "If you want to know who betrayed you guys, look in that direction."

"Rae? No. She'd never——"

"Well, *someone* told. If it wasn't me or you, or the guys, who does that leave?"

"W-we should be quiet. Sound travels."

"Really? Wow. Now you give science lessons, too. Did Derek teach you that?"

"Tori?"

"What?"

"Shut it."

She did, for about five seconds, then said, "Shouldn't Liz have checked in by now? How do you know she's still out there?"

"She comes and goes. That's why I needed that sweatshirt to——"

Liz dashed through the tarp and stooped over us. "Tell her to *shhh*!"

"I already did," I whispered. "Repeatedly."

"Well, they've heard, and they're on their way. It's your aunt and a guy with a gun."

I relayed this to Tori in whispers.

"What? Why are we sitting here then?" She darted for the side.

I grabbed her arm.

"Hey!" she said, loud enough to make Liz wince.

"Which way are they coming from?" I asked Liz.

She pointed left. I crawled to the right side and lifted the tarp.

Liz hurried out. "I don't see them now."

I squinted against the sun. There was a building about twenty feet away, but I couldn't see a door. I leaned out for a better look. To my left was a cluster of rusty barrels. We could hide between—

"Chloe!" Liz yelled. "He's right—"

A *thump-thump* on the trailer bed cut her off.

"Back up!" Liz said. "Back up!"

"What's going on?" Tori whispered. "Move!"

When I tried to back up, Tori shoved me and I flew out from under the trailer, doing a face plant in the dirt.

"Well, that made it easy," said a voice.

I rolled onto my back. There, on the trailer bed, stood Mike—the man who'd shot at us Saturday night.

"Lauren?" he said. "Better give me that gun. I'll handle this."

Gaze still fixed on me, he jumped to the ground. He put out his hand as Aunt Lauren came around the back of the trailer, rifle in her hands.

"I'm sorry, Chloe," she said.

She aimed the gun at me and I scuttled back.

"N-no. I—I won't fight. I—"

She swung the gun and fired at Mike. The dart hit his arm. He stared at it. Then his knees gave way.

Aunt Lauren ran over and helped me up. "Tori, get out of there. He radioed the others when we heard you."

I backed away, my gaze on Aunt Lauren as I motioned for Tori to be ready to run. Aunt Lauren grabbed my arm; but when I pulled away, she released her grip and stepped back.

"Why do you think I shot him?" she said. "Why did I let Tori get away from me so easily? I'm trying to help. We'll find the boys, then we'll find Kit—Simon's dad."

A weird ringing sounded in my ears. I think it was my heart, shouting for joy. Aunt Lauren had realized she was wrong. She still loved me. She was going to make it up to me, fix my problems like she always did, and make everything okay.

Could I have imagined anything more perfect?

No, and that's why I took another slow step back, fingers at my side, waving for Tori to get ready to bolt. I'd been tricked too often to fall for a fairy-tale ending now.

"Chloe, please." Aunt Lauren held out the insulin pouch. As I reached for it, she caught my hand. "I made a mistake, Chloe. A huge mistake. But I'm going to fix it." She handed me the pouch. "Now head that way." She pointed toward the factory. "Stick to the shadows. I need to hide him under the truck."

Aunt Lauren caught up and we circled the warehouses, heading toward the front gates. She swore no one from the Edison Group was covering the front. Though we hadn't seen employees wandering around outside, the group wouldn't risk getting too close to the factory.

And if she was lying and leading us into a trap? I hoped Tori's spells would get us through.

At the far side of the yard, we paused behind a warehouse to catch our breaths.

"Okay, girls," Aunt Lauren said. "There's a delivery gate over there. It's closed, but you both should be able to squeeze through. Head right two blocks, then along the street to the end. You'll see a Seven-Eleven."

I nodded. "I know where it is."

"Good. Go around the back of the store and wait. I'll meet you there."

Tori sprinted off, but I stood there, looking at Aunt Lauren.

"Chloe?"

"Tori didn't turn us in, did she?"

"No. Now—"

"It was Rae, wasn't it?"

Aunt Lauren paused, and I saw the answer in her eyes. "I'm not the only one who mistakenly thought she was doing the right thing, Chloe."

I started to turn away. She caught my arm and held out a folded envelope.

"An explanation and some money." When I didn't take it, she leaned around and put it into my back pocket. "If you decide to keep running, I won't blame you. But, please, give me a chance. One last chance."

I nodded. She pulled me into a hug and kissed my cheek, then let me go. Tori had already rounded the corner of the building, disappearing from sight when Liz shrieked behind me.

"Chloe!"

I spun so fast I lost my balance. Aunt Lauren gestured for me to keep going, but I saw only the figure behind her. Tori's mom.

I shouted a warning, but Mrs. Enright's hand flew out. A bolt shot from her fingertips. It hit Aunt Lauren with a horrible sizzling pop, knocking her off her feet. Blood flew from her lips, spraying the concrete as she fell.

thirteen

I STARTED TO RUN to Aunt Lauren. I made it a few feet before Tori's mom locked me in a binding spell. I dimly heard her say something, but I didn't know what it was. My ears were filled with my own silent screams as I stared at Aunt Lauren, motionless on the ground. Finally Mrs. Enright's voice came through.

"I should probably ask where my darling daughter is."

"Right here," said a voice behind me.

Mrs. Enright's head lifted. Her brow furrowed. Her lips parted. Then she jolted backward, hit by a spell from Tori. My binding broke. I lurched toward Aunt Lauren, but Tori grabbed my arm.

"We have to go," she said.

"No. I—"

Mrs. Enright recovered, hands flying as she launched a

spell. Tori yanked me out of the way and it hit the wall, blasting a blackened crater.

"You can fight her," I said. "Stop her, and I'll get the gun—"

"I can't."

Tori heaved on my arm. I pulled away. She muttered "Fine," let go, then raced off, disappearing around the corner. Tori's mom lifted her hands again. Then a voice shouted, distracting her, "They're over here!"

I took one last look at Aunt Lauren and ran.

There was no way we were getting to that delivery gate now. I soon realized why Aunt Lauren had sent us ahead—so she could watch our backs because we'd be exposed to any employees entering the side yard and we couldn't afford to raise any alarms.

We peered around the corner of the next building, saw that open expanse, heard voices coming, and knew we'd never make it.

"Now what?" Tori said.

I didn't answer.

"Come on!" she whispered. "What's the plan?"

I wanted to grab her and shake her and tell her there was no plan. I couldn't even wrap my head around the concept. My aunt might be dead. *Dead.* That's all I could think about.

"Chloe!" she whispered. "Hurry! What are we going to do?"

I longed to tell her to leave me alone. Come up with her own plan. Then I saw her eyes, bright with fear fast turning into panic, and the words died in my throat.

She'd just learned Liz was dead. She'd seen my aunt possibly killed by her mother. Neither of us was in any shape to think, but one of us had to.

"Your aunt said the Edison Group won't come close to the front," she said. "If we run for it—"

"They'll make an exception. Or find a way to cut us off. But . . ." I looked around. My gaze stopped on the huge building dominating the yard. "The factory."

"What?"

"Stay close to me."

I knew of two doors—the emergency exit we'd escaped from Saturday night and the main entrance Derek had broken into. The main doors were closest. As we headed for them, I whispered to Liz, asking her to run ahead and scout the way. If someone was coming, she'd whistle.

The door was in an alcove. I darted in and I pressed against the wall while Liz zipped through the door. She was back in a second.

"There's a guard dead ahead," she said. "I'll distract him. You open the door a crack and listen for my whistle. You know a place to hide, right?"

I nodded. When we were here Saturday, Derek had us opening all the doors, searching for an exit, and I remembered a storage room that would be perfect.

When Liz gave the all clear, I eased open the door. Tori danced impatiently behind me, though I'd asked her to watch for anyone approaching.

Inside, Liz was at a closed door twenty feet away. The guard stood beside her, staring down at the knob as it slowly turned one way, then the other.

We slipped past. I could hear the distant rumble and thump of machinery and the laughs and shouts of workers. This section, though, was quiet.

We made it to the side hall easily, as the guard stood transfixed by that mysterious turning doorknob.

Liz raced up behind us. "Where to?"

I gestured to the adjoining hall. She sprinted ahead, turned the corner, and whistled the all clear. Our luck held, and we made it safely into the storage room. As its door closed, the guard's voice echoed down the empty halls.

"Hey, Pete, come here! You gotta see this. The knob was turning by itself. I tell you, ever since Dan did a nosedive into the saws, this place has been haunted."

He was right. Saturday night, I'd seen the ghost of a man jump into those saws. Then he'd reappeared and done it again. Was that some kind of penance? Aunt Lauren had done bad things, maybe even committed murder. If she was dead, would she go to Hell? Was she—?

I swallowed hard.

"What now?" Tori whispered.

I looked around. The room was the size of a classroom and full of boxes.

"Find a place in the back," I said. "There's lots of dust, which means they don't come in here very often. We'll hide—"

Liz ran through the door.

"They're coming!"

"Wha—?"

"Dr. Davidoff and Sue. She saw you by the doors."

Thanks to Tori, who'd kept such a good watch . . .

"Are they inside?" I asked.

"Not yet."

"Is who inside?" Tori asked as Liz took off. "What's going on? What'd she say?"

I told her, then opened the door a crack.

"What are you doing?" she said, tugging my sleeve. "Are you nuts? Close that!"

Tell her to be quiet, and she got louder. Tell her to stay back, and she pushed me into the line of fire. Tell her to watch for our pursuers, and she hovered at my shoulder instead. Open the door to listen, and she wanted to drag me back inside.

Ah. The beginning of a beautiful friendship.

Friendship? We'd be lucky if we survived a temporary partnership.

I told her I was trying to listen. When she argued, I glared; and for once in my life, it actually worked. Her mouth shut and she backed into the room, sulky and glowering, but silent.

"Can I help you?" the guard's voice echoed down the hall.

"Yes, we're looking for two teenage girls," Dr. Davidoff replied. "We believe they came in here. They're runaways from a nearby group home. They're fifteen years old. One's about five six, short dark hair. The other is five feet, reddish-blond hair."

"With red streaks," Sue added. "Painted red streaks."

The guard chuckled. "Sounds like my kid, only hers are blue. Last week they were purple."

"Teenagers," Dr. Davidoff said with a fake laugh. "These two of ours are always slipping away. You know what girls are like. Running off to see their boyfriends and buy new lip gloss. They don't mean any harm, but we worry about them."

"Sure. If I see them, I'll give you a shout. You got a card?"

"We're quite certain they're in here."

"Nope. This is the only door that opens from the outside, and I've been at my post all shift."

"I understand. But perhaps if we could take a look—"

A chair squeaked and I pictured the beefy man rising. "This is a factory, folks. Do you have any idea how many safety regulations I'd be breaking if I let you poke around?"

"We'll wear hard hats and safety glasses."

"This isn't a public building. You can't come in here

without an appointment and an escort."

"May we speak to the plant manager, then?"

"He's out. Meeting. All day. I told you, no one got past me. Your girls aren't in here. But if you really want to check, that's fine. Get the cops and I'll let you in."

"We'd prefer not to involve the police."

"Well, you're gonna have to, 'cause it's the only way you're getting past me."

After the guard chased them off, we holed up to wait for dark. We each found a separate spot, far enough apart that we had an excuse for not chatting. That was fine with me at first. Like Tori and I would have anything to chat about. But after a while, even bickering would have been better than this silent waiting with nothing to do but think. And cry. I did a lot of that, as quietly as I could. I'd taken out the envelope so often it was covered in tearstains. I wanted to open it, but I was terrified that whatever was in it wouldn't be a good enough explanation, that it *couldn't* be good enough, and I so desperately needed it to be.

Finally, I couldn't take it anymore. I ripped it open. Inside was money, but I shoved that into my pocket without counting it, then unfolded the letter.

Aunt Lauren started by explaining how necromancy worked. In necromancer families, not everyone saw ghosts. Most didn't. Aunt Lauren didn't. Nor had my mom or their parents. But my uncle had. My mother's twin brother,

Ben—I'd never known she'd even had a twin. Aunt Lauren wrote.

Ben died long before you were born. Your mom would have showed you pictures, but you were too young to understand. After she was gone . . . there just didn't seem any point in bringing it up. He started seeing ghosts when he was a little older than you are now. He went away to college with your mom, but it was too much for him. He came home. Your mom wanted to quit and come back, too, to keep an eye on him. He insisted she stay at school. I said I'd watch over him, but I didn't really understand what he was going through. When he was nineteen, he died in a fall. Whether he jumped or whether he was running from ghosts, we never knew.

Did it matter? Either way, his powers had killed him. I kept telling myself ghosts couldn't hurt me, but in my gut I knew I was wrong, and here was the proof. Just because you can't reach out and push someone off a roof, doesn't mean you can't kill him.

Your mom had been looking for help for Ben before he died. Our family had some connections in the necromancer world, and eventually someone gave her a contact name for the Edison Group. Only Ben went off the roof a month before she got the message. Later, when I started med school, I contacted them. If they were scientists, they could use doctors; and if I could help people like Ben, that's what I wanted to do. Your mom wasn't involved. Not then. That didn't come until she wanted to have a child.

She'd planned to have kids even after what happened to her brother?

As if in answer to my question, Aunt Lauren wrote:

You have to understand, Chloe, it's like any other genetic disorder. It's a risk we accept. If we have a child and she has the power, then we deal with that. Your mother wouldn't take that risk, though. Not after Ben. She wanted to adopt, but with your father, that wasn't an option. There were . . . things in his past. The agencies didn't consider him a suitable parent. Your mother was miserable. She wanted children so badly. She looked into other alternatives, but they all cost money and at that time, your parents were living in a rat-infested hole downtown. Every penny they earned went to your father's new business. Then I told her about a break-through with the Edison Group. A team had isolated the genes that conferred powers for necromancers. By testing the potential carrier of that gene code and the proposed human parent, we could determine the

likelihood that a child of that union would be a necromancer. Jenny was so excited. I ran the tests on her and
your dad . . . and it was almost certain that any child
they had would be a necromancer. I tried to persaude
her to consider other options, maybe artificial insemi-
nation with another biological father. But she was so
tired and so *crushed* that she just didn't have the energy
to consider alternatives. And she suspected I was trying
to come between her and your dad, because I'd made
it clear I didn't think he was right for her. We didn't
talk for almost a year. Then, I called her with the most
amazing news. A breakthrough, here at the lab. We
couldn't give her a child who wasn't a necromancer, but
we could eliminate the dangers that killed our brother.
She could have a child who could speak to the dead on
her own terms.

But it hadn't worked out that way, as I knew. When I
started seeing ghosts so abruptly, Aunt Lauren said she'd told
herself nothing was wrong. I wasn't one of the failures—I just
needed time to adjust to my new powers. The Edison Group
had insisted I go to Lyle House, though, and she'd agreed,
still expecting they'd discover I was fine, and then I could be
told the truth.

She'd kept believing that until she learned that I'd
raised zombies at Lyle House. Still, she told herself it was
okay—we'd deal with it. The group had promised that no

matter what happened, I wouldn't be killed. A necromancer wasn't dangerous, they told her, so there was no reason to terminate me.

Still worried, she'd started digging for answers, just like I had, and she learned the same thing I had—that they'd lied. Apparently, they'd lied about a lot of things, she said, though she didn't go into detail.

That's what changed everything for me, Chloe. I know it's horrible to admit I only realized my mistakes when my own niece's life was in danger. Until then I'd done what I thought was right—the greater good and such. But, in doing that, I forgot my oath as a doctor, to first do no harm. I did harm and I'm sure I'll pay the price, but I won't let you pay it with me. That's why I had to get you out.

Three final paragraphs. In the first, she said that if I was reading this letter, then she hadn't gotten away with me. If I'd left her behind, she understood. If she'd been killed, that was the price she'd paid. And if she'd been taken by the Edison Group, I wasn't to go back for her. I was to keep going and find Simon and his dad, Kit. She had no idea what had happened to Kit. She'd searched the Edison Group files and she was convinced they weren't involved in his disappearance, but that was it.

She also told me to make sure I wore my necklace—always.

I remembered how quick she'd been to get it back for me when I went to Lyle House without it. In the letter, she didn't say much about it, only that it was supposed to ward off ghosts. But it didn't. Or maybe it *was* working, and if I lost it, I'd start seeing a lot more ghosts, my powers running unchecked.

The next bit was about my dad. He didn't know anything, not even about me being a necromancer. So if I escaped and she didn't, I needed to stay away from him.

Then came the final paragraph. Three more sentences.

> She wanted a child so badly, Chloe. And you are just as wonderful as she imagined. You were the center of her world.

Tears burned my eyes, that old never-quite-healed ache flaring. I took a deep, shuddering breath, folded the letter, and put it back in my pocket.

We'd been there over an hour when Liz came racing in with the news. "She's not dead. Your aunt. She's okay."

From the excitement on Liz's face, you'd think she'd just learned her own aunt had survived. It didn't matter that Aunt Lauren was part of the group that murdered her. All she cared about was that this news would please me. Looking at her glowing face, I realized that as good as I tried to be, I could never be as selfless as Liz.

My relief was cut short by a fresh worry. What would they

do to Aunt Lauren now that she'd helped us escape? Now that she'd betrayed them. Thinking of that reminded me of another betrayal. Rae's.

I'd trusted her. I'd vouched for her to the guys, persuaded them to let her join us, and she'd turned us in.

Rae was the one who'd insisted that the boys weren't coming back. She was the one who suggested I go to Aunt Lauren, who'd talked me into it when I'd hesitated.

I remembered the night we'd left, lying in our beds trying to sleep. She'd been so excited about her powers and not the least concerned about what lay ahead of us. Now I knew why she hadn't been worried.

Aunt Lauren said Rae honestly thought she was helping me. Betrayal as tough love, forcing me onto the path chosen for me, certain she was right and I was just too stubborn to see it.

Now both she and my aunt were trapped with the Edison Group. Once the glow over her new life faded, Rae would see the cracks and pick away at them until she realized the truth. I hoped she didn't. I prayed both of them would just hold tight and do whatever the Edison Group wanted until I could return. And I *would* return.

Finally Liz popped in to tell me that Dr. Davidoff and his crew had given up, assuming Tori and I had snuck past the front gates and were long gone. They'd left a guard behind, keeping watch from some hidden spot, in case Derek showed up, following my trail.

At five, the whistle blew, the workday ending. By five thirty, the building was empty. Still we waited. Past six, past seven . . .

"It must be dark out by now," Tori whispered, crawling over to me.

"Dusk, not dark. We'll give it another hour."

At eight, we left.

fourteen

WE SNUCK PAST THE night guard, who was busy reading *Playboy* in the lunchroom. Liz stayed with him to make sure he didn't hear us. He didn't.

Luckily Tori and I had the good fortune to dress in dark clothes that morning—Tori in a navy American Eagle sweat suit and leather jacket, me in jeans and a green shirt. I only wished I had more than this thin jacket. With the sun gone it was freezing, made worse by an icy blast that had to be coming straight across the river from Canada.

Once inside the warehouse, we wouldn't have to worry about the wind. Getting there, though, was taking forever. Liz was having trouble finding the Edison Group guard, so we had to go the long way around, scooting from hiding place to hiding place, to reach the real rendezvous point—the warehouse where Rae and I had waited for Derek and Simon.

As it had been the other night, the warehouse door was latched but not locked. Unless you knew a hot black market in cardboard boxes, crates, and wooden pallets, there was nothing inside to steal. All that worthless junk made it the perfect place to hide . . . and meant there were a million spots for the guys to leave a note.

After a few minutes of banging around in the dark, I gave up.

"We'll have to wait until morning," I said.

No response. I squinted around for Tori.

"This is my stop," she said, somewhere to my left.

"Hmm?"

"This is where I get off." Her voice was oddly monotone, like she was too tired to put any bite into the words. "My adventure, as fun as it's been, ends here."

"Just hold on until morning. If there isn't a note, we'll figure something out."

"And if there is a note? I wanted to join your escape, Chloe, not your crusade to find Simon's dad."

"B-but he'll—"

"Save the day?" She managed a sarcastic lilt. "Rescue us from the mad scientists, cure us, and take us to a land of lollipops and unicorns?"

My voice hardened. "Finding him might not solve anything, but right now, we're a little short on options. What are you going to do instead? Go back to the Edison Group and say you're sorry, it was all a mistake?"

"I'm doing what I planned all along. We needed each other to get out. But that's all I wanted from you. I'd help you find the note, but I won't stay until morning to do it. I'm going home, to my dad."

That shut me up, if only because I was afraid I'd say something I'd regret, like ask if she meant her dad or her father. Did she know there was a difference? I doubted it.

"So your dad. . . . He's human?"

"Of course. He doesn't know anything about this. But I'm going to tell him."

"Is that such a good idea?"

"He's my *dad*," she snapped. "When he hears what my mom did . . . ? Everything's going to be okay. My dad and me get along great. Better than him and my mom. They hardly even talk. I'm sure they only stay together because of us kids."

"Maybe you should wait a day or two. See what happens."

She laughed. "And join your band of superheroes? Sorry, but I'm allergic to spandex." Her sneakers scuffed on the concrete as she turned away. "Say bye to Liz for me."

"Wait!" I tugged off my shoe. "Take some money."

"Save it. I don't plan to ever get the chance to repay you."

"It's okay. Just take—"

"Keep your money, Chloe. You'll need it more than I will." She took a few steps, then stopped. For a moment, she stood there, then she said quietly, "You could come with me."

"I need to get Simon his insulin."

"Right. Okay then."

I waited for a good-bye but heard only the slap of her sneakers, then the creaking of the door as she left.

When Liz returned from patrol, she said she'd seen Tori leaving. I explained, then braced for a chewing out. Why had I let Tori take off? Why hadn't I gone after her? But all Liz said was, "I guess she didn't want to hang around," and that was that.

We were both quiet for a while, then Liz said, "I'm sorry I didn't believe you. About me being dead."

"I handled it wrong. I should have made it easier for you."

"I don't think there's any way to make that easier."

We sat side by side in the darkness on a piece of cardboard I'd dragged over. My back rested against a crate. I'd stacked more around me, like a play fort. A small, dark, cold fortress.

"Why'd they kill me?" Liz asked.

I told her about the experiment and the genetic manipulation and what the file said about terminating us if we couldn't be rehabilitated.

"But I *could* have been rehabilitated," she said. "If they'd just *told* me what was going on, I wouldn't have been freaking out about poltergeists. I would have taken lessons, pills, whatever they wanted."

"I know."

"So why? *Why?*"

The only answer I had was that we didn't matter to them. We were subjects in an experiment. They'd try rehabilitation because we weren't animals, but Lyle House had been only a token effort, to prove to themselves that they'd made some attempt to save us.

They said they killed us because we were dangerous. I didn't believe that. I wasn't dangerous. Brady wasn't dangerous. Maybe Liz and Derek, but they weren't monsters. Derek had been willing to stay at Lyle House just so he wouldn't hurt anyone else.

They played God and they failed, and I think what they were really scared of wasn't that we'd hurt people but that other supernaturals would find out what they'd done. So they killed their failures, leaving only the successes.

That's what I thought. "I don't know" was what I said, and we sat quietly for a while longer.

Next time, I was the one to break the silence. "Thank you. For everything. Without you, Tori and I would never have gotten away. I want to help you in return—help you cross over."

"Cross over?"

"To the other side. Wherever ghosts are supposed to go. The afterlife."

"Oh."

"I'm not sure why you haven't gone. Have you . . . seen anything? A light maybe?"

A small laugh. "I think that's only in movies, Chloe."

"But you vanish sometimes. Where do you go?"

"I'm not sure. I still see everything here, but you can't see me. It's like being on the other side of a force field, where I can see— Well, I guess they must be other ghosts, but they seem to be just passing through."

"Where do they come from?"

She shrugged. "I don't talk to them. I thought maybe they were other shaman spirits, but I . . ." Her gaze dropped. "I didn't want to ask. In case they weren't."

"Can you ask them now? Find out where you're supposed to be?"

"I'm fine."

"But—"

"Not yet. Just not yet, okay?"

"Okay."

"When you do find Simon and Derek, I'm going to take off for a while. I want to visit my nana, see how she's doing, and my brother, maybe my friends, my school. I know they can't see me. I'd just like to see them."

I nodded.

Liz wanted me to sleep. I closed my eyes to make her feel better, but there was no chance of drifting off. I was too cold, too hungry.

When she slipped out to patrol, I stretched and shifted. The chill of the concrete came right through my cardboard mat. I was crawling over to grab more layers when Liz reappeared.

"Good, you're awake."

"What's wrong? Is someone coming?"

"No, it's Tori. She's in front of the warehouse. She's just sitting there."

I found Tori crouched between the warehouse and a Dumpster, staring at the rusty bin, not even blinking.

"Tori?" I had to touch her shoulder before she looked at me. "Come inside."

She followed me without a word. I showed her the spot I'd made, and she settled in, crouching in her strange way.

"What happened?" I asked.

It took a moment for her to answer. "I called my dad. I told him everything. He said to stay where I was, and he'd come and get me."

"And you changed your mind. That's okay. We'll—"

"I went across the street to wait," she said, as if I hadn't spoken. "I was in an alley, so no one would see me before he got there. The car pulled up and I started to step out and—and I didn't. I kept telling myself I was being stupid, that I'd been around you too long, getting all paranoid, but I needed to see him first, to be sure. It was his car—my dad's. It stopped right where I said I'd be. It idled there, all the windows up, too dark to see through. Then a door opened and . . ." Her voice dropped. "It was my mom."

"She must have intercepted the call," I said. "Maybe they switched cars. Or she got to his car first, knowing you'd be looking for it. He was probably on his way, in *her* car and—"

"I snuck away and called my house again, collect. My dad answered, and I hung up."

"I'm sorry."

More silence. Then, "Not even going to say 'I told you so'?"

"Of course not."

She shook her head. "You're too nice, Chloe. And I don't mean that as a compliment. There's nice, and then there's *too* nice. Anyway, I'm back." She reached into her pocket, and pulled out something. "With food."

She handed me a Snickers bar.

"Thanks. I thought you didn't have any money."

"I don't. Five-finger discount." Her sneakers squeaked on the concrete as she shifted farther onto the cardboard mat. "I've watched my friends do it plenty of times. But I never did. Know why?" She didn't wait for an answer. "Because I was afraid of getting caught. Not by the store or the cops. I didn't care about that. All they do is give you a lecture, make you pay it back. I was afraid of my mom finding out. Afraid she'd be disappointed in me."

A crackle as she unwrapped her candy bar, then broke off a piece. "Not really an issue now, is it?" She popped the chunk into her mouth.

fifteen

ONCE MY STOMACH HAD something in it—even a candy bar—exhaustion took over. I wasn't asleep long before the dreams came—nightmares of never finding the guys, of Mrs. Enright killing Aunt Lauren, of Tori hog-tying me and leaving me for the Edison Group to find. . . .

I awoke to the sound of voices. I leaped up, breath jamming in my throat, searching the darkness for men with guns.

Beside me, Tori was snoring.

"Liz?" I whispered.

No answer. She must have been out on patrol.

After a moment, I decided I'd dreamed the voices. Then the sound came again—a *psst-psst-psst,* too faint to make out the words. I strained to hear but could only catch that papery whisper. I blinked hard. The unending darkness became a landscape of black jagged rocks—boxes and crates. Only a pale moonglow made it through the thick grime coating the windows.

I caught a whiff of something musky, animal-like. Rats? I shivered.

The sound came again. A papery rustling, like the wind through dry leaves. Maybe that's what it was.

Dry leaves in April? When the nearest tree is hundreds of feet away?

No, it sounded like a ghost. Like the scary movie version, where all you hear is a wordless whispering that creeps down your spine and tells you there's something lurking just around—

I shook myself, then stood and stretched my legs. I scuffed my sneakers against the cardboard carpet a little more than necessary, hoping Tori might stir. She didn't.

I exhaled, cheeks ballooning. I'd been doing well so far, facing my fears and taking action. This wasn't the time to bury my head and plug my ears. If my powers were abnormally strong . . .

Uncontrollable . . .

No, not uncontrollable. Dad would say that everything can be controlled if you have the willpower and the will to learn.

The whisper seemed to come from the next room. I picked my way through the maze of boxes and crates. As careful as I was, I kept knocking my knees against them, and each rap made me wince.

With every step I took, the whispering seemed to move farther away. I was clear across the warehouse before I realized the sound *was* moving away. A ghost was luring me.

I stopped short, my scalp prickling as I peered through the darkness, boxes looming in every direction. The whisper snaked around me. I whirled and crashed into a stack of crates. A sliver jabbed into my palm.

I took a deep breath, then asked, "Do you w-want to talk to me?"

The whispers stopped. I waited.

"No? Fine, then I'm going back—"

A giggle erupted behind me. I spun, smacking into the crates again, dust flying into my mouth, my nose, my eyes. As I sputtered, the giggle turned to a snicker.

I could see enough to know no living person was attached to that snicker.

I marched back the way I'd come.

The whispers followed, right at my ear now, escalating to a guttural moan that made goose bumps rise on my arms.

I remembered what the necromancer's ghost at Lyle House had said—that he'd followed me from the hospital, where he'd been dealing with ghosts pestering mental patients. I guess if you're a sadistic moron who's been stuck in limbo for years, haunting mental patients—or young necromancers—might seem like a fun way to pass the time.

The moaning turned to a weird keening, like the wailing

souls of the tormented dead.

I wheeled toward the noise. "Are you having fun? Well, guess what? If you keep it up, you're going to find out that I'm a lot more powerful than you think. I'll yank you out of there whether you want to show yourself or not."

My delivery was pitch-perfect—strong and steady—but the ghost just gave a derisive snort, then resumed keening.

I felt my way to a crate, brushed dust off the top, and sat. "One last chance or I'm pulling you through."

Two seconds of silence. Then the moaning again, right at my ear. I almost toppled off the crate. The ghost snickered. I closed my eyes and summoned, careful to keep my power on low, just in case his body was nearby. I might get some satisfaction from slamming him back into his rotting corpse, but I'd regret it later.

The moaning stopped. At a grunt of surprise, I smiled and amped it up, just a little.

The figure started to materialize—short, chubby guy old enough to be my grandfather. He twisted and writhed like he was caught in a straitjacket. I pulled harder. . . .

A dull thump nearby made me jump.

"Liz?" I called. "Tori?"

The ghost snarled. "Let me go, you little—"

Another thump drowned out the nasty name he called me—or most of it. Then came a weird skittering noise.

"Let me go or I—"

I closed my eyes and gave the ghost one big mental shove.

He gasped and sailed backward through the wall, like he'd been thrown out of a spaceship air lock. I waited to see if he'd return. He didn't. I'd cast him to the other side, wherever ghosts live. Good.

Another thump. I scrambled to my feet, the ghost forgotten. I crept past a stack of crates and listened. Silence.

"Tori?" I whispered. "Liz?"

Um, if it's not *them, maybe calling their names isn't such a bright idea.*

I eased along the crates until I reached a gap. Through it, I saw the pale rectangle of a window. The grime was smudged, like someone had haphazardly rubbed it away.

The scratching sound came again. Then the smell hit, like that musky odor in the other room, only ten times worse. The skittering came again—like tiny claws on concrete.

Rats.

As I pulled back, the window darkened. Then *thump*. I looked up too late to see what it was. Was someone throwing stuff at the window? Maybe the boys, trying to get my attention.

I hurried forward, forgetting the rats, until I saw a dark blob on the shadowy floor, moving slow, like it was dragging something. That must be what I smelled—a dead animal that the rat was taking back to the nest.

When something brushed the top of my head, I yelped, clapping my hands over my mouth. A shadow flew past and hit the window with that familiar thump. As it fell, I noticed thin, leathery wings. A bat.

The dim shape flapped its wings against the concrete, making a scratchy, rustling noise. Weren't bats supposed to fly by echolocation? It shouldn't hit a window trying to escape.

Unless it was rabid.

The bat finally launched itself again. It fluttered away, weaving and bobbing like it was still dazed. It headed for the ceiling, then turned and came straight at me.

As I stumbled back my foot slipped, and I fell with a bone-jarring crack that set my injured arm on fire. I tried to leap up, but whatever I'd stepped on was stuck to my sneaker, sending me skidding again.

The thing on my sneaker was slick and cold. I pulled it off and raised it into the moonlight. Pinched between my fingers was a rotting wing. The bat I'd seen still had both of its wings, so there must be another one in here, dead.

I threw the wing across the room and frantically wiped my hand on my jeans. The bat swooped again. I ducked, but my foot slid out and I fell. As I hit the floor, a horrible smell enveloped me, so strong I coughed. Then I saw the bat, less than a foot away, teeth bared, long fangs white against the dark.

The cloud cover shifted, the light streaming into the room, and I realized I wasn't looking at fangs but at white patches of skull. The bat was decomposing, one eye shriveled, the other a black pit. Most of the flesh was gone; only hanging bits remaining. The bat had no ears, no nose, just a bony snout. The snout opened. Rows of tiny jagged teeth flashed, and it started to shriek, a horrible garbled squeaking.

My shrieks joined it as I scrambled back. The thing pulled itself along on one crumpled wing. It was definitely a bat—and I'd raised it from the dead.

With my gaze fixed on the bat creeping toward me, I forgot about the other one until it flew at my face. I saw it coming—then saw its sunken eyes, bloody stumps of ears, and bone showing through patchy fur. Another zombie bat.

I slammed back into the crates. My hands sailed up to ward the bat off, but too late. It hit my face. I screamed then, really screamed as the rotted wings drummed me. The cold body hit my cheek. Tiny claws caught in my hair.

I tried to smack it away. It dropped. As I clapped my hands to my mouth, I felt something tugging at my shirt. I looked down to see the bat clinging to it.

Its fur wasn't patchy at all. What I'd mistaken for spots of bone were wriggling maggots.

I pressed one hand to my mouth, stifling my screams. With my free hand, I swatted at it, but it clung there, rows of teeth opening and closing, head bobbing like it was trying to see me.

"Chloe? Chloe!" Liz raced through the outside wall. She stopped short, eyes going huge. "Oh my God. Oh my God!"

"G-get it off. P-please."

I whirled, still swatting at the bat. Then I heard a sickening crunch as I stepped on the other one. When I wheeled, the one clinging to me fell off. As it hit the floor, Liz shoved the top crate off a stack and it fell on the fallen bat, the thud drowning out that horrible bone-crunching noise.

"I—I—I—"

"It's okay," she said, walking toward me. "It's dead."

"N-n-no. It's . . ."

Liz stopped. She looked down at the bat I'd stepped on. It lifted one wing feebly, then let it fall. The wing twitched, claw scratching the concrete.

Liz hurried to a crate. "I'll put it out of its misery."

"No." I held out my hand. "That won't work. It's already dead."

"No, it's not. It's—" She bent for a closer look, finally seeing the decomposing body. She stumbled back. "Oh. Oh, it's— It's—"

"Dead. I raised it from the dead."

She looked at me. And her expression . . . She tried to hide it, but I'll never forget that look—the shock, the horror, the disgust.

"You . . . ," she began. "You can . . . ?"

"It was an accident. There was a ghost pestering me. I—I was summoning him and I must have a-accidentally raised them."

The bat's wing fluttered again. I dropped beside it. I tried not to look, but of course I couldn't help seeing the tiny body crushed on the concrete, bones sticking out. And still it moved, struggling to get up, claws scraping the concrete, smashed head rising—

I closed my eyes and concentrated on freeing its spirit. After a few minutes, the scratching stopped. I opened my eyes. The bat lay still.

"So what was it? A zombie?" Liz tried to sound calm, but her voice cracked.

"Something like that."

"You . . . You can resurrect the dead?"

I stared at the crushed bat. "I wouldn't call it resurrection."

"What about people? Can you . . . ?" She swallowed. "Do that?"

I nodded.

"So that's what Tori's mom meant. You raised zombies at Lyle House."

"Accidentally."

Uncontrollable powers . . .

Liz continued. "So it's . . . like in the movies? They're just empty, re-re— What's the word?"

"Reanimated." I wasn't about to tell her the truth, that necromancers didn't reanimate a soulless body. We took a ghost like Liz and shoved her back into her rotting corpse.

I remembered what the demi-demon said, about me nearly returning the souls of a thousand dead to their buried shells. I hadn't believed her. Now . . .

Bile filled my mouth. I turned away, gagging and spitting it out.

"It's okay," Liz said, coming up beside me. "It's not your fault."

I looked at the box she'd shoved onto the other bat, took a deep breath, and walked to it. When I reached to move it, she said, "It's dead. It must be—" She stopped and said in a small, shaky voice. "Isn't it?"

"I need to be sure."

I lifted the box.

sixteen

HE BAT WASN'T DEAD. It was— I don't want to remember it. By that point, I'd been so stressed out that I couldn't concentrate, and freeing the bat's spirit had taken . . . a while. But I did it. And I was glad I'd checked. Now I could relax . . . or so I thought.

"You should sleep," Liz said after I'd lain there with my eyes open for almost an hour.

I glanced at Tori, but she was still snoring—hadn't even stirred since I'd come back.

"I'm not tired," I said.

"You need to rest. I can help. I always helped my nana sleep when she couldn't."

Liz never talked about her parents, only her grandmother, and I realized how little I knew about her.

"You lived with your nana?"

She nodded. "My mom's mom. I didn't know my dad. Nana said he didn't stick around."

Considering he'd been a demon, I supposed that was how it worked.

Liz was silent a moment, then said quietly, "I think she was raped."

"Your mom?"

"I heard stuff. Stuff I wasn't supposed to hear, Nana talking to her sisters, her friends, and later to social workers. She said Mom was wild when she was young. Not *really* wild, just smoking and drinking beer and skipping classes. Then she got pregnant, and that made her different. She got older. Pissed off. Things I heard—I think she was raped."

"That's awful."

She pulled her knees up and hugged them. "I never told anyone that. It's not the kind of thing you share. Kids might look at you funny, you know?"

"I'd never—"

"I know. That's why I told you. Anyway, for a few years, everything was okay. We lived with Nana, and she looked after me while Mom worked. But then Mom had this accident."

My gut chilled as I thought of my own mother, killed in a hit-and-run. "What kind of accident?"

"The cops said she was at this party, got drunk, and fell down the stairs. She hit her head really hard and when she got out of the hospital, it was like she was a whole different person. She couldn't work, so Nana did and Mom stayed home with me, but sometimes she'd forget to feed me lunch or she'd get really mad and hit me and say it was all my fault. Blaming me because she wasn't happy, I guess."

"I'm sure she didn't—"

"Mean it. I know. Afterward she'd cry and tell me she was sorry and buy me candy. Then she had my little brother, and she started getting into drugs and getting arrested for stealing stuff. Only she never went to jail. The court always sent her to a mental hospital. That's why, at Lyle House, I was so scared—"

"Of being sent to one. I should have helped. I—"

"You tried. It wouldn't have mattered. They'd already made up their minds." She went quiet for a moment. "Mom tried to warn me. Sometimes she'd show up at my school, high on dope, going on about experiments and magic powers, and saying I had to hide before they found me." Another pause. "I guess she wasn't so crazy after all, huh?"

"No, she wasn't. She was trying to protect you."

She nodded. "Okay, enough of that. You need to rest up so you can find the guys. Nana always said I was good at helping people fall asleep. Better than any pills. You know why?"

"Why?"

She grinned. "'Cause I can talk your ear off. Now, let's see, what can I talk about that'll bore you to sleep? Oh, I know. Guys. Hot guys. I have this list, see? The ten hottest

125 ◆

guys ever. Actually, it's two lists, ten each, 'cause I needed one for real guys—guys I actually know—and one make-believe list, for guys in movies and bands. Not that they aren't real guys, because of course they're real . . ."

I finally drifted off and didn't wake until the roar of a truck sent me jerking up, limbs flailing.

Light streamed through the windows. I checked my watch. Eight thirty. No sign of Liz. Was she on patrol? Or had she left already?

Tori was still sound asleep, snoring softly.

I shook her shoulder. "It's morning. We need to search for the note."

Tori opened her eyes, muttered that there probably wasn't any note, the guys were long gone, and we were screwed. A ray of sunshine, our Victoria.

But after moaning about not having lifted breath mints or a hairbrush or breakfast she did rise and help me.

We'd been searching for about a half hour when Tori said, loud enough to be heard by anyone walking past the windows, "The taggers in this town really have too much time on their hands."

I hurried over to shush her. "Taggers?"

She waved at the surrounding stacks of crates and I saw what she meant. A crate in every stack had been tagged with graffiti. "My dad's store gets hit every month, but he never had one this fancy."

She pointed to one almost hidden in shadow. Where the others were typical tags—nicknames and symbols—this was a sketch in black marker of a teenage guy with a paw print tattoo on his cheek, brandishing Wolverine-like claws.

I grinned. "Simon." When Tori gave me a *huh?* look, I said, "It's Simon."

"Uh, no. It's a guy with a paw on his face."

"It's Simon's *work*. This is one of his comic-book characters."

"I knew that."

"Help me lift the crate."

She didn't move. "Why?"

"Because the note"—I heaved the top crate off by myself—"will be under it."

"Why would he put—?"

Sure enough, under the crate was a folded piece of paper. We both grabbed for it. I won.

Simon had drawn three pictures. In the top left corner, like a salutation, was a ghost. The middle had a big sketch of Arnold Schwarzenegger as the *Terminator*. The third in place of a signature, was a lightning bolt surrounded by fog. Beside the drawing, someone had scrawled in inch-high letters *10 A.M.*

Tori snatched it from me and turned it over. "So where's the message?"

"Right there." I pointed from picture to picture. "It says: Chloe, I'll be back, Simon."

"Okay, that's just weird. And what's that mean?" She pointed to the time.

"That would be Derek, making sure I know *when* they'll be back."

"Only once a day?"

"Every time they sneak in here, it's a big risk. Anyway, the time isn't really important. If I pick up the message, Derek will smell me. He can follow my trail."

Her nose wrinkled. "Like a dog?"

"Cool, huh?"

"Uh, no." She made a face. "So they weren't kidding about him being a werewolf. Explains a lot, don't you think?"

I shrugged and checked my watch. "We've got just over an hour to wait, so—" I swore under my breath, making Tori arch her brows in mock-surprise.

"We can't let the guys come back," I said, "not with that Edison Group guard patrolling."

There wasn't an Edison Group guard patrolling. There were two. I sent Liz to check all possible entry points. She returned, naming four: the main gate, the front delivery gate, the back delivery gate, and the entire surrounding fence.

I doubted Derek would climb the fence again. He'd be exposed up there where anyone could see him. If I were him, I'd pick the same entry point as the Edison Group had yesterday—that rear gate.

But I also knew Derek well enough to admit that I *didn't* know him well enough to guess his strategy with any real confidence. So we had to split up and cover all three entrances. I needed to stay close to Liz, so she could communicate with me. That meant Tori got the back. I could only pray she'd actually remember to watch.

By nine thirty we were in position. The factory yard was at the edge of a residential area—a neighborhood of older homes including, a block away, Lyle House. Derek and I had come this way Saturday night when we escaped and I still remembered the general layout. The roads ran north-south, with the factory yard down at the southern end.

My spot was across the street from the factory, behind one of the end houses. No one was home—the driveway was empty and the windows dark.

I crouched behind a shed watching the front delivery gate, ready to whistle at the first sign of the guys. At 9:45 an SUV passed in front of the factory, moving at a crawl: it was the same Edison Group vehicle Derek and I had run from on Saturday night.

As it rolled past, I saw Mike in the driver's seat. Beside him sat Tori's mom, watching out the side window. The SUV continued to the corner, then made a right, heading for the back of the factory yard.

I waited until it was out of sight, then leaped up. As I moved, a shadow loomed over me. My fists flew up, but before I could turn, hands grabbed me, one clamping over my mouth, the other around my waist, yanking me back behind the shed.

"It's me," a deep voice rumbled.

The hands released me and I turned. There stood Derek, all six foot something of him. Maybe it was just the thrill of seeing him, but he looked better than I remembered. His black hair was still lank, and his face was still dotted with acne. But he looked . . . better.

"I am so glad to see you," I said, grinning up at him.

His snort said the feeling wasn't necessarily mutual. Maybe I should have been a little disappointed, but I was too relieved to care. At this moment, Derek's trademark scowl was better than any smile.

"I am so glad—"

"Got that," he said. "Stop bouncing, Chloe, before they notice you."

"They're gone. That's why—" I looked behind him and my grin faded. "Where's Simon? H-he's okay, isn't he?" I fumbled to pull out the insulin pouch. "I know he needs this. It was—"

"That's his backup. He had another one in his pocket."

"Oh. Right. Um, good. So where—?"

"Around back. I smelled Tori so I thought it was a trap and—"

"Tori! Her mom— The car— We have to warn her."

"What?"

I wheeled, motioning for him to follow. I crossed the yard, darting from hiding place to hiding place as I headed for the road the SUV had taken. Derek tried to keep up, his harsh whispers of "Chloe, get back here!" mingled with harsher curses when I slid into spots he couldn't fit.

Finally, as I dashed along a row of hedges, he caught me by the jacket collar and swung me off my feet, letting me dangle there like a puppy.

"I know a better route. I've been here for two days, checking things out as I waited for you." He plunked me down but kept his grip on my collar so I couldn't take off. "Now what's this about Tori and her mom?"

"No time. Just— Liz. We need Liz."

"Liz is alive?"

I hesitated, reminding myself how much he'd missed. "No. I mean . . . her ghost. I was right about her being dead. She's been helping me, though, and we need her to scout the way."

I broke from his grip and dashed to a break in the hedge. I slid sideways into it and peeked out. Liz stood in the middle of the road two blocks down. I gave a whistle that I thought was just fine, but Derek sighed, put his fingers in his mouth, and whistled loud enough to make my ears ring. I couldn't tell whether it got Liz's attention—he made me duck while he listened, in case it got anyone else's attention. After a moment, he let me peek around the hedge.

"She's coming," I said.

Derek nodded. He scanned the yards around us, making sure all was clear.

"You wanted to lead," I said. "So lead. She'll catch up."

He didn't move. When I tried to walk away, he caught my sleeve.

"I gotta know what I'm walking into."

"Two Edison Group guards discreetly patrolling the yard—"

"Edison Group?"

"And Tori's mom, plus the guy who shot at you Saturday night. But of all of them, Tori's mom is the one to watch."

"Tori's mom? Edison Group? What's—?"

"Derek?"

"What?"

I looked up, meeting his gaze. "Do you trust me?"

I honestly had no idea what the answer would be, but he didn't hesitate, just grunted, "Course."

"Then, yes, I know you want details. But we don't have time. Not if Simon's back there and Tori's mom's on her way. She's a witch, and she's not afraid to use her spells. Good enough?"

He looked off across the yard. Maybe he did trust me, but for Derek, not having all the facts was like sticking a blindfold on him and telling him to follow.

"Stay behind me," he said, and we took off.

seventeen

LIZ SCOUTED THE WAY, running ahead and whistling us onward. Derek's mouth stayed set in that way that let me know he wasn't happy . . . which was pretty much his normal expression, so I ignored it.

The SUV had gone down a service road beside the factory. Along it were smaller industrial buildings, with more at the back, which is where we'd entered with the Edison Group yesterday and where Tori now waited. It was also where the SUV had headed.

We were still in the residential blocks to the north of the factory yard, now standing behind a minivan at the neighborhood's edge. As we peered around it, we could see the SUV parked behind another vehicle. Tori's mom, Mike, and the balding driver stood beside it, talking.

"Where's Simon?" I whispered.

133 ◆

"On the other side of them. Tori?"

"I left her over there—" I pointed. "She went around back to watch the rear entrance. Hopefully, she's lying low and staying put."

"If it was you, yeah. Tori?" A derisive snort. I'd have basked more in the compliment if I didn't know Derek considered Tori only slightly smarter than plankton.

"We can slip across this road and cut through the next yard," I said. "Then we can circle—"

Derek caught my arm again as I started to move—at this rate, it was soon going to be as sore as my injured one.

"Dog," he said, jerking his chin toward the fenced yard. "It was inside earlier."

Expecting to see a Doberman slavering at the fence, I followed his gaze to a little puff of white fur, the kind of dog women stick in their purses. It wasn't even barking, just staring at us, dancing in place.

"Oh, my God! It's a killer Pomeranian." I glanced up at Derek. "It's a tough call, but I think you can take him."

A glare. "That's not—"

The wind changed and the dog went rigid. Derek swore, and pulled me backward. The dog gave one low, piercing whine. Then it went nuts, jumping and twisting and barking, a whirlwind of white fur battering itself against the fence.

Derek yanked me behind the minivan. We were out of the dog's sight, but it continued yelping and snarling, the wire fence twanging with each hit.

"It smelled me," Derek said. "The werewolf thing."

"Do they always do that?"

He shook his head. "I used to just make them nervous. They'd steer clear, maybe bark a bit. Now?" He waved toward the racket. "I get this. We need to shut it up."

"I'll— Wait. Liz!"

She was already running over.

"Could you distract that dog?" I asked her. "I think he wants to play fetch."

Her brow furrowed. Then she smiled. "Right. I can do that."

"Play *fetch*?" Derek whispered as she took off. "What—?"

I motioned him to the end of the van and pointed. There, on the other side of the fence, a stick levitated, then shook. Liz was holding it, but Derek could see only the stick. The dog watched it fly, then spun back to the fence, barking and jumping again. Liz retrieved the stick, and tapped it on the dog's back. Once she had his attention, she threw it. This time, he chased.

I looked up at Derek, who was staring at the dog.

"Remember Liz thought she had a poltergeist? Turned out she is the poltergeist. She's a half-demon with the power of telekinesis."

"Huh." He turned to stare again, slowly shaking his head, as if wondering why *he* hadn't figured that out. Probably because he didn't know half-demons could be telekinetic, but for Derek, that wouldn't be an excuse.

"Coast is clear!" Liz shouted. "And this pooch is getting bored!"

Derek and I got across the street. We headed for the service road on the other side, leading through the industrial buildings bordering the factory. Then Derek stopped.

"Tori," he said.

I peered past him. "Where? I don't see . . ." I noticed his face lifted to the breeze. "Not see, smell, right?"

He nodded and led me to where she was huddled behind a wall, peeking around the other side.

"It's us," I whispered.

She saw Derek and without so much as a hello, leaned to look behind him. "Where's Simon?"

"He's—"

"Is he okay? Why isn't he here?" She glared up at Derek. "Where'd you leave him?"

"Passed out in an alley." Derek frowned in thought. "Not sure where, though . . ."

"He's kidding," I said as Tori sputtered.

"We need to get moving." Derek hooked a thumb at Tori while looking at me. "She's your responsibility."

"Excuse me?" Tori said.

Derek didn't even glance her way. "Make sure she keeps up. And shuts up."

* * *

As we headed out, Liz returned to say the Edison Group was in the factory yard, having slipped in the rear way again. We found the spot where Derek had left Simon, behind a building with faded For Sale signs on the boarded-up windows.

"Well, where is he?" Tori demanded.

"Huh. Must have broken his chain."

"He means Simon's a big boy and he's free to move around." I turned to Derek. "Can you track him?"

"Yeah."

He dropped to a crouch. It was a long way from stooping to sniff the ground, but Tori still stared.

"Please tell me he isn't doing what I think he's doing," she said.

Derek scowled—not at Tori but at me. "There'd better be a good explanation for this," he said with a pointed look her way.

"Not really," I murmured.

He took a deep breath and pushed to his feet. "Stay here."

Tori waited until he was gone, then shuddered. "Okay, Derek always weirded me out, but that wolf man stuff is seriously creepy. Suits him, I suppose. A creepy power for a creepy guy."

"I thought he looked better."

She stared at me.

"What? He does. Probably because he's starting his wolf changes and he's not stressed out about being in Lyle House. That must help."

"You know what would really help? Shampoo. Deodorant—"

I raised my hand to cut her off. "He smelled fine, so don't start that. I'm sure he's wearing deodorant and—for once—it's working. As for showers, they're a little hard to come by on the street, and we won't look much better soon."

"I'm just saying—"

"Do you think he doesn't *know* what you're saying? News flash—he's not stupid."

Derek was all too aware of the impression he made. At Lyle House, he'd showered twice a day, and it still hadn't fixed the puberty smackdown.

She went back to watching for Simon. I stayed where I was, ten feet away, better hidden, while keeping an eye on her *and* on that corner, waiting for—

A soft poke at my shoulder blade startled me.

"Still jumpy, I see."

I spun to see Simon, Derek hanging back behind him.

Simon grinned, the sight as familiar as Derek's scowl. "Got my note, I hear," he said.

I pulled it out and waved it.

He plucked it from my fingers and tucked it into my

jacket pocket. Then he caught my hand, his thumb rubbing my knuckles, and the back of my throat ached with the relief of seeing him, finally actually seeing *both* of them after all the worry and the nightmares . . .

If I'd had the courage, I would have hugged him. Instead, I just said, "I'm really glad you found us," my voice cracking.

Simon squeezed my hand. His lips lowering to my ear, whispering, "I—"

He went rigid, head lifting.

"Hey, Simon," Tori said behind me.

"What is she doing here?"

Derek jabbed his thumb at me. "Ask her. I'm not getting any answers."

"It's a long story," I said.

"Then it'll have to wait," Derek said. "We need to get away from here."

Simon whispered to me, "But is everything okay?"

"No," Tori said. "I kidnapped her and forced her to escape with me. I've been using her as a human shield against those guys with guns, and I was just about to strangle her and leave her body here to throw them off my trail. But then you showed up and foiled my evil plans. Lucky for you, though. You get to rescue poor little Chloe again and win her undying gratitude."

"Undying gratitude?" Simon looked at me. "Cool. Does

that come with eternal servitude? If so, I like my eggs sunnyside up."

I smiled. "I'll remember that."

"Enough yapping," Derek said. "Move out."

eighteen

IN THE MOVIE VERSION of our flight, we'd have run straight into a trap. Everyone would have been taken captive . . . except me, being the heroine. I'd be smart enough to avoid capture, so I could plot a daring rescue to free my friends. But it wouldn't be easy. Or quiet. Tori and Simon would blow up a city block with magic. Derek would throw a few trucks at our pursuers. I would recruit a platoon of zombies from a conveniently located cemetery.

But as cool as all that would have looked on the big screen, I was really more in the mood for a quiet getaway. And that's exactly what we got. The Edison Group never left the factory yard.

We walked at least three miles. When we were far enough from the factory to stop skulking, Derek led us into the commercial section on the other side of the neighborhood, where four teens wouldn't look so out of place on a school day.

"I know you guys love this cloak-and-dagger stuff," Tori said finally, "but can't we just grab a taxi?"

Derek shook his head.

I cleared my throat. "A cab would be risky, but if there's a shorter route to where we're going, my feet would really appreciate it."

Derek stopped short. I smacked into his back—not for the first time, since he insisted on walking in front of me. I'd been tripping on his heels and mumbling apologies the whole way. When I'd slow down to let him get farther ahead, he'd snap at me to keep up.

"We're almost there," Simon said.

He was beside me—sticking to the curbside, walking as close as Derek. While normally I wouldn't complain about Simon being so close, I had the weird sensation of being blocked in.

As we started forward again, I tried dropping back with Tori, who lagged behind, but Simon put his fingers on my elbow and steered me back into place.

"Okay," I said. "Something's up. What's with the walking blockade?"

"They're protecting you," Tori said. "Shielding you from the big bad world."

Neither of the guys said a word. Whatever it was, they weren't telling me. Not yet.

* * *

Our destination was some kind of unused industrial building in a neighborhood so rundown that even the gangbangers and the homeless seemed to steer clear.

Just as we were about to go inside, Liz called to me. She stood by the missing front door like she couldn't cross the threshold. I asked whether there was magic keeping her out, but she said no, she just needed to talk to me. So I waved Derek and Simon on, telling them I had to speak to Liz.

She'd been quiet since I'd met up with the others, staying out of sight. Now she crouched on the dirt patch beside the building to tug up one purple and orange sock.

"You know, I really loved these socks, but another day of having to look at them, and I'm going barefoot for eternity." She tried to smile, but after a moment's struggle, gave up and straightened. "I'm taking off now. You don't need me anymore."

"No, I—I mean, if you want to, sure, but—"

"That came out wrong. I just . . ." She lifted her foot, adjusting the sock again. "I should go. But I'll be back."

"I don't have your shirt. We'll need to set up a rendezvous point or something."

She laughed, almost genuine now. "No more rendezvous points. I'll find you. I always do. It just . . . might be a while. I've got stuff to do. And you . . ." She looked toward the building, and the wistfulness in her eyes stabbed through me. "You've got stuff to do. You and the others."

"Liz, I—"

"It's okay. You do your thing, and I'll catch up."

"I'll miss you."

She reached out, and I swore I felt her fingers brush mine. "You're sweet, Chloe. Don't worry about me. I'll be back." Then she disappeared.

The others were waiting just inside the door. We picked our way through the debris, walking single file in the near dark behind Derek.

As we moved, the hairs on my neck rose, and a dull throbbing started in the back of my skull. I slowed. Now it was Tori's turn to smack into me.

"Come on, *move*," she said. "Oh, that's right. Chloe's afraid of the dark. Simon, you'd better hold her hand or—"

"Knock it off." Simon pushed past Tori and came up beside me. "You okay?"

"There's . . . something here. I can feel it."

"Ghosts?"

"I don't think so. It's like what I felt in the crawl space at Lyle House."

Derek swore.

I turned to peer at him in the darkness. "What?"

"There's a body."

"*What?*" Simon said, with Tori echoing, shriller.

"There's a dead body somewhere in here. I smelled it yesterday, after we'd settled in."

"And you didn't bother telling me?" Simon said.

"It's a body. Long dead. Some homeless guy. It's a good place otherwise."

"*Otherwise?* A pitch-black hideaway filled with trash, dead bodies, and rats. You know how to pick 'em, bro."

"R-rats?" I said, thinking of the bats.

"Great," Tori muttered. "She's scared of rats, too."

"As long as I'm here, they're staying away," Derek said.

It wasn't the *live* rats I was worried about.

He continued. "But I didn't think about the body. Chloe? Is it a problem?"

It was. I should say something about the bats, how I'd accidentally raised them while dealing with that ghost. But I looked at everyone, how tired they seemed, all impatiently waiting to find a place to rest and talk, find out what I knew. I could handle this. As long as I didn't try summoning Liz, I wouldn't raise this body.

So that's what I said.

"But it bothers you being near it," Simon said. "We should—"

"I'm sure safe places aren't easy to find." I forced a smile. "It'll be good experience. I need to learn to recognize the feeling."

"Oh, of course," Tori said. "Chloe's going to *learn* from it. Do you ever quit? You're like a perky little Energizer bunny—"

Simon turned to snap something at her, but Derek waved us on. We reached a room in the middle, with no windows.

Derek turned on a lantern. It cast enough wavering light to see by. Earlier, the guys had set up crates to sit on, and laid newspaper over the filthy floor. Two new backpacks were hidden behind the crates alongside a neat stack of cheap blankets. Not exactly the Hilton—or even Lyle House—but a lot better than where we'd slept last night.

As we sat, Derek pulled a handful of energy bars from his pocket, and gave one to me.

"Oh, right. You must be starving." Simon reached into his pockets. "I can offer one bruised apple and one brown banana. Convenience stores aren't the place to buy fruit, as I keep telling someone."

"Better than these. For you, anyway, Simon." Derek passed a bar to Tori.

"Because you aren't supposed to have those, are you?" I said. "Which reminds me . . ." I took out the insulin. "Derek said it's your backup."

"So my dark secret is out."

"I didn't know it was a secret."

"Not really. Just not something I advertise."

In other words, if kids knew he had a chronic illness, they might treat him differently. He had it under control, so there was no reason for anyone to know about it.

"Backup?" Tori said. "You mean he didn't need that?"

"Apparently not," I murmured.

Simon looked from her to me, confused, then understanding. "You guys thought . . ."

"That if you didn't get your medicine in the next twenty-four hours, you'd be dead?" I said. "Not exactly, but close. You know, the old 'upping the ante with a fatal disease that needs medication' twist. Apparently, it still works."

"Kind of a letdown, then, huh?"

"No kidding. Here we were, expecting to find you minutes from death. Look at you, not even gasping."

"All right, then. Emergency medical situation, take two."

He leaped to his feet, staggered, keeled over, then lifted his head weakly.

"Chloe? Is that you?" He coughed. "Do you have my insulin?"

I placed it in his outstretched hand.

"You saved my life," he said. "How can I ever repay you?"

"Undying servitude sounds good. I like my eggs scrambled."

He held up a piece of fruit. "Would you settle for a bruised apple?"

I laughed.

"You guys are weird," Tori said.

Simon sat on the crate beside me. "That's right. We are totally weird and completely uncool. Your popularity is plummeting just by being near us. So why don't you—"

"Chloe?" Derek interrupted. "How's your arm?"

"Her—?" Simon swore under his breath. "Way to keep showing me up. First, food. Now her arm." He turned to me. "How is it?"

"Fine. All stitched and bandaged."

"We should take a look," Derek said.

Simon helped me pull off the jacket.

"Is that all you're wearing?" Derek said. "Where's your sweater?"

"They didn't give us a chance to grab anything. I have money. I'll buy one."

"Two," Simon said. "It's freezing after the sun goes down. You must have been a Popsicle last night."

I shrugged. "I had other things on my mind."

"Her aunt and Rae," Tori said.

"W-we'll get to that," I said, as Simon looked at me. "There's a lot to catch up on. You guys start."

nineteen

"BACK TO THE BEGINNING, then," Derek said, settling onto his crate. "The last time we saw you, you were running for the warehouse with Rae. Our distraction worked and we got away, but we couldn't go back for a while, in case they were watching. When we got there, you guys were gone."

"Rae convinced me to leave." She'd said that when she was alone with Simon, Simon hadn't mentioned me at all—only worried about his brother. I knew now that wasn't true—she'd known it would make me feel bad, maybe bad enough to leave with her, and now I was embarrassed that it had worked. "She . . . said stuff. She got me to leave to get my arm checked by Aunt Lauren, and then . . ."

I took them through the last two days, step by step, revelation by revelation. When I finally finished, they all sat there, silent, even Tori.

"So Brady and Liz are dead," Simon said slowly. "And, I guess, that other girl—the one who was shipped out earlier."

"Amber," Tori said. "Her name was Amber."

I nodded. "She was on the list. All three of them."

Another moment of silence.

"Rae and Aunt Lauren are still there," I said finally. "I know Rae betrayed us, and my aunt was one of them, but I-I need to get them out. I don't expect any help with that—"

"No, you're right," Simon said. "Rae screwed up, but she sure doesn't deserve to die for it."

"I know we can't rescue them alone." I snuck a look at Derek. When he nodded, I felt a pinch of disappointment, like I'd been hoping he'd say that we could handle it. He was right, of course. We couldn't.

"Once we find your dad, I want to go back," I said. "I guess now we know why he took you guys and ran."

"Because he decided genetically engineering his son hadn't been such a bright idea after all?" There was a bitterness in Simon's voice that surprised me. All this time, I hadn't thought of that—I'd been too focused on Simon's father as "the good guy." But he'd put his son in the experiment, like all the other parents.

"They tried to do the right thing," I said, remembering my aunt's letter. "They thought it would make our lives easier. The Edison Group sold them this dream, and when it started to go wrong, your dad got out. Aunt Lauren tried, too."

I touched the letter in my pocket. "Just too late."

"And then there are those of us whose parents never regretted it," Tori said. "Whose mothers have turned out to be total evil bitches. But, hey, at least now no one can say I don't come by it honestly." She ripped the last bit of wrapper from her energy bar. "I don't buy this crap about us being failures, though. They wanted stronger supernaturals. That's what we are. They just need to teach us how to control it."

"You go back and tell them that," Simon said.

"What about you?" Tori waved at Simon. "Your powers work fine. You didn't even get counseling at Lyle House."

"Simon isn't on the list. They consider him a success."

"Whatever that means." Simon shifted on his crate. "The experiment's so-called successes seem to have weaker powers, but maybe they just haven't kicked in yet. When they do, we could have the same problems."

Tori nodded. "Ticking time bombs."

Exactly what the demi-demon had said . . .

I hadn't mentioned the demi-demon. An unnecessary complication and a chance for Derek to tell me I'd been stupid even to listen to her. As for what she said, about going back, freeing her? Not something I wanted to consider right now. If we did go back, we'd have Simon's dad and he'd find a way to stop the Edison Group *without* freeing any demons.

"My dad will fill in the blanks," Simon said.

"Great," Tori said. "We can save Chloe's aunt and Rae and get all our questions answered . . . just as soon as you find your missing dad. How's that going?" She looked at our surroundings. "Not so well, I see."

Anger flared in Simon's eyes, but he blinked it away. "We're working on it."

"How?"

"Later," Derek said. "Right now, we need to get Chloe warmer clothes—"

"Chloe, Chloe, Chloe. Stop worrying about poor little Chloe. She hasn't frozen yet. What about your dad? Any clues? Hints?"

"Not yet," Simon said.

"So what have you been doing for the last two days?"

His anger flared, and this time he let it, turning on her so fast she shrank back. "We've spent every waking minute of them on three things: surviving, finding Chloe, and finding our dad. What have *you* been doing?"

"I was locked up."

"So? That didn't stop Chloe. What do you have to add, Tori? Did you find out *anything*? Or just piggyback on her escape?"

"Tori helped me," I said. "Without her—"

She whipped around to face me. "Don't you defend me, Chloe Saunders."

Silence. Then Derek said, "Where can we take you, Tori? To a grandparent? Friend? You're out now and you're safe, so I'm sure there's someplace you'd rather be."

"No."

I opened my mouth to tell them what had happened with her dad, but her glare shut me up.

"She doesn't have any place to go," I said. "Like me."

"There must be someone," Derek said, "maybe not in Buffalo, but we'll buy you a bus ticket."

"Preferably on one leaving in the next hour?" she said. "I'm not going anywhere. I'm joining your little gang of baby heroes on the quest to find Superdad."

Simon and Derek exchanged a look.

"No," Derek said.

"No? Excuse me, it was *Rae* who betrayed you guys. Not me. I helped Chloe."

"And was it Rae who tormented her at Lyle House?"

"Tormented?" A derisive snort. "I didn't—"

"You did everything you could to get Chloe kicked out," Simon said. "And when that didn't work, you tried to kill her."

"Kill her?" Tori's mouth hardened. "I'm not my mother. Don't you dare accuse—"

"You lured her into the crawl space," Derek said. "Hit her over the head with a brick, bound and gagged her, and locked her in. Did you even check to make sure she was okay? That you hadn't cracked her skull?"

Tori sputtered a protest, but from the horror in her eyes, I knew the possibility hadn't occurred to her.

"Derek," I said, "I don't think—"

"No, *she* didn't think. She could have killed you with the

brick, suffocated you with the gag, given you a heart attack from fright, not to mention what would have happened if you hadn't gotten out of your bindings. It only takes a couple of days to die from dehydration."

"I would *never* have left Chloe to die. You can't accuse me of that."

"No," Derek said. "Just of wanting her locked up in a mental hospital. And why? Because you didn't like her. Because she talked to a guy you *did* like. Maybe you're not your mother, Tori. But what you *are* . . ." He fixed her with an icy look. "I don't want it around."

The expression on her face . . . I felt for her, whether she'd welcome my sympathy or not.

"We don't trust you," Simon said, his tone softer than his brother's. "We can't have someone along that we don't trust."

"What if I'm okay with it," I cut in. "If I feel safe with her . . ."

"You don't," Derek said. "You won't kick her to the curb, though, because it's not the kind of person you are." He met Tori's gaze. "But it's the kind of person I am. Chloe won't force you to leave because she'd feel horrible if anything happened to you. Me? I don't care. You brought it on yourself."

Now that was too harsh. Simon squirmed, mouth opening.

I beat him to it. "Where is she going to go? She doesn't have any money. Anyone she runs to will almost certainly call her parents."

"I don't care."

"We can't do that," Simon said. "It's not right."

I knew Derek didn't lack empathy—he couldn't forget what he'd done to that kid who attacked Simon. But it was like he held some weird list of checks and balances, and if you got on the wrong side, like Tori had, he had no problem "kicking you to the curb," to face whatever fate waited.

"No," I said.

"It isn't up for negotiation. She's not coming."

"Okay." I stood and brushed off my jeans. "Come on, Tori."

When Simon rose, I thought he was going to stop me. Instead, he followed me to the door. Tori caught up, and we made it into the next room before Derek jogged out, catching my arm with a wrench that yanked me off my feet.

I winced and peeled off his fingers. "Wrong one."

He dropped my arm quickly, realizing he'd grabbed my injured one. A long minute of silence, then, "Fine." He turned to Tori. "Three conditions. One, whatever your problem is with Chloe, get over it. Go after her again, you're gone."

"Understood," Tori said.

"Two, get over Simon. He's not interested."

She flushed and snapped, "I think I've figured that out. And number three?"

"Get over yourself."

TWENTY

ONCE THAT BIT OF ugliness was over, I was—for the first time in my life—excited about going shopping. I couldn't wait to get out of this damp, dark, cold place, reminding me too much of the basements I hated. Get away from that dead body, the vibes from it keeping my nerves on edge. Get warm clothing, get real food, and a real *bathroom*, with soap and running water and a toilet. Don't ask what I'd been doing about "bodily needs" until now—the answer is really better left unsaid.

"If we get far enough from here that it's safe, I want to try using my bank card," I said. "My account is probably locked, but it's worth a shot. We can always use more money."

"We have some," Derek said.

"Okay. If you don't think it's safe for me to try."

"You aren't going out, Chloe. We are. You're staying here."

"Where you'll be safe," Tori said. "We wouldn't want you to break a nail using your card."

"Tori . . ." Derek said, turning. "You've been warned. Leave her alone."

"That slam was directed at you, wolf boy."

His voice dropped another octave, almost a growl. "Don't call me that."

"Please. Can we stop the bickering?" I stepped between them. "If I haven't proven by now that I'm careful and can look after myself—"

"You have," Simon said. "*This* is the problem." He handed me a newspaper clipping. I read the headline, then slowly lowered myself onto a crate, gaze fixed on the article.

My father was offering a half-million-dollar reward for information leading to my safe return. There was a picture of me—last year's school photo. And there was one of him, at what looked like a news conference.

The night after my breakdown at school, my father came to see me in the hospital. He'd flown back from Berlin, and he'd looked awful—exhausted and unshaven and worried. He looked even worse in the newspaper article, circles under his eyes, lines etched in his face.

I had no idea what the Edison Group had planned to tell my dad about my disappearance. They must have fed him a story, maybe said I'd been transferred and he couldn't visit me yet. They meant to cover up my disappearance, but they'd been too slow.

They were trying to cover their tracks, though. According to the nurses and my roommate, Rachelle Rogers—interviewed for the story—I'd run away.

Did my dad believe that? I guess he did. The article quoted him as saying he'd handled my situation badly—that he'd handled a lot of things with me badly—and he desperately wanted the chance to start over. When I read that, tears plopped onto the paper. I shook them off it.

"Half a million?" Tori read over my shoulder. "The Edison Group must be footing the bill, to get us back."

Simon pointed to the date. Yesterday morning, when we'd still been in their custody.

"Okay," Tori said. "They told her dad to make this big deal of her being gone so no one asks questions. He offers money he'll never have to pay, because he knows where she is."

I shook my head. "My aunt said he doesn't know anything about the Edison Group." I stared at the article, then folded it quickly. "I have to warn him."

Derek stepped into my path. "You can't do that, Chloe."

"If he's doing this"—I waved the paper—"he's putting himself in danger and he doesn't know it. I have to warn—"

"He's not in danger. If they could have beat him to the media, maybe. But now, if anything happened to him, it would only attract more attention. He's obviously not questioning their story about you running off so they'll leave him alone . . . as long as he doesn't find out the truth."

"But I have to let him know I'm okay. He's worried."

"And he's going to have to worry a little longer."

"Do we know for sure he's not in on it?" Tori said. "What did your aunt say? Did she trick your mom into the genetic modification? Or was your mom involved?"

I took out the letter and ran my fingers over it. Then I told them what it said—the parts that would matter to them.

"Anything about your dad?" Derek asked.

I hesitated, then nodded.

"What did she say?"

"That he wasn't involved, like I said."

"Which means it should be safe for Chloe to contact him, right?" Simon said.

Derek searched my face. Then said, in a low voice, "Chloe . . ."

"She said— My aunt said to stay away from him."

I guess Derek trusted me not to run to the nearest pay phone and call my dad because all three went shopping after that.

Both my aunt and Derek thought I should stay away from my dad. Derek said it would endanger him; Aunt Lauren probably figured it would endanger me.

I loved my dad. Maybe he worked too much, wasn't home enough, didn't quite know what to do with me, but he tried his best. He'd said he'd stick around while I was at Lyle House, but when a business emergency called him away, I hadn't been mad at him for leaving. He'd made arrangements to take a month off after my release instead, and that was more important to me. He thought I was safe at Lyle House, under my aunt's care.

He must think that I'd been so hurt and angry that I'd run away. Now his schizophrenic daughter was wandering the streets of Buffalo. I wanted to call him, just to say "I'm okay." But Derek and Aunt Lauren were right. If I did that, it might not be okay . . . for either of us.

To distract myself from thoughts of my father, I decided to check out the dead body. After what happened with the bats, if there was a way of honing my corpse-sense, I needed to start training now, so I'd know about nearby dead bodies *before* I accidentally slammed their ghosts back into them.

It did seem to work like radar. The closer I got, the stronger the feeling got. Which made finding the body sound easy, but it wasn't. The "feeling" was only a vague sense of unease, a prickle on the back of my neck and a dull headache; and when it seemed to increase, it was impossible to tell whether I was detecting the body, my nerves, or a draft.

I couldn't tell what kind of business had once run out of this place. Buffalo is full of abandoned buildings and houses. Drive down I-90 and you see them—crumbling buildings, boarded-up windows, empty yards. This one was no bigger than a house, with rooms like a house, though the outside didn't look like one. The inside was filled with junk—moldy cardboard boxes, pieces of wood, broken furniture, piles of garbage.

I'm sure I could have found the body without using my powers—there were only eight rooms. But I used them anyway, for practice. I finally found it in one of the back corners. From the doorway, it just looked like a pile of rags. When I got closer, I saw something white sticking out from under those rags—a hand, the flesh nearly rotted away, leaving only bone. The closer I got, the more I saw—a leg, then a skull, the corpse mostly skeletonized. Whatever smell it gave off, my human nose wasn't good enough to detect it.

The rags, I realized, were actually clothes, and not all that ragged, just crumpled around what remained of the body. The corpse wore boots, gloves, jeans, and a sweatshirt with a faded logo. A few strings of graying hair hung below the hat, and the clothes and body didn't identify it as male or female, but I instinctively thought of it as "him."

At some point last winter, this person had crawled in here to escape the cold, curled in this corner, and never gotten up. We couldn't have been the first ones to find him. Had everyone else just steered clear, like we were doing? No thought of informing the authorities, getting him out and identified and buried?

Was he on a missing person's list? Was someone waiting for him to come home? Had they offered a reward, like my dad?

Not quite as much, I was sure. A *half-million* dollars. That would bring out every crank in Buffalo. What was Dad thinking?

He wasn't thinking. He just wanted me home safe.

I blinked away tears. Great. Even examining a corpse couldn't stop me from worrying about my dad.

What about this guy? Someone had to be concerned about him. If I could contact his ghost, maybe I could relay a message. But I couldn't risk accidentally summoning him back into his corpse, like I had with the bats.

A tap on my shoulder sent me spinning.

"Sorry," Simon said. "I thought you heard me coming. I see you found our roomie. Trying to communicate?"

"Trying *not* to communicate."

"Looks like he's been here awhile." He crouched beside the corpse. "We could play CSI, figure out how long he's been dead. I don't see any bugs."

"Wrong time of year."

He winced. "Duh, right. It's still too cold in here. He definitely died a few months ago, meaning no bugs. I should have known that. Derek did a science fair experiment a couple years ago on bugs and decomposition." He caught my look. "Yeah, gross. Kind of interesting, too, but I wouldn't ask Derek about it. He was pissed. Only placed second in the city finals."

"Slacker." I backed up as he straightened. "I'm done here, though, so I'd better get farther away. Me and corpses don't mix." I considered telling him about the bats. I wanted to tell someone, talk it over, get advice, but . . . "I was just seeing whether I could use my powers to find it."

"I'm guessing the answer is yes."

I nodded and we left the room.

"We can find another place to stay," he said. "Derek's fine with that. Really."

"I'm okay. Speaking of Derek, where is he?"

"Still shopping. He sent me back to hang with you." He leaned down to my ear. "I think he just wanted to spend more time with Tori."

I laughed. "Want to take bets on who makes it back alive?"

"Derek. No contest. Last I saw, he was ordering her to go find more blankets. By now, he's probably on his way here, leaving her to find her own way and hoping she doesn't."

"How mad is he? About her being with us?"

"Mad? I'd rate it a five. Annoyed? An eleven. He'll get over it. We all have to. At least until she gets bored and remembers a long-lost aunt in Peoria."

When we got back to our spot, Simon set out a spread of the best a convenience store had to offer—juice, milk, yogurt, apples, wheat crackers, and cheese slices.

"All the food groups . . . except one." He handed me a candy bar. "Dessert."

"Thanks."

"Now, if you'll excuse me a moment, I'll spare you the

sight of blood and needles before dining."

"It's okay. That stuff doesn't bother me."

He still turned around, to test his blood, then give himself a shot.

"And I thought annual flu shots were bad," I said. "Do you have to do that every day?"

"Three times for the needle. More for the testing."

"Three needles?"

He put the pouch away. "I'm used to it. I was diagnosed when I was three, so I don't ever remember not getting them."

"And you'll always have to do that?"

"There's a pump I can use. Stick it on my leg and it monitors my blood sugar and injects insulin. I got one when I turned thirteen. But . . ." He shrugged. "I had a deal with my dad, that I could only have one if I didn't use it as a license to eat whatever I wanted. Too much insulin isn't good. I screwed up."

"Too many of these?" I waved the candy bar.

"Nah. Too many carbs in general. I'd go out for pizza with the team, and I wouldn't want to have only two slices if everyone else was scarfing down six. You get razzed about being on a diet, being such a girl . . ."

"Now there's an insult."

"Hey, I was thirteen. I know it was stupid, but when you're always the new kid, you just want to fit in. I guess you know what that's like. You've probably been in as many schools as we have."

"Ten . . . no, eleven."

"It's a tie. Cool." He took a bite of his apple. "Now that I'm approaching the very mature age of sixteen, though, I've gotten over that. Dad and I were negotiating for me to get the pump back again when he disappeared."

"Simon?" Tori's voice echoed through the building.

"So much for peace and quiet," he muttered, then called, "We're back here."

TWENTY-ONE

DEREK RETURNED BEARING SHOPPING bags and cash. I'd given him my bank card and PIN, and he'd found an ATM without a camera. My card still worked. He'd withdrawn my limit of four hundred dollars. We couldn't do this again—every time I used it, the bank would know I was still in Buffalo, and Derek was afraid the Edison Group might be able to find that out.

He handed me the cash and receipt, discreetly folded. Tori snatched the receipt and opened it.

"My God, is this your bank account or college fund?"

I took it back. "My dad direct-deposits my allowance. After fifteen years, it adds up."

"And he just lets you access it?"

"Why wouldn't he?"

"Um, because you could spend it. No, wait. Let me guess.

You're too responsible for that."

"She's smart," Simon said.

"Is that what you call it? I was thinking more . . ." She yawned.

My cheeks heated.

"Enough," Derek growled.

"Yeah, don't forget who gave you money for this." Simon nudged Tori's shopping bag.

Tori's jaw twitched. "It was twenty bucks for food and a blanket, and I'm keeping tabs. I'll pay her back. I'm responsible, too. Just not"—she waved at my receipt—"disgustingly responsible."

I took my bag from Derek. "So what did I get?" I reached inside. "A backpack. Two sweaters. Thank—"

The sweaters unrolled, and Tori choked on her mouthful of soda, laughing.

I turned, slowly and calmly, to her. "Your choices?"

She lifted her hands. "Uh-uh. I offered to pick something out, but Derek insisted." She turned to him. "No wonder you were gone so long. Must have had a hard time finding ones that ugly."

He'd bought me two identical gray hooded sweatshirts, made from the tacky polyester found only in the cheapest discount stores, the kind that shimmers like plastic and picks at your skin.

"What?" Derek said.

"They're fine. Thanks."

Tori reached out and caught the tag, then laughed. "I thought so. They're *boys'*. Size twelve boys."

"So? The women's cost more. I figured it wouldn't make a difference with Chloe."

Tori looked at me. Then she looked at my chest and started to laugh.

"What?" Derek said.

"Nothing," Tori sputtered. "You're just being honest, right?"

"Tori?" Simon said. "Shut up. Chloe, we'll grab something else for you tomorrow."

"No, Derek's right. These will fit. Thanks." Cheeks burning, I mumbled something about trying them on and fled the room.

When dusk began to fall, we settled in for the night. It was only eight o'clock and Tori complained bitterly. Derek told her she was free to stay awake, as long as she didn't use the lantern batteries and could still wake up at dawn. We weren't living in a world of light switches anymore. We had to use the sun when we could and sleep when we couldn't.

That was fine by me. I wasn't in the mood for a slumber party. Simon had tried cheering me up, but that only brought me down all the more. I didn't want to *need* to be cheered. I wanted to roll with the punches, bounce back smiling.

I couldn't stop thinking about Aunt Lauren. I thought of Rae, too, and my dad, but most of all I thought of Aunt

Lauren. I could tell myself Dad and Rae were safe for now. The Edison Group wouldn't bother my father as long as he knew nothing about them. And Rae was well on her way to "rehabilitation," according to that file. But with Aunt Lauren, I could find no such rationalization for the Edison Group to keep her alive. Every time I opened my eyes, I expected to see her ghost standing in front of me.

Even when I managed to force myself not to worry, the only alternative was more mundane concerns and a general feeling of disappointment.

I'd found the guys. I'd brought Simon his insulin. I'd single-handedly uncovered the secrets of the Edison Group. My reward? Having Tori take potshots at me every chance she got, trying to make me look bad in front of Simon.

If there was any point in my life when I should have been anything *but* dull and boring, it was now. I could talk to the dead. I could *raise* the dead. In the last week, I'd plotted and schemed enough to win a spot on *Survivor*.

Yet all I could picture was Tori yawning.

It was nice having Simon defend me, but it wasn't any more than he might do for a little sister. I kept thinking of that—the way he'd come to my defense, the way he'd squeeze my hand, the way he'd lean in and whisper to me—and I wanted to read more into it. But I couldn't.

And so what? With everything that was going on, was I really feeling sorry for myself because a cute guy wasn't interested in me "that way"? That made me worse than boring. It made me the silly twit Derek seemed to think I was.

Speaking of Derek . . . and I'd really rather not . . . had I forgotten what he could be like? No, I'd just forgotten what it felt like to be on the receiving end. Between him and Tori, at least I'd come out of this with a thicker skin. Or lose every ounce of self-confidence I had.

A night for tossing and turning, lost in nightmares of Aunt Lauren and my dad and Rae. I kept waking up, gasping and sweating, everyone around me sound asleep. I'd gulp cold air and calm down enough to join them only to have the nightmares return.

Finally my sleeping brain found a distraction in the same place my waking brain had: thoughts of the dead body in the other room. No objective, sympathetic examination of his situation this time, though. I dreamed of dragging that poor spirit back to his shell, screaming and cursing me.

Then the dream changed and I was back in the crawl space. The musty, awful stench of death surrounded me. I felt Derek behind me, the heat of his body radiating, as he whispered, "Chloe, come on."

Come where? I was trapped in the crawl space, with those horrors crawling toward me, cold skeletal fingers touching me, the stink of them making my stomach churn.

Derek shook me, and I tried to push him away, tell him he wasn't helping—

"Chloe!"

I jerked awake, the dream evaporating. Above me, green eyes glinted in the darkness.

"Derek? What—?"

He clamped his hand over my mouth. His lips moved to my ear. "Are you awake now? I need you to do something for me."

The urgency in his voice knocked any sleepiness from my head. I squinted at him in the darkness. Were his eyes feverish? Or was that just their usual weird glow, like a cat's in the dark?

I pulled his hand away. "Are you Changing again?"

"What? No. I'm fine. Just listen, okay? Remember the body in the other room?" He spoke slowly, carefully.

I nodded.

"You're going to think about that body for me, okay? About the spirit that was in it. You need to release the—"

"Release? I—I didn't summon—"

"Shhh. Just concentrate on releasing it without waking the others. Can you do that?"

I nodded. Then I tried to sit up. Something heavy held my legs to the floor. I pushed onto my elbows. Derek lunged so fast all I saw was his dark form coming down on me, hands going to my shoulders, slamming me back into the ground, pinning me down.

I freaked. I didn't stop to wonder what he was doing. My

brain just registered a guy on top of me in the middle of the night, and instinct kicked in. I lashed out, arms and legs flailing. My nails caught his cheek, and he fell back with a grunt of pain.

I scrambled up, legs still weighted down . . . and now I saw why. A corpse was crawling up me.

It was the one from the next room, little more than a skeleton, covered in clothing and strips of leathery flesh. Greasy hanks of hair patchworked its skull. Its eyes were empty pits. Its lips were long gone, leaving a skull's permanent grin of rotted teeth.

When I let out a whimper, it stopped and tried to hold its head upright, skull swaying from side to side, eye sockets searching blindly, jaws opening with a guttural *gah-gah-gah*.

I let out a bona fide "Scream Queen" shriek that rang through the room.

I kicked and fought, trying to get out from under the thing. Derek grabbed me by the armpits and yanked me out. He slapped his hand over my mouth, but I could still hear my scream, echoing around me. He growled for me to shut up and as I tried to obey, I realized it wasn't me screaming now.

"What is that?" Tori shrieked. "What *is* that?"

The flick of a flashlight. A beam shining in our eyes. And then she *really* screamed, loud enough to make my ears ring. The corpse reared up, mouth opening, screaming back, a high-pitched wail.

Simon woke up, too. When he saw the corpse, he let out a string of profanity.

"Shut her up!" Derek snarled to Simon, jabbing a finger at Tori. "Chloe! Calm down. You need to calm down."

I nodded, gaze fixed on that thing. I tried to remind myself it wasn't a "thing" but a person, yet all I could see was a skeleton held together by bits of flesh, that eyeless head swaying, those teeth clicking—

I inhaled, in and out, fast.

"Calm down, Chloe. Just calm down."

There was nothing calming about his tone, just an impatient snap, telling me to stop freaking out and get to work. I pulled from his grasp.

"You need to—" he began.

"I know what I need to do," I snapped back.

"What is that thing?" Tori gibbered. "Why is it moving?"

"Get her out of here," Derek said.

As Simon hauled Tori away, I tried to relax, but my heart was racing too fast for me to focus. I shut my eyes, only to feel something on my foot. My eyes opened to see fingers reaching for my leg.

I scuttled back. A filthy rag-covered arm reached out, finger bones scratching the newspaper on the floor as it tried to propel itself forward, too broken to lift itself. How could it even move? But it did. Just like the bats, inch by inch, coming toward me—

"You called it," Derek said. "It's trying—"

"I didn't call anything."

"Somehow you summoned it, and now it's trying to find you."

I concentrated, but at the first touch on my leg, I skittered to the side. The thing paused, skull wobbling, then those empty eye sockets locked on me as it turned in my new direction.

"You have to release it," Derek said.

"I'm *trying*."

"Try harder."

I squeezed my eyes shut and formed a mental image of the corpse. I pictured the ghost trapped inside and imagined drawing it out—

"Concentrate," Derek whispered.

"I am. If you'd shut up—"

The corpse stopped, like it could hear me. Then it reached out, blindly, searching. It found my leg and its finger started feeling its way toward my knee. I steeled myself against the urge to pull away. It needed to find me, so I let it. Ignore that and focus on—

"What did you do the last time?" Derek asked.

I glared over at him.

"I'm trying to help," he said.

"You'd help a lot more if you'd shut—"

His glare matched mine. "You need to release it, Chloe.

With all that screaming, someone's bound to have heard us, and you've got about five minutes before they burst through that door and see a corpse crawling—"

"Is that supposed to *help* me?"

"I didn't mean—"

"Out."

"I just—"

"*Out!*"

He retreated. I closed my eyes and envisioned the skeleton, the trapped spirit—

A bony finger touched the bare skin where my shirt had twisted away from my jeans and I jumped, eyes flying open to see it right there, the skull a few inches from my face, bobbing and weaving.

The coarse scraggly hair brushed my throat and I whimpered. It went still. Then the skull moved closer still. I could smell it now, the faint stench of death I hadn't noticed earlier, churning my stomach, the thought of someone in there, trapped in that rotting—

It moved closer.

"Stop. P-please stop."

It went still. We hung there, eyeball to eye socket as I took short quick breaths, calming myself without inhaling its stink too deeply.

I waited for its next move, but it didn't make one.

I'd told it to stop, and it had.

I remembered those gruesome old pictures on the Internet of necromancers leading armies of the dead. I remembered the book Dr. Davidoff had given me about the powers of necromancers.

The power to communicate with the dead. The power to raise the dead. The power to control the dead.

"M-move back," I said. "P-please."

It did, slowly, teeth clacking. A guttural sound rose from its chest. A growl.

I knelt. "Lie down, please."

As it did, it lifted its face to me, skull moving from side to side like a snake, its growl a rattling hiss. I heard that hiss and I looked into those empty eye sockets and I felt hate. Waves of loathing rolled off the corpse. It wasn't obeying me because it wanted to, but because it had to. It was an enslaved spirit, summoned by a necromancer, slammed back into little more than a skeleton, forced to make it move to obey the will of its master.

I swallowed hard. "I-I'm sorry. I didn't mean to call you back. I wasn't trying to."

It hissed, head still moving, as if it would love nothing more than to show me what death felt like.

"I'm so sor—"

I swallowed my words. The ghost trapped in there didn't want apologies. It wanted freedom. So I closed my eyes and concentrated on making that happen, which was a lot easier when I didn't have to worry about it creeping up my legs.

As I visualized tugging the spirit out, the chattering stopped so fast I peeked, thinking I'd accidentally commanded it to be silent. But the skeleton had collapsed in a motionless heap by my feet. The ghost was gone.

so far I visualized tipping the sofa out the clattering... ...thinking I'd accidentally com... ...that the Menina had collapsed in a... ...lamp in my face. The ghost was gone.

twenty-two

I TOOK A DEEP, shaky breath, rubbed my face, and looked up to see Derek's figure filling the doorway.

"If you think someone might have heard, we should grab our things and go," I said, my voice remarkably steady. "We'll leave him where he is, so he'll be found and buried."

As I spoke, I had this crazy idea that Derek might actually be impressed by how I'd finally handled it. But he just stood there, fingering the scratch on his cheek.

"I'm sorry about that," I said. "I panicked when you—"

"I gave you the option of leaving earlier. I said if that"—he gestured at the corpse—"was a problem, we'd find another place."

"And I thought it wasn't a problem, as long as I didn't summon any ghosts."

"But you did."

"I was *asleep*, Derek."

"What were you dreaming?"

I remembered and went still.

"You dreamed that you summoned him, didn't you?"

"I—I didn't mean—" I rubbed my face. "Normal people can't control their dreams, Derek. If you can, then I guess you really are smarter than the rest of us."

"Of course, I can't. But it was a bad situation—you being close to a dead body. You should have known that from the crawl space."

I did know that, especially after the incident with the bats. My gut had told me to leave, but I hadn't had the nerve to admit my fear. I was afraid of being weak. Afraid of being mocked by Tori, of pissing off Derek, of disappointing Simon. In trying to be strong, I'd been stupid.

I wanted to own up to my mistake and tell Derek about the bats. But when I saw his expression—the intolerant arrogance that said he was right and I was a silly little twit—there was no way I was admitting anything.

"Everything okay?" Simon stood behind Derek, trying to see past him.

"It's . . . he's gone," I said. "The ghost."

"Good, because I think I heard someone coming."

"And when were you going to warn us?" Derek snapped.

"I wasn't going to barge in and interrupt Chloe." He turned to me. "Are you okay?"

"Of course she's okay." Tori came up behind Simon.

"*She's* the one who summoned that thing. She should be asking if we're okay, after being woken in the middle of the night and totally traumatized."

"You weren't too traumatized to grab your hairbrush," Simon said.

"As a weapon, okay? I—"

I stepped between them. "Did someone mention we're in danger of being discovered? Let's grab our stuff and move."

"You're giving orders now, Chloe?" Tori said.

"No, I'm making suggestions. If you choose to ignore them, that's fine. Stay behind and explain the dead body to whoever's coming."

"Yes," said a voice behind me. "Maybe you should explain that, little girl."

A figure stood across the room, only his outline visible in the dark. I turned back to the others, but no one had moved. They were all just looking at *me*.

"Chloe?" Simon said.

A man stepped from the shadows. His long hair was only streaked with gray, but his face was so lined he looked eighty. My gaze dropped to his sweatshirt, emblazoned with a Buffalo Sabres logo. Then I looked at the skeleton on the floor, twisted just enough for me to see the same logo, faded almost to nothing on the tattered shirt.

"Chloe?" he said. "Is that your name, brat?"

"I-I'm sorry," I said. "I didn't mean to summon you."

Simon jumped in front of me. "Look, ghost, I know you

can hear me. It was an accident."

The man lunged through Simon. I fell back with a yelp. Simon spun, but Derek yanked him aside.

"Who's Chloe talking to?" Tori asked.

"The ghost she summoned," Simon said.

"Grab your backpacks," Derek said. "We need to get going."

As Simon and Tori took off, Derek followed my gaze, figuring out where the ghost stood. "She didn't mean to raise you. She apologized, and we're leaving, so it won't happen again. Go on back to your afterlife."

The ghost strode over to glare up at Derek. "You going to make me?"

"He can't," I said. "And he can't hear you either. I *am* sorry. Very—"

He wheeled on me. I shrank away again, but Derek put his hand against my back, stopping my retreat.

"He can't hurt you," Derek whispered. "Stand firm and tell him to go."

"I'm very sorry." I straightened and moved forward. "I didn't mean to summon you. It was an accident—"

"Accident! That was no accident. You and your punk friends thought it would be funny to drag me back into that— that thing." He pointed at the corpse. "You think I haven't dealt with kids like you before? Drive me out of my sleeping spot for kicks. Roll me for my boots. Now you come here, conducting your satanic rituals . . ."

"Satanic? No. W-we—"

"Did you hear that?" said a distant voice. "Someone's in there."

Derek swore, then gave me a shove toward the back of the building. Simon and Tori raced in.

"Two men," Simon said. "Cops, I think. Coming up the front—"

"Back door," Derek said. "Move."

The front door banged open. Simon spun and headed for the rear. We followed.

"Hey!" the ghost yelled. "Where do you think you're going?"

A shove from Derek kept me moving.

"Oh no, you don't, little girl," the ghost said. "I'm not done with you yet. You're going to pay for that stunt. . . ."

He snarled threats right on my heels as we snuck out the back door.

twenty-three

"**I**S HE GONE?" TORI asked as I approached.

I nodded and inhaled. The icy night air burned my lungs. I didn't feel the cold, though——I was wearing my shirt, one of the new sweatshirts with the hood up, and the oversized jacket on top. Sweat dripped down my face as I struggled to catch my breath. I'd separated from the others a couple of blocks back, thinking that without a group, I might lose him easier. I'd been right.

We didn't know who'd come to investigate the noises. Maybe cops like Simon thought, maybe street people——we hadn't stuck around long enough to find out.

Now we stood in a parking lot, between a minivan and a pickup. Music boomed from a nearby club. That had surprised me——a packed parking lot and a busy bar so late at night on a weekday. Then I'd checked my watch and realized it wasn't even midnight yet.

"You shouldn't have taken off like that," Derek said.

"I told you what I was doing. It worked, didn't it?"

"You can't—"

"Ease off," Simon murmured. "We need to find a new place to sleep."

"Thanks to someone," Tori said.

"It isn't Chloe's fault."

"Sure it is. Even Derek said so."

"He didn't mean—"

I held up my hands. "I take all blame. Can we please stop bickering? I know everyone's on edge, but if we're going to get through this—"

"If you start a speech about how we all need to overcome our differences and work together, I'm going to hurl," Tori said.

"Well, I would, but I'm afraid this genetically modified supernatural would be eaten by a genetically modified shark."

Simon burst out laughing. "*Deep Blue Sea.*" He looked at Derek. "You didn't see it. Samuel L. Jackson is giving this group of survivors the speech about how they have to stop fighting and to work together. In the middle of it, the shark comes up behind him and eats him. Best death scene ever."

"And a fitting one for anyone who makes that speech, which is why I'm not going to."

"But you're right," Simon said. "Time to call a moratorium on the bickering."

"Moratorium?" Tori said. "Oooh, big word. Showing off, Simon?"

We all turned to look at her.

"What?" she said.

"No bickering means no jabs, no insults, no snark, no baiting," Derek said. "And it means we probably won't hear another word from you for days."

"As for this situation," I said, "I take the blame, so I'll fix the problem. Stay here and I'll find us a place——"

Derek caught the back of my jacket. "You still have a pissed-off ghost looking for you and a huge reward on your head. Stay here with Tori. Simon and I will find a new spot."

Before they took off, Derek turned back to me. "I mean it, stay right here."

"Even if the owners of these"——Tori rapped the vehicles on either side——"come out?"

Derek ignored her. "She's your responsibility, Chloe."

When they were gone, Tori turned to me. "Why do you let him get away with that? He treats you like a little kid."

I said nothing, just started walking away from the spot where Derek told me to stay.

She smiled. "That's more like it."

I led her to a strip of gravel between two buildings. Then I lowered myself to the ground. "This is safer, but still close enough."

She stared at me. "You're kidding, right?"

I pulled my jacket sleeves over my hands to keep them warm.

"You actually listen to him?"

"Only when he has a point."

She towered over me. "You're going to let a guy order you around like that? Make the girls sit on their butts while the men go hunt up a cave to sleep in, maybe drag back some food for us to eat?"

"Yep."

"Well, I'm not. I'm going to show those guys that a girl can do this just as well as they can."

I leaned back against the wall and closed my eyes. She stomped off. I opened my eyes, watching her get farther away.

Derek said to stay. And he said to look after her. Conflicting requests at the moment. I know he'd tell me to forget Tori and take care of myself. But I couldn't do that.

"Hold up," I said as I jogged behind her.

"If you're going to whine at me about pissing off Frankenstein, save it."

"I'm not here to give you crap. I'm helping you find a spot. As long as we don't go far, Derek can track us." As she stepped onto the sidewalk, I made sure my hood was still on, then hurried out and caught her sleeve. "We can take quiet roads, but I need to avoid people as much as I can."

"I don't. I'm not the one with stalker ghosts and a half-million bucks on my head."

"Yes, but if the Edison Group wants us back badly enough, they might have gone public to flush us out. We both need to be careful."

We reached the end of the street. As she started turning left, I stopped her again.

"This way," I waved to the darker end of the street. "Look for a good spot in an alley. The wind's coming from the north, so we need a northern barrier. A corner or alley end or recessed delivery door would be best, so we can see anyone coming. And the worse the lighting, the better. We want dark and we want secluded."

"You're as bossy as Derek, you know that? The only difference is you give your orders nicely."

But, apparently giving orders nicely was a strategy that worked, because she made no attempt to take off or take over, just came with me as we checked spot after spot.

Behind a row of stores we found a long, narrow alley with a wall on one side and a solid six-foot fence on the other.

"This looks promising," I said.

"Uh, yeah. If you're Oscar the Grouch." She waved at a row of trash bins.

I lifted a lid and pointed at shredded paper inside. "Recycling. There aren't any restaurants around here, so the garbage won't smell."

I continued down the alley. It dead-ended at a wall.

"This is great," I said. "Three sides, the bins block part

187 ◆

of the entrance. We can shift boxes around and put paper down to sit on."

"And maybe, if we're lucky, find a cardboard box big enough to crawl inside so we can pretend we're homeless people."

"Right now, Tori, we *are* homeless people."

That shut her up. I stopped near the end of the alley and let out a laugh.

"Come here."

She sighed. "What now?"

I waved for her to come over.

"Oh." She reached out to thaw her hands in the hot air blowing from the vent.

I grinned. "We've even got heating. How perfect is that?"

"Too perfect," said a girl's voice. "Which is why this spot is taken."

Three girls were walking toward us down the alley. All were about our age. One was blond and dressed in oversized fatigues. Another had dreadlocks. The third girl wore a battered brown leather jacket, and when she stepped into a patch of moonlight, I saw a thick scar running from her eye to her chin.

"See that?" the dreadlocked girl pointed to a tag on the wood fence. "That's our mark. That means this spot is ours."

"We d-didn't see it. Sorry. We'll go."

I started to walk away, but Tori pulled me back. "No, we

won't go. You can't *reserve* an alley, mark or no mark. It's first come, first served. You want this one? Be here earlier tomorrow."

"*Excuse* me?"

The scarred girl pulled a switchblade from her pocket. It snapped open with a twang. Tori glanced at the knife but didn't budge, her gaze locking with the girl's.

"Check it out," the scarred girl said to her friends. "This chick's going to challenge us for our spot. How long you been on the streets, girl?" She looked Tori up and down. "Since about nine this morning, I'll guess. What happened? Mommy and Daddy said you couldn't see your boyfriend on a school night?"

The girls snickered. Tori flexed her fingers, preparing to cast. I caught her wrist. She tried to shake me off. I got her to notice the matching knives now in the hands of the other two, but her gaze returned to the scarred girl, and all her rage from the last twenty-four hours bubbled up. The boxes near the girls quavered and rustled. Papers swirled behind them. The girls never turned, dismissing it as the wind.

I clasped Tori's wrist tighter and whispered, "Too many."

To my surprise, her hand relaxed. Expecting a trick, I held on, but she shook me off, saying "Fine. We're going."

"Good idea," the scarred girl said. "Next time, girls, if you see that"—she pointed at the tag—"steer clear. At least until you have the hardware to play."

We started to pass, but the scarred girl's hand flew out,

smacking Tori's chest and stopping her.

"Life out here isn't what you girls think it is. You've got a lot of lessons to learn."

"Thanks," Tori grunted, and tried to keep walking, but the scarred girl stopped her again.

"The thing about lessons? If they're going to sink in, they've gotta come with consequences. So I'm going to help you remember this one. Give me your jacket."

She held out her hand. Tori stared at it.

"Mine's getting old," the girl said. "I like yours better."

Tori snorted and tried to pass again.

The girl stepped in front of her, knife raised. "I said I want your jacket."

"And *her* shoes." The girl with the dreadlocks pointed at me.

"Fine, the jacket and the shoes," the scarred one said. "Take 'em off, girls."

The girl in fatigues stepped forward. "I want the little one's jeans, too. Never had a pair of Sevens." She smiled, flashing a jeweled tooth. "Gonna make me feel like a movie star."

"Yeah, if you can get them on," the dreadlocked girl said.

"Forget the jeans," the scarred girl said. "Jacket and shoes. Now."

Tori needed her jacket, and I definitely needed shoes. I

bent to undo one of my sneakers, pretending to have trouble with my balance, hopping, then waving Tori over to help. To my relief, she came. I leaned against her, tugging at my shoe, and whispered, "Knock back."

Tori frowned.

I flicked my fingers. "Knock back. One, two, three." I nodded to each girl in turn.

Tori shook her head. "Binding."

"Too many. Knock back."

"Come on, girls," the scarred girl said.

Tori gave an exasperated sigh and bent, as if helping me undo my shoe. Then she shot up, her hands flying out, hitting the scarred girl with—

The girl froze. So much for my advice.

At first the other two didn't notice. They just looked at their leader impatiently, waiting for her to prod us again.

"On my count," Tori whispered. "One, two . . ."

"Hey, what's—?" the girl in fatigues began.

Tori's hands shot up, but the girl kept coming. And the scarred girl stumbled, the spell breaking. She advanced, knife raised. Her friends fell into position, flanking her. Tori tried again, but apparently she'd used up all her juice because nothing was happening.

"Whatever trick that was," the scarred girl said. "It was really dumb. You have three seconds to strip out of everything. Both of you."

"I don't think so," Tori said. "Now, back off."

Tori flicked her fingers. The girl didn't even sway.

"I said, *back off*!"

She flicked again. The girls kept coming. I spun, only to discover the problem with a blind alley—if the entrance is blocked, you're trapped. When the girl in fatigues lunged for me, I ran anyway, Tori at my side.

At the end, I deked fast, hoping to catch my pursuers off guard and dodge around them. It worked on the one in fatigues. But the dreadlocked girl saw my feint and blocked me.

I ducked her knife, but she kicked me in the back of my knee. My leg buckled, and I dropped. I scuttled out of her way. I caught sight of Tori, her hands raised as if in surrender. Then one hand shot out, grabbing for the scarred girl's knife hand. The blade flashed and laid open the sleeve of Tori's leather jacket.

Tori let out a strangled howl of outrage, as if it had sliced through her arm instead. Her hands flew up. The scarred girl jolted back to avoid a punch, but Tori's hands went straight up over her head, then slammed down.

An invisible wave smacked me, and the next thing I knew I was lying on my back. Sneakers slapped the concrete and I looked up to see Tori running over.

"Are you okay?" Seeing I was conscious, she didn't wait for an answer. "Get up!"

I wobbled partway up, my leg still throbbing from the

dreadlocked girl's kick. I looked around quickly. She lay a few feet away.

Tori yanked me all the way to my feet. The girl in fatigues lay crumpled at the foot of the wall. She let out a soft moan. The scarred girl was on all fours, conscious but dazed.

Seeing the dreadlocked girl's blade on the ground, I snatched it up and ran to the girl in fatigues, telling Tori to take the scarred girl's knife as I looked for this one's. It had fallen a couple of feet away. I grabbed it. Tori was already running down the alley. I ignored the pain in my leg and raced to catch up.

"Did you grab her knife?" I asked.

"Why? You have two."

"That's not why I—"

"Hey!" a shout from behind us. "Hey!"

I glanced over my shoulder to see the scarred girl coming after us, knife in hand. *That's* why I wanted all three.

twenty-four

I SLAPPED ONE OF the knives into Tori's hand and told her to run. She did, sprinting ahead, her long legs soon leaving me behind, which was *not* what I'd meant. But we had enough of a head start. We just needed to get—

I glanced back at my pursuer and missed the curb. I stumbled and tried to recover, but my injured knee gave out and I sprawled onto a strip of grass. I dug in with both hands, ready to scramble up, but the girl landed on my back and the wind flew from my lungs.

We fought—if you could call my frantic kicking and flailing a fight. Soon she had me pinned on my back, knife at my throat. That stopped me.

"I—I—I—" I swallowed. "I'm sorry. Do you want my jacket? My shoes?"

Her face twisted in disgust. "You don't have anything I want, blondie."

She wrenched down my hood and yanked a handful of my hair. I winced and bit back a yelp.

"Red streaks?" A humorless laugh. "You think that makes you tough? Makes you cool?"

"N-no. If you want my shoes—"

"They'd never fit me. I wanted your friend's jacket, but she's long gone. Nice friend you've got there. Never even looked back." The girl eased up, knife still at my throat. "It was a taser, wasn't it?"

"What?"

"What she did to me back there. She tasered me, then my girls. I bet you thought that was funny."

"N-no. I—"

"I said I was going to teach you a lesson, and since you don't have anything I want . . ."

She lifted the knife until the point was an inch over my eye. I saw that tip coming down and went nuts, writhing to get free, but she had me securely pinned with her arm on my neck, cutting off my air as I struggled, and all I could do was watch that point coming straight for my eye. A whimper burbled up from my gut. She laughed and lowered the blade to rest on my cheekbone.

The tip pressed in. I felt the jab of pain, then hot blood trickling down my cheek.

"This is no life for pretty girls, blondie. A cute little thing like you? I'll give you a week before some player has you turning tricks. Me? I'm lucky. I don't have to worry about that." She tilted her face, showing me her badly scarred cheek. "I'm going to do you the same favor."

The knife bit in, digging deeper. I closed my eyes against the pain, then felt the girl leap off me with a snarl of rage.

As I scrambled up, I realized it wasn't *her* snarling. And she wasn't leaping off me—she was sailing up, eyes wide, knife dropping point down in the earth as Derek wrenched her into the air. He swung her straight at the wall.

I screamed "No!" I thought it was too late, much too late, but at the last moment he checked himself, so abruptly that he stumbled. The girl flailed and kicked. Her foot made contact. Derek didn't seem to notice. He looked around, saw the fence and, with a grunt, heaved her over it. She crashed onto the other side.

I was almost on my feet, unsteady, shaking. He grabbed my collar and yanked me up.

"Move!"

I found the fallen knife and snatched it. He shoved me forward so hard I stumbled. Then I started running. He got in front, leading me. We'd gone about a quarter mile when he spun, meeting my gaze with a look that made me shrink back. He grabbed my upper arm and held me still.

"Did I tell you to stay put?"

"Yes, but—"

"Did I tell you to stay put!" he roared.

I glanced around, afraid we'd be heard, but we were behind a row of stores, all the windows dark.

"Yes." I kept my voice low and even. "You did. But you also told me to watch out for Tori, and she took off."

"I don't give a rat's ass about Tori. If she walks away, let her. If she steps in front of a bus, let her."

When I looked up at his eyes, I saw the terror behind the rage and knew who he was really mad at—himself, for almost throwing that girl into the wall, just like the boy in Albany.

Saying nothing, I pried his fingers from my arm. He pulled back, clenching and unclenching his hand.

"If she takes off, let her go," he said, quieter now. "I don't care what happens to her."

"I do."

He stepped back, rubbing absently at his forearm. When he saw me watching, he stopped.

"It's an itch," he said. "A normal itch."

"Have you had any other symptoms? Fever or——"

"No," he snapped. "Don't change the subject. You need to be more careful, Chloe. Like earlier, with that body. You need to think about what could happen."

He was right. But seeing him scratching reminded me that I wasn't the only one who'd been careless, who'd ignored a potential threat.

"And what about you?" I pointed as he scratched his arm again. "The werewolf who hasn't had his first Change yet, but knows he's developing fast. Yet when you started getting restless, feverish, itchy, it never occurred to you that you might be Changing early? You let it slide . . . until it starts on the night we're supposed to escape."

"I wasn't going with you guys—"

"But if I hadn't stayed to find you, Simon wouldn't have left. You could have botched the escape because you didn't know what was happening to you."

"I *didn't*."

"Like I didn't know I could raise the dead in my sleep. But did I chew you out? Did I even mention how close I came to getting caught because I stayed to help?"

He looked away, jaw working, then said, "I tried to help you, too. And got this." He gestured to the scratch on his cheek.

"Because I woke up with a guy pinning me to the floor! I know you were trying to keep me from seeing that zombie crawling on me. A good plan, poorly executed. Then you totally lost patience and kept barking orders."

"I was trying to help."

"And what if I'd done that to you? Yelled at you to finish Changing before we got caught?"

He looked away again. "I . . . About that night. I haven't said . . ." He squared his shoulders. "We need to get back. Simon will be worried about you."

We walked about twenty steps in silence, me trailing him. When his shoulders bunched, I knew he was thinking about it again, and I prayed he'd let it go. Please just let it—

He spun on me. "Next time when I tell you to stay, I mean stay."

"I'm not a dog, Derek."

I kept my voice steady, but his jaw tensed, green eyes flashing. "Maybe not, but you obviously need someone to look after you, and I'm tired of doing it."

"Don't."

"Don't what?"

"Didn't we agree to stop bickering?"

His face darkened. "This isn't—"

"You're mad at yourself and you're taking it out on me."

I meant to be reasonable, but he exploded, coming at me so fast I backpedaled and hit a chain-link fence.

"I'm mad at *you*, Chloe. You took off. You got in trouble. I had to rescue you."

He kept coming at me. I pressed against the fence, the links whining in protest.

"And stop doing that," he said. "Backing away, giving me that look."

"Like you're scaring me? Maybe you are."

He stepped back so fast he wobbled and caught himself, and the look on his face— It vanished in a second, the scowl returning.

"I'd never hurt you, Chloe. You should know—" He stopped. Paused. Then wheeled and started walking away. "Next time? Handle it yourself. I'm done taking care of you."

I wanted to fly after him, yell that I hadn't asked him to take care of me, didn't need it, didn't want it. Not if this was the price—his rage, his guilt, his scorn.

Tears prickled. I blinked them away and waited until he was far enough that he wouldn't turn on me again. Then I followed him to Simon.

Tori was already there. She didn't say a word to me, as if mentioning what happened would mean explaining why she'd left me behind.

No one said much of anything. We were all too tired and too cold. Our new spot was a delivery bay. Safe, but the north wind blew right in. We huddled against the walls with our thin blankets pulled around us, and tried to sleep.

twenty-five

I WOKE TO THE smell of sausage and eggs and squeezed my eyes shut to savor the dream, knowing when I opened them, I'd be lucky to get bruised fruit and an energy bar.

"Rise and shine," a voice whispered.

A paper bag rustled. Then sausage-scented steam bathed my face. I opened my eyes to see Simon holding a familiar take-out bag in front of me.

"McDonald's?"

"Shhh."

Simon pointed at Tori, still snoring beside me, then quietly retreated from the delivery bay, motioning for me to follow.

He led me into an alley, where a fire escape ladder hung, then he boosted me onto it. We climbed up to the roof of a three-story building.

I walked to the edge and looked out. There was a park to the east, glistening with dew, the sun still rising behind it, tinting the sky pink.

"Nice, huh?" Simon said. "That park wasn't quite so empty last night or we would have slept there." He set down the bag and drinks on the rooftop. "So is this okay for breakfast? Up here?"

I looked at the view again. After last night, this was better than the fanciest breakfast in the fanciest restaurant. It might be the most thoughtful thing anyone had ever done for me.

"It's perfect," I said. "Thank you."

"Good. If it wasn't, I'd have blamed Derek."

"Derek?"

"He suggested we come up here and helped me pull down the ladder. Breakfast was my idea, though. We saw the Mickey D's last night and I thought you might like a bickering-free breakfast."

Derek picked the spot? Had he been hoping I'd be blinded by the morning sun and stumble off the edge?

"Pancakes or sausage McMuffin?" Simon asked as I settled onto the rooftop.

"Which do you want?"

"I've got mine." He lifted a wrapped sandwich. "I thought I'd buy you both and, whichever you don't want, Derek will eat. Nothing goes to waste with him around."

I took the McMuffin.

He lifted two cups. "OJ or a strawberry milkshake?"

"I didn't think you could get milkshakes in the morning."

He grinned. "I can."

When I took the shake, his smile grew. "I thought you might like that."

"Thanks. This"—I waved at the food and the spot—"is really nice."

"And well-deserved after your cruddy night. By the way, there's a cut on your cheek. We should get that cleaned up later. I know Derek gave you the gears last night—more than once."

"It's okay."

"No, it's not. Going at you about raising that zombie? That was out of line, even for Derek. He's been . . ."

"Crankier than usual?"

"Yeah. I think it's because he Changed—or couldn't Change—but that's no excuse to vent at you, not after what you did for him."

I shrugged and took a long draw of my milkshake.

"About what you did that night, staying with Derek while he was trying to Change . . ." Simon shook his head. "I don't know how you kept your cool. Finding him like that when you didn't even know he was a werewolf."

"I figured it out."

Simon took a bite of his sandwich and chewed, looking out at the sky before saying, "I wanted to tell you. Especially after he forced *you* to admit you were seeing ghosts. We argued; he won, as usual. But if we thought you could ever have stumbled on him like that, we'd have warned you. Even knowing what he is, I doubt I could have stuck around, much less helped. It took guts." He caught my gaze. "It really took guts."

I'm sure I turned crimson. I glanced away and chomped into my sandwich.

"I appreciate what you did for him, Chloe. Derek appreciates it, too, though I'm sure he hasn't said so."

I swallowed my mouthful and changed the subject. "So, about your dad . . . You never did tell me how he disappeared."

He laughed. "Enough about Derek, huh? Unfortunately, Derek is where this story starts. It was after he broke that kid's back. When it got a mention in the Albany paper, Dad decided it was time to move on. He must have known the Edison Group was still trying to find us. We should have left right away. But . . ."

Simon picked a burned piece off his muffin. "This happened a lot. At the first hint of trouble, we'd pack and move. Derek and I didn't understand why, so we'd complain." He paused. "No, *I'd* complain. After growing up in that lab, Derek was happy as long as the three of us were together. I hated moving. It always seemed I'd just made new friends, just made the team, just met a girl . . ."

"I know what that's like. Well, except the part about meeting girls."

"Yeah, but I bet you never complained. You're like Derek. You make the best of things. I bitched and moaned, so Dad always tried to make it easier on me. That day, I had a basketball game I was hyped about, so when Dad saw the article after we'd gone to school, he called Derek's cell. He told him not to mention it to me, but that he'd meet us after school and we'd take off. He never showed."

"And you haven't seen him since?"

Simon shook his head. "We got home, found the car packed, the keys in the kitchen. He'd taken his wallet or had it in his pocket when . . . whatever happened, happened."

"You think someone kidnapped him?"

"I don't know. Derek couldn't find anyone's scent in the house. It was like Dad just walked away, which he'd never do. Derek wanted to take off. Again I screwed up. I thought there was some logical explanation—maybe Derek misunderstood Dad's message. The next morning, I gave in and we left, but it was too late. They caught up with us the next day."

"The Edison Group?"

"They said they were child services. We believed them. They took us back to the house to see if Dad had returned, and when he wasn't there, they said that we had to go into a group home until they figured stuff out. Since we'd been born in Buffalo, that's where they put us. Which should have seemed weird, but we didn't know better. So that's how we ended up in Lyle House."

Simon continued, explaining that, since we'd escaped,

he'd been casting some kind of seeking spell his dad taught him, but he couldn't detect him. Using library computers, Derek had searched on their dad's name and aliases, but found nothing.

"And now, with all this about the Edison Group, and Liz and Brady and Amber murdered . . ." He looked out over the parking lot. "I'm starting to think it might be a waste of time. That he's not out there. That they killed him."

"But Aunt Lauren was sure the Edison Group wasn't involved in your dad's disappearance. And she seemed certain he'd still be alive. Do you know any other place he could be? Or anyone who might know something?"

"I thought about going back to Albany, maybe talk to people he worked with, our neighbors, someone who might have seen something that day . . ."

"We could do that. We have enough money."

"Derek doesn't want to."

"He wants to stay here?" That didn't sound like Derek.

"No, he just doesn't see any point in going back—and says it's probably dangerous. But there is someone we could go to. This friend of my dad's. Andrew Carson. He lives outside New York City. Dad said if we were ever in trouble and he wasn't around, we should go to Andrew."

"Have you called him? Maybe he knows something about your dad."

"That's the problem. Dad put his number on our cell phones, but they took those when we were tossed in Lyle

House. We know his name and where he lives—we've been there plenty of times. But when we tried looking him up on a computer, we couldn't find anything."

"His number must be unlisted. Or he's using an alias."

"Or he's not there anymore. It's been a few years since we saw him. He and Dad had a falling-out."

"Maybe you shouldn't contact him then."

Simon crumpled his wrapper. "I shouldn't say 'falling-out.' A disagreement. Dad and Andrew kept in touch; we just didn't go visit him anymore. He was still our emergency contact. So we *should* go see him, like Derek says. I'm just . . . not ready to give up on finding Dad. But with you and Tori here, and your picture everywhere, Derek's ready to buy the bus tickets."

"How about another solution? I need to get out of Buffalo. You need to talk to this guy. What if Tori and I go find Andrew while you and Derek look—"

"No. I don't trust Tori with you, especially after last night. Derek wouldn't go for it either."

I wasn't so sure. He might jump at the chance to get rid of me.

Simon continued, "Even if Tori's *not* homicidal, she's careless and reckless. Worse than me, which is saying a lot. We'll find another way."

twenty-six

F OR MOST OF THAT day, both Derek and Tori steered clear of me, like I had a bug they didn't want to catch. I didn't see a lot of Simon either. He went off with Derek to the library, still trying to find their dad or his friend Andrew. Tori tagged along. I stayed put in a lovely dank alley Derek had chosen for me. Simon left me with a movie magazine, snacks, a hairbrush and soap, and promised they'd get me to a bathroom after dark.

It was mid-afternoon when I heard footsteps tromping down the alley and I scrambled up to meet Simon. Derek might be bigger, but it was Simon who made all the noise. Derek was only loud when . . .

Derek stomped around the corner, scowling.

. . . when he was mad.

He had a newspaper rolled in his hand, bearing down on me like a puppy that had piddled on the carpet.

"Bad Chloe," I muttered.

"What?"

I'd forgotten his bionic hearing. "Bad Chloe." I gestured at the rolled-up paper and put out my hand. "Get it over with."

"You think this is funny?"

"No, I think it's tiresome."

He slapped down the paper. In the bottom corner of the front page was the headline "Missing Girl Spotted" with a picture of me. I skimmed the short paragraph, then turned to the rest inside.

It had happened last night, when Derek had been yelling at me after my run-in with the street girls. The windows around us may have been dark, but a woman had been watching from an apartment over a shop, drawn by Derek's voice. She'd seen "a girl with light hair and red streaks" being yelled at by "a large, dark-haired man." So now police speculated that I might not be a runaway but a kidnap victim.

"Well?" Derek said.

I folded the paper carefully, my gaze down. "Guess you shouldn't have yelled at me in public."

"What?"

"That's what caught her attention. You chewing me out."

"No, what caught her attention was your hair. If you'd kept your hood up like I said—"

"Of course. Totally my fault. After nearly getting my face

carved up, how dare I forget my attacker yanked down my hood. Bad Chloe."

"So this is a joke?"

I looked up at him. "No, it's not a joke. It's a serious problem. The joke is this." I waved from him to me. "You've been sulking all day, brooding—"

"Brooding?"

"Just itching for me to screw up so you can rip me a new one, your favorite pastime. You couldn't just come back and calmly say we have a problem that we need to discuss. Where's the fun in that?"

"You think I enjoy—"

"I have no idea what you enjoy, if anything. But I do know what you'd like. Me, gone."

"What?"

"I've served my purpose. I got Simon out of Lyle House. Sure, you were willing to make a half-assed effort to find me, so it looks good for Simon—"

"Half-assed?"

"You showed up hours late. Left a hidden note. Came by once a day. Yes, half-assed."

"No. Ask Simon. I was worried—"

"I'm sure you faked it well. But, unfortunately, I found you and, worse, I showed up with Tori in tow and a price on my head. So it's time to activate the backup plan. Make me so miserable and unwelcome that I slink away."

"I'd never—"

"No, you won't." I met his gaze. "Because I'm not going to slink away, Derek. If I'm too much of an inconvenience to keep around, then at least have the guts to tell me to get lost."

I brushed past him and walked away.

I didn't get far. I bumped into Simon and Tori, and Derek caught up with us. And then he got his way. Not about driving me off—he still had to work at that. But this new development gave him all the ammunition he needed to persuade Simon it was time to go to their father's friend's place. The bus left at four. First, though, the half-million-dollar runaway needed a disguise.

Derek took me to a restroom in the park I'd seen from the roof. The building was locked for the off-season, but he easily broke the locks and got me in. He made sure the water hadn't been turned off, then slapped a box of hair color on the counter.

"Gotta get rid of that," he said, pointing at my hair.

"I could just keep my hood—"

"Already tried."

He walked out.

I strained to see by the bit of light coming through a row of tiny, filthy windows. It was hard to read the instructions, but it looked similar to the red dye I'd used, so I applied it the same way. I couldn't tell what color Derek had chosen. It looked black, but the red dye had, too, so that didn't mean much. I didn't think too much about it until I washed out the dye, looked in the mirror, and . . .

My hair was black.

I hurried to the door and propped it open to get better light. Then I went back to the mirror.

Black. Not sleek glossy black like Tori's hair, but dull, flat black.

Before now, I hadn't been thrilled with my latest haircut. I'd had my long straight hair chopped shoulder length in a layered style that had turned out wispy and waiflike. Still, the worst I could have said was that it made me look "cute"—not what a fifteen-year-old girl wants to be called. In black though, it was not cute. It looked like I'd hacked my hair off with kitchen shears.

I never wore black because it drained any color from my pale skin. Now I saw there was something that washed out my face even worse than a black shirt.

I looked like a Goth. A *sick* Goth, white and hollow-eyed.

I looked dead.

I looked like a necromancer. Like those ghastly pictures of them on the Internet.

Tears sprang to my eyes. I blinked them back, grabbed some tissue, and started awkwardly trying to daub leftover dye onto my pale eyebrows, praying it would make a difference.

Through the mirror, I saw Tori walk in. She stopped.

"Oh. My. God."

It would have been better if she'd laughed. Her look of horror, then something like sympathy, meant it was as bad as I thought.

"I told Derek to let me pick the color," she said. "I *told* him."

"Hey," Simon called in. "Everyone decent?"

He pushed open the door, saw me and blinked.

"It's Derek's fault," Tori said. "He—"

"Don't, please," I said. "No more fighting."

Simon still shot a glare over his shoulder as Derek pushed open the door.

"What?" Derek said. He looked at me. "Huh."

Tori hustled me out the door, brushing past the guys with a whispered "jerk" for Derek.

"At least now you know never to go dark again," she said as we walked. "A couple years ago, I let a friend dye mine blond. It was almost as bad. My hair felt like straw and . . ."

And so, Tori and I bonded over hair horror stories. We put our differences aside and by the time we were on the bus, we were painting each other's fingernails.

Or not.

Tori did try to cheer me up. For her, this situation seemed to warrant more sympathy than having a dead guy crawling over me. But the closer we got to the bus station, the lower

213 ◆

her mood dropped, coinciding with a rising discussion of finances—how much did we have, how much would the tickets cost, should I try to use my bank card again . . .

I did use an ATM we passed. Derek figured that was okay—if they thought we were still in Buffalo, that was good, considering we were leaving. He didn't expect my card would work though. It did. I suppose that made sense. The bank or police might have told my dad to lock it, but he wouldn't cut off my only source of money, even if he thought it could make me come home.

That, of course, made me think about him and how much he must be worrying, and what he was going through. I wanted so badly to contact him, but I knew I couldn't. So all I could do was think about him, and think about Aunt Lauren, and feel awful about everything.

To get my thoughts off my family, I concentrated on my companions. I knew not having money bugged Tori. So I tried to give her a couple hundred. It was a mistake. She lashed out at me, and by the time we reached the station, we weren't talking again.

Simon and Tori bought the tickets. I wondered whether they'd catch any flak—unaccompanied teens buying one-way tickets to New York City—but no one commented. I guess we could just be traveling alone. We were old enough to do that.

Not that *I'd* ever traveled alone. Not even on a city bus. That got me thinking about who I normally traveled with—Aunt Lauren and Dad. When I tried to stop worrying about them I only thought about someone else I was leaving behind: Liz.

Liz said she could find me, but I was sure she'd meant "in Buffalo." How long would she search for me? Could I summon her without her green hoodie . . . from hundreds of miles away? I'd need to try really hard, and that wasn't safe.

Maybe she'd move on to the afterlife. That was probably a good thing. But at the thought of never seeing her again, my mood sunk lower than Tori's until, by the time the bus arrived, it was as black as my new hair.

Simon had gone to grab sodas for the trip. Tori was already out the station door. When I struggled to get my backpack on, Derek grabbed it and threw it over his shoulder, which would have been nice if I knew he wasn't just hurrying me along.

"Stop sulking," he said as he walked beside me. "It's just hair."

"That's not—" I shut up. Why bother?

Simon jogged up to join us in the passenger line. He handed me a Dr Pepper.

"You okay?"

"Just thinking about my dad and Liz. I wish I could have told them we're leaving."

Derek leaned down to my ear. "Smile, okay?" he whispered. "You look like you're being kidnapped, and people are staring."

I glanced around. No one was paying any attention to us. Simon shouldered past his brother, whispering, "Ease off."

He waved me to the first empty seat. "This okay?"

I nodded and turned in.

"There's more at the back," Derek said. "We can't sit together up here."

"No, we can't." Simon slid in beside me.

twenty-seven

I STARED OUT THE bus window as we left the city.

"We'll be back for them," Simon said.

"I know. I'm just . . . off today."

"I don't blame you. You had a crappy night. And a crappy day before that. And a crappy week before that."

I smiled. "At least it's consistent."

"And I know that"—he pointed at my hair—"isn't making you feel any better, but if you wash it enough when we get to Andrew's place, it'll come out."

"Have some experience, do you?"

"Me? *Pfft.* Never. I'm a guy. A guy guy. We do not color our hair. We don't even use conditioner if we can help it." He ran his fingers through his hair. "This? Totally natural."

"I never said—"

"Well, it wouldn't be the first time. Or the hundredth. When a guy looks Asian and has blond hair, everyone presumes it's a dye job."

"But your mother was Swedish."

"Exactly. Blame genetics, not chemicals." He leaned over and whispered. "But I did color it once. Temporary stuff like you've got. For a girl."

"Aha."

He put his chair back, settling into it. "It was a couple of years ago. I liked this girl, and she kept going on about this other guy, how his hair went so blond in the summer, how hot that looked."

I sputtered a laugh. "So you dyed—?"

"Shut up. She was cute, okay? I bought this washout highlight stuff, then spent all weekend outside, kicking around a ball with Derek. Sunday night, I color my hair. Monday morning I go to school and, hey, look what happened from me being out in the sun all weekend."

"Seriously?"

"I couldn't admit I dyed my hair for a girl. How lame would that be?"

"I'd think it was sweet. So did it work?"

"Sure. She went to the dance with me the next weekend. Then I came home, washed my hair until the color was out, and vowed never to do that again for a girl until I knew her well enough to be sure she was worth it."

I laughed, then said, "Thanks." When he arched his brows, I added, "For cheering me up."

"I'm good at it. With Derek, I get lots of practice." He reached into his backpack. "I have something else that might cheer you up. Or scare the crap out of you."

He pulled out a new sketch pad and flipped through it. A few pages in, he turned it so I could see.

"Hey, that's me," I said.

"So it looks like you? Or does the corpse crawling toward you give it away?" He handed the sketch pad to me. "I drew it this morning when Derek was doing his computer searches. I was thinking about last night."

In the picture, I was kneeling on my blanket, the corpse in front of me. Thankfully, he hadn't opted to draw the part where I'd been screaming in mortal terror, but later, when I thought he'd been outside with Tori.

I had my eyes closed, hands raised. The corpse was rearing up, seeming to follow my hands like a cobra dancing before a flute. All I could remember was how terrified I'd been, but in Simon's sketch, I didn't look terrified—I looked calm, confident. I looked powerful.

"I know that might not be a moment you care to have immortalized," he said.

I smiled. "No, it's cool. Can I have it?"

"When it's done. I need to color it when I get some pencils." He took the pad back. "I thought it might be interesting to do a kind of graphic journal about us. What's happening."

"Like a comic?"

"I was avoiding that word, for fear of sounding like a total geek. But, yeah, like a comic. Just for us, of course. A project to take our minds off stuff. It'll be way cooler on paper than it feels when we're living it." He took a long drink of his Diet Coke, then recapped the bottle slowly. "You could help, if you wanted. You know screenwriting and scripts for comics aren't much different."

"Like a movie told in stills."

"Right. I'm not good at the writing part. I know this is a true story, so it's not like I need to make stuff up, but I suck at knowing what parts to put in and what to leave out."

"I could help with that."

"Great." He opened his pad to the page after his picture of me. There were a few rough sketches on it. "I was trying to figure out where to start. . . ."

For the next few hours, I plotted and Simon drew. When I started yawning, he closed the sketchbook.

"Take a nap. We still have five hours to go. We'll have lots of time to work on this after we get to Andrew's place."

"Will we be staying with him?"

Simon nodded. "He's got the extra room. It's just him—no wife or kids. He'll take us in, no problem." He put away the sketch pad, then slowly zipped up his backpack. "There's another thing I've been thinking. I know it's not exactly a good time, but once we get settled in, I thought maybe you and I could—"

A shadow loomed over us.

Simon didn't bother looking up. "Yes, Derek?"

Derek leaned over the seat, one hand on the back for balance as the bus swayed. He seemed distracted, almost anxious.

"We're coming up to Syracuse soon."

"Okay."

"I need something to eat. I'm starving."

"Sure. I figured we'd jump off and grab dinner."

"I can't. Not here." When Simon looked confused, Derek lowered his voice. "Syracuse?"

"I don't think they're going to be hanging out at the bus station."

"Is something wrong?" I asked.

"Nah." Simon looked up at his brother. "I'll grab some food, okay?"

Derek hesitated. He didn't look anxious, really. More unhappy. Because Simon was annoyed with him?

As I watched Derek lurch back to his seat, I thought about that. Simon and Derek weren't just foster brothers— they were best friends. From the way Simon talked, though, he obviously had other friends, teammates, girlfriends. . . . I doubted Derek had any. For him, it was just Simon.

Was that why he wanted to get rid of me? It made sense, but it felt wrong. At Lyle House, Derek had never seemed jealous of any time Simon spent with me. Derek just went off and did his own thing. If anyone followed, it was Simon.

Maybe he wasn't jealous. Just feeling ignored.

It bothered me enough that when we stopped in Syracuse, I offered to take the food back out to Derek while Tori and Simon stretched their legs.

I meant to suggest that Derek and I switch seats. When I got there, Derek was staring out the window.

"Everything okay?" I asked.

He turned sharply, like I'd startled him, then nodded and took the food with a mumbled thanks.

I slid into the empty aisle seat. "Did you used to live here?"

He shook his head and looked out the window again. I took that as a sign he wasn't in the mood for conversation and was about to suggest the seat switch when he said, "We lived just about every place else in the state except here. We can't. There are . . . others here."

"Others?"

He lowered his voice. "Werewolves."

"In Syracuse?"

"Near it. A Pack."

"Oh."

Was that how werewolves lived? In packs, like wolves? I

wanted to ask, but was afraid he'd think I was mocking him.

So I said, "And that's a problem? If they smelled you?"

"Yeah." He paused, then added grudgingly, "We're territorial."

"Oh."

"Yeah."

He kept looking out the window. I could see the reflection of his eyes, still and distant, lost in thoughts he obviously didn't care to share. I started to get up.

"When I was a kid," he said, without looking my way. "When I lived in that place where you were locked up, the others were like that. Territorial."

I lowered myself into the seat again. "The other werewo—" An elderly woman approached in the aisle and I said instead, "Subjects?"

"Yeah." He turned then. "They had this pack, I guess you'd call it, and they'd claim stuff, like the sandbox, as their territory, and if—"

His chin lifted, gaze moving to the front of the bus.

"Simon's coming," he said. "He's looking for you. Better go."

I was going to say that was okay, I wanted to hear more. Chances to hear something personal from Derek were fleeting, but this one had already passed.

"You go," I said. "Sit with him the rest of the way."

"Nah, I'm good."

"Really, I—"

"Chloe?" He met my gaze. "Go." His voice softened. "Okay?"

I nodded and left.

I fell asleep and dreamed of Derek—about what he'd said, about what the demi-demon had said about him, about the other werewolf subjects. I dreamed of Aunt Lauren at the facility, saying she wanted Derek put down like a rabid dog, and of Brady saying how Aunt Lauren had tried to get him to blame Derek for their fight.

The memories and the images swirled until I felt someone shaking my shoulder. I woke up to realize the bus had stopped. Derek was in the aisle, leaning past Simon, who was asleep.

I was about to ask what was wrong. Then I looked at Derek and I knew. His eyes glittered, and his skin glistened with sweat; his hair was plastered down with it. I could feel the heat of his hand through my shirt.

I shot up. "You're—"

"Yeah," he whispered. "We're outside Albany. Truck stop. I gotta get off."

I reached to wake Simon, but Derek stopped me. "I just wanted to tell you, in case I don't get back on. I'll be fine. I'll meet you at Andrew's."

I grabbed my sweatshirt and jacket. "I'm coming with you."

I was sure he'd argue, but he only nodded, face averted,

murmuring. "Yeah. Okay."

"You go ahead," I said. "I'll talk to—"

I looked at Simon, but didn't need Derek to tell me not to wake him. Better to tell the person who'd never insist on following us—Tori. So I did that, then hurried after Derek.

twenty-eight

I CAUGHT UP WITH Derek at the edge of a wooded patch beside the truck stop.

"I need to get in as deep as I can," he said. "Follow my path. It's muddy."

I could smell the rain, the damp chill of it lingering in the night air. Dead and decaying leaves slid underfoot. A dog barked somewhere. Derek paused, tracking the sound, then nodded, like it was far enough away, and continued walking.

"If I finish this," he began. "If I seem even close to finishing, you need to take off."

When I didn't answer, he said. "Chloe . . ."

"You aren't going to turn into some bloodthirsty monster, Derek. It'll still be you, just as a wolf."

"And you know that based on how much experience with werewolves?"

"Okay, but—"

"You could be right. Dad said it would be like that—still me in wolf form—but after what those guys did? Playing with our genes? I have no idea what will happen. So you're getting out of here when the time comes or you aren't sticking around at all."

"Okay."

He glanced back at me, fevered eyes glowing. "I mean it, Chloe."

"So do I. You're right. We don't know what will happen, and we can't take chances. As soon as you sprout fangs and a tail, I'll run screaming for the truck stop."

"You can skip the screaming part."

"We'll see."

We walked until the floodlights from the parking lot barely pierced the trees. The moon was shrouded in cloud. Whether it was a full moon or a half-moon, I didn't know. It didn't matter. A werewolf's Changes had nothing to do with moon cycles. When it happened, it happened, whether the timing was convenient or not.

Derek slowed, scratching his arm through his shirt. "There's a log here, if you want to sit and wait. I'll get a little deeper in—I'm sure it's not the prettiest sight."

"I've seen it before."

"If it goes further, it'll be worse."

"I'm fine."

When we entered a small clearing, Derek pulled off his

sweatshirt. Under his T-shirt, his back muscles rippled, like snakes were trapped under his skin. Having seen this before, it didn't bother me, but it did remind me of something.

"On second thought, maybe I can't watch. Unless you brought a change of clothes, you really should get undressed this time.

"Right. Hold on."

He disappeared into the brush. I turned around. A couple minutes later, the leaves crackled as he came out.

"I'm decent," he said. "Got my shorts on. Nothing you haven't seen."

My cheeks flamed at the memory, which was stupid, because seeing a guy in his boxers shouldn't be any different than seeing him in swim trunks. I'd even seen guys in their underwear, pranking at camp by running around our cabins, and I'd laughed and hooted with the other girls. But none of the guys at camp had looked like Derek.

I turned slowly, hoping it was too dark for him to see me blushing. He wouldn't have noticed anyway. He was already on all fours, his head down, breathing in and out, like an athlete preparing for a run.

I blamed the note Simon left, the image of the Terminator still lingering in my brain, but that's what Derek looked like, that scene where the Terminator first arrives, and he's crouched, naked—not that Derek was totally naked or as pumped as Schwarzenegger, but he didn't look like a sixteen-year-old kid either, with a muscular back, bulging biceps, and . . .

And that was enough of that. I looked away to scan the forest and took a few deep breaths of my own.

"Sit here." Derek pointed to a clear spot beside him where he'd laid out his sweatshirt.

"Thanks." I lowered myself onto it.

"If it gets too bad, go. I'll understand."

"I won't."

He looked at the ground again, eyes closed as he inhaled and exhaled. His back spasmed and he winced, then stretched, his breathing deeper.

"That's a good idea. Stretch and work it out—" I stopped. "Okay, I'll shut up now. You don't need a coach."

He gave a low rumble that it took me a moment to recognize as a laugh. "Go ahead. Talk."

"If there's anything I can do— I know there probably isn't, but . . ."

"Just be here."

"That I can manage." I realized his skin hadn't rippled in a while. "And we might not even have to worry about it. It seems to be passing. False start, maybe. We should give it a few more minutes, then—"

His back shot up, body jackknifing as he let out a strangled cry. He managed two panting breaths before convulsing again. His arms and legs went rigid. His back arched to an unnatural height, spine jutting. His head dropped forward. His skin rippled and his back went even higher. A long whimper bubbled from his throat.

His head flew up and, for a second, his eyes met mine, wild and rolling with pain and terror, even more than the first time because then, as scared as he'd been, he'd known this was natural, that his body would take him through it safely. Now, knowing about the mutations, he had no such guarantee.

His fingers dug into the moist earth, the tips disappearing, the backs of his hands changing, tendons bulging, wrists thickening. He let out another cry, swallowing the end of it as he tried to keep quiet. I reached out and lay my hand on his. The muscles bulged and shifted. Coarse hair sprouted and pushed against my palm, then retreated. I rubbed his hand and moved closer and whispered it would be okay, he was doing fine.

His back arched and he gulped air, and in that moment of silence, footsteps clomped along the path into the woods.

"Are you kids in there?" It was the bus driver, his words harsh in the still forest, his figure backlit by the truck stoplights. "Someone saw you kids head in here. You've got one minute to come out or the bus leaves."

"Go," Derek whispered, his voice guttural, barely recognizable.

"No."

"You should—"

I met his gaze. "I'm not going. Now *shhh*."

"Ten seconds!" The bus driver yelled. "I'm not holding up the bus so you kids can screw around in the forest."

"If he comes closer, you go in there." I pointed at the thicket. "I'll stop him."

"He won't."

Sure enough, Derek barely got the words out before the figure began retreating. A few minutes later, the bus lights receded from the lot.

"That's okay," I said. "I have money. We'll catch—"

Derek convulsed again. This time his head shot up and he spewed vomit into the bushes. Wave after wave of convulsions rocked him, each one emptying his stomach until vomit dripped from every branch and the sickly smell mingled with the sharper stink of his sweat.

Hair sprouted and retracted and he kept convulsing and vomiting until there was nothing left to throw up, and still his stomach kept trying, with horrible dry heaves that were painful to hear. I rose onto my knees and rested my hand between his shoulder blades, rubbing and patting the sweat-slick skin there as I whispered the same words of reassurance, not even sure he could hear them anymore.

His back muscles twisted and shifted under my hands, the knobs of his spine pressing against them, his skin soaked with sweat and covered with coarse dark hair that wasn't retracting, but growing longer.

Finally Derek stopped heaving and shuddered, his whole

body trembling from exhaustion, his head lowered almost to the ground. I rubbed his shoulder.

"It's okay," I said. "You're doing great. You're almost there."

He shook his head and made a sound that must have been "no," but it was too guttural to be more than a growl.

"That's fine," I said. "You will or you won't. You can't rush it."

He nodded. His head was down, face averted, but I could still see the changes, his temples narrowing, hair shortening, the tops of his ears sticking out as they shifted higher onto his skull.

I absently rubbed his back, then halted. "Do you want me to stop? Move away and give you more room?"

He shook his head as he struggled to catch his breath, sides and back heaving. I massaged the spot between his shoulders. His skin stopped moving and his spine retracted. His shoulders felt different, though. Set different, the muscles bunched and thick, almost hunched. The hair felt more like fur now, like my friend Kara's husky, with a coarse top layer, softer underneath.

Derek said werewolves changed into actual wolves. I'd found that hard to believe. In fact, I'd heard that the reason the "wolfman" type of werewolf had been so popular in early Hollywood was because of the difficulty of changing a human into a wolf. If they couldn't do it with makeup and prosthetics, surely the human *body* couldn't do it. But looking at Derek, shivering and gasping as he rested mid-Change, I saw I'd been wrong. I still couldn't quite wrap even my vivid imagination around what I was seeing, but there was no doubt he was changing into a wolf.

"It seems to have stopped again," I said.

He nodded.

"That's probably it, then. For now, this is as far as—"

His body went rigid. The muscles under my hand moved, but slowly, like they were settling, preparing to reverse the transformation . . .

His back shot up, limbs straightening, head dropping and there was this . . . sound—an awful popping and snapping, like bones crackling. Then his head flew up and the crackling was drowned out by an inhuman howl. His head whipped from side to side and I saw his face then, the nose and jaw lengthening to a muzzle, neck thick, brow receding, black lips pulled back to show teeth sharpened to fangs.

One eye caught mine, and the absolute terror in it chased mine away. I could not be afraid. I could not be freaked out. I could not make this worse for him in any way. So I met his gaze, unblinking, and kept rubbing his back.

After a moment, the muscles under my hand relaxed and he went still, the silence broken only by labored heaves as he panted, the sound more canine than human. His back rose and fell with the deep breaths. Then another massive convulsion seized him, and I was sure that was the final jolt, that the transformation would finish. Instead, the fur between my fingers receded. He convulsed again, gagging, threads of bile dripping from his jaws. He shook them off, then turned his face away.

Derek hacked and coughed for a minute, his limbs trembling. Then, slowly, they slid out from under him, like they couldn't bear his weight any more, and he collapsed, panting and quivering, his fur a dark shadow of stubble, his body almost returned to a human shape, only the thickened neck and shoulders remaining.

After one more deep, shuddering sigh, he rolled onto his side, toward me, legs drawn up, one hand draped over his face as it finished the reversal. I huddled there, trying to keep my teeth from chattering. Derek wrapped his hand around my bare ankle, where my sock had slid down into my sneaker.

"You're freezing."

I didn't feel cold. The shivering and goose bumps seemed more from nerves, but I said, "A little."

He shifted, then took my knee and tugged me closer, sheltered from the bitter wind. The heat of his body was like a radiator and I stopped shivering. He wrapped his hand around my ankle again, his skin rough, like a dog's paw pads.

"How're you doing?" he asked, his voice still odd, strained and raspy, but understandable.

I gave a small laugh. "I should be asking you that. Are you okay?"

"Yeah. That must be what'll happen for a few times. A partial Change, then back to normal."

"Practice runs."

"I guess so." He moved his hand down under his eyes. "You didn't answer my question. Are you all right?"

"I didn't do anything."

"Yeah. You did." He looked at me. "You did a lot."

His eyes met mine, and I looked into them and I felt . . . I don't know what I felt. A strange nameless something I couldn't even identify as a good something or a bad something, could only feel in my gut, jumping and twitching, until I turned away and looked out over the forest.

"Yeah, we gotta go," he said, starting to rise.

"Not yet. Lie down. Rest."

"I'm"—he sat up and swayed, as if light-headed—"*not* fine. Okay. Just give me a sec."

He lay back down, eyelids bobbing as he fought to keep them open.

"Close your eyes," I said.

"Just for a minute."

"Mmm-hmm."

I don't know if they were even fully closed before he fell asleep.

twenty-nine

I HUDDLED THERE UNTIL the sweat dried from his skin and he began to shiver, still sleeping. Then I unwrapped his fingers from my ankle. He let go, only to grasp my hand instead. I looked down at his hand, so huge around mine, like a kid's clutching a toy.

I was glad I'd been here for him. Glad someone was—I don't think it would have mattered who. Even if there'd been nothing I could do, just having me there seemed to help.

I couldn't imagine what he was going through—not just the agony but the uncertainty. Was this normal for young werewolves? Starting to Change, then reversing? Or was it something the Edison Group had done? What if he couldn't ever finish it? Would his body keep trying, putting him through this hell again and again?

I knew he would already be worrying about the same

thing. That didn't excuse his outbursts, but maybe it helped me understand him and not take it so personally when he lashed out at me.

I slipped my hand from his, and he shifted with a grunt but didn't wake, just tucked his hand under his other arm and shivered. I hurried to where he'd left his clothing. When I returned, I checked the sweatshirt I'd been sitting on, but it was a damp, mud-caked mess. I decided to give him my jacket instead—it had to be close to his size—but it soon became apparent I wasn't getting *any* clothes on him.

It didn't matter that they were baggy—all Derek's clothing was, like he thought he'd be less intimidating if he looked chubby instead of muscular. Still, I couldn't get his jeans past his knees and even then I was sure I was going to wake him. So I settled for draping the clothing over him. I was fussing with the jacket, making sure it was the fleece side against him, when I caught a movement in the trees. I hunkered down beside Derek and went still.

When I didn't hear anything, I peeked over Derek and saw a man through the trees. His face was rigid with anger as he walked fast. Something moved near the ground ahead of him. A truck stop visitor taking his dog for a walk?

I glanced at Derek. If the dog smelled him, we were in trouble. I pushed up to a crouch and crept forward as quietly as I could. I saw a flicker of yellow fur through the thick bushes. The man waved his hand with a flash of silver, like he was holding a chain leash. He looked furious. I couldn't blame him. It was cold and wet and muddy, and his dog seemed to be insisting on doing its business in the deepest part of the small forest.

When the man's foot flew out in a kick, though, my sympathy vanished, and I tensed, a shout of outrage on my lips. Then I saw it wasn't a dog in front of him. It was a girl with long blond hair, wearing a light-colored shirt and jeans, crawling on all fours, like she was trying to get away from the man.

He kicked her again and she twisted, scuttling forward awkwardly, like she was too badly hurt to get up and run. Her face turned my way and I saw she wasn't any older than me. Mascara raccoon-ringed her eyes. Dirt streaked her face. Dirt and blood, I realized, the blood still dripping from her nose, staining her shirt.

I sprang to my feet and as I did, the man raised his hand. Silver flashed—not a leash, but a knife. For a second, all I could see was that knife, my mind stumbling back to the girl in the alley, the knife tip over my eye. The terror I'd fought so hard to hide shot through me.

The man grabbed the girl's long hair. He wrenched her head up and that jolted me from my frozen terror. My mouth opened to call out, yell anything, just get his attention so she could escape.

The knife sliced through the air, heading straight for the girl's throat and I let out a cry. The knife passed through, seeming not to have left a mark, and I was sure he'd missed.

Then her throat opened, splitting, gaping, blood gushing, spurting.

I fell back, hands flying to my mouth to stifle another scream. He thrust the dying girl aside with a snarl of disgust. She collapsed to the ground, blood still spurting, mouth moving, eyes rolling wildly.

The man turned toward me. I ran, tripping and stumbling through the undergrowth. I had to get to Derek, wake him, warn him. It seemed to take forever, but I finally made it. As I dropped beside him, I caught a glimmer out of the corner of my eyes and I turned to see the man . . . back where I'd first seen him, in exactly the same position, heading the same way.

His mouth opened, saying something, but no words came out. Why couldn't I hear him? The forest was so silent my panting breaths sounded like a train, but I couldn't even hear the man's footsteps. I realized that the whole time I'd never heard a thing.

I waited for the flash of silver I'd seen earlier, and it came, in exactly the same place. Then he kicked the girl . . . in the same spot.

I reached into the pocket of my jacket, still wrapped around Derek, and pulled out the switchblade I'd taken from the girl in the alley. I was pretty sure by now that I wasn't in danger, but I wasn't taking chances. I crept toward the silent figures moving through the woods. The man kicked the girl a second time, but again the blow made no sound, her fall made no sound, *she* made no sound.

Ghosts. Like the man in the factory.

No, not ghosts. Ghosts might not make noise moving, but I could hear them talk. I could interact with them. These were just images. Metaphysical film clips of an event so horrible it was imprinted on this place, endlessly looping.

The man grabbed the girl by her hair. I squeezed my eyes shut, but I still saw it, the memory imprinted on *me* now, replaying on my eyelids.

I swallowed and retreated. Back in the clearing, I hunkered down beside Derek, drawing my knees up, my back turned to the scene playing out in the woods. But it didn't matter that I couldn't see it. I knew it was there, unfolding behind me, and it didn't matter if I hadn't *really* watched a girl die. In a way, I *had*.

A girl my age had been murdered in these woods and I'd seen her last terrified moments, watched her bleed to death in this forest. A life like mine had ended here, and it didn't matter how many times I'd seen deaths in movies, it wasn't the same, and I wasn't ever going to forget it.

I huddled there, shivering, surrounded by darkness. I'd hated the dark since childhood. I know why now—I used to see ghosts in the dark when I was little, brushed off by my parents as bogeymen. Now, knowing that the "bogeymen" were real didn't help at all.

Every whisper of wind sounded like a voice. Every animal rustling in the forest was a poor creature I'd raised from the dead. Every creak of a tree was a corpse clawing up from the cold ground. Each time I closed my eyes, I saw the dead girl. Then I saw the dead bats. Then I saw the girl, buried in this forest, never found, waking in a shallow grave, trapped in her rotted corpse, unable to scream, to struggle. . . .

I kept my eyes open.

I thought of waking Derek. He wouldn't complain. But after what he'd just been through, it seemed silly to say I couldn't bear being out here with a murder reenactment playing behind me. I did nudge him a few times, though, hoping he'd wake up.

But he didn't. He was exhausted and he needed his rest, and even if he did wake up, what could we do? We were trapped at this bus stop until morning.

So I sat and I tried not to think. When that failed, I recited multiplication tables, which only reminded me of school and made me wonder whether I'd ever go back; and that reminded me of Liz, of how much she'd hated math, and I wondered how she was and where she was and . . .

I switched to reciting favorite movie dialogue, but, again, it only reminded me of my other life, then my dad and how worried he must be. I drove myself nuts trying to figure out some safe way to get him a message, getting more and more frustrated when I couldn't.

I finally settled on something that always comforted me—singing "Daydream Believer." It was my mom's favorite song, the one she'd sung me to sleep with whenever I had nightmares. I only knew one verse and the chorus, but I whispered them under my breath, over and over and . . .

"Chloe?"

Fingers touched my shoulder. I blinked and saw Derek crouched beside me, still in his shorts, his face dark with worry.

"S-sorry. I drifted off."

"With your eyes open? Sitting up? I've been trying to snap you out of it for a while."

"Oh?" I looked around and saw it was day. I blinked harder and yawned. "Long night."

"You've been sitting here awake all night?" He lowered himself to the ground. "Because of what happened with me? I know that couldn't have been easy to watch—"

"That's not why."

I tried to duck having to explain, but he kept pushing, and it came down to telling the truth or letting him think that watching him Change had put me in a state of shock. I told him about the girl.

"It wasn't real," I said as I finished. "Well, it was—once. But I was just seeing some kind of ghostly replay."

"And you watched that, all night?"

"No, it's"—I waved my hand over my shoulder—"back there. I didn't look."

"Why didn't you wake me up?"

"You were tired. I didn't want to bother you."

"Bother me? That is the stupidest—" He stopped. "Wrong word. Stubborn, not stupid . . . and yelling at you right now isn't helping, is it?"

"Not really."

"Next time, wake me up. I don't expect you to tough out something like that, and I'm not impressed that you did."

"Yes, sir."

"And next time you don't tell me, I *will* yell at you."

"Yes, sir."

"I'm not your drill sergeant, Chloe. I don't *like* getting on your case all the time."

I wasn't touching that one.

"I don't mean to . . ." He sighed, shook his head, and got to his feet. "Give me a minute to get dressed, and we'll head into the truck stop, warm up, and get some breakfast."

He took his clothes and headed for the thicket, still talking. "The main bus station is in the city. I'm hoping we'll have enough for cab fare. When we get inside, we'll call and get the bus rates and schedule, so we'll know how much money we have left over."

"I've got"—I pulled bills from my pocket—"eighty. I left the rest in my backpack. I don't like carrying it all around."

"Most of mine is in my backpack, too, which I forgot on the bus." He cursed himself under his breath.

"You were in no shape to be remembering anything last night. I should have thought to grab mine."

"But *you* were worried about *me*. Never mind, we'll have

enough. I've got about a hundred . . ."

A pause. Then the sound of hands slapping fabric, like he was patting his pockets.

He swore. "It must have fallen out. Where did you get my jeans from?"

"Right where you left them, folded by the tree. I checked the pockets first. There was just an energy bar wrapper."

"I know I had—" He stopped and swore again. "No, I moved the money to my jacket, which I left on the bus."

"Eighty dollars should cover the bus to New York and breakfast. We'll walk, then catch a city bus to the station."

He strode from the bushes, muttering, "Stupid, stupid."

"Like I said, you had other things on your mind. We both did. And neither of us is used to playing fugitive yet. We'll learn. For now, let's get inside. I'm freezing."

Thirty

WHILE DEREK WAS IN the bathroom I called the bus station and got fares and a schedule. The guy was even nice enough to tell me which city buses we needed to take to get there.

When Derek came out of the bathroom, his sweatshirt was damp and clean, and his hair was wet and glistening, like he'd wiped down the shirt and washed his hair in the sink.

"Good news first or bad—" I stopped. "Dumb question. Bad, right?"

"Yeah."

"We've got a two-mile walk to the nearest bus stop, plus one transfer to get to the terminal. The good news? The fare is sixty dollars for two students to New York, so we have enough for breakfast."

"And deodorant."

I was going to say that didn't matter, but from the set of his jaw, it mattered to him, so I nodded and said, "Sure."

We bought deodorant and a cheap comb. And, yes, we shared them. Money was too tight to get silly about that.

The smell of bacon and eggs from the restaurant set my mouth watering, but our cash wouldn't stretch to cover a hot breakfast. We grabbed cartons of chocolate milk, two energy bars, and two bags of peanuts, then headed out for our hike to the bus stop.

After about a half mile of silence, Derek said, "You're quiet this morning."

"Just tired."

Another hundred feet.

"It's last night, isn't it?" he said. "If you want to talk about it . . ."

"Not really."

Every few steps, he'd glance my way. I wasn't in the mood to share, but my silence was obviously bugging him, so I said, "I keep thinking about when I first saw that girl in trouble. When I thought it was real. I was going to do something—"

"What?" he cut in.

I shrugged. "Yell. Distract him."

"If it was real, you shouldn't have even *thought* of

getting involved. The guy had a knife. He was obviously ready to use it."

"That wasn't really the point," I murmured, watching my toe kick a pebble along the roadside.

"Okay. So the point was . . ."

"I saw that knife and I froze. All I could think about was that girl in the alley, the one who held a knife on me. If last night *had* been real, I might have let someone die because I was too freaked out to do anything."

"But it wasn't real."

I looked up at him.

"Okay," he said. "Again that wasn't your point. But what happened in that alley—you still hadn't had time to slow down and . . ." He gestured, searching for a word. "Process it. You talked to Simon about it, right?"

I shook my head.

He frowned. "But you *did* tell him what happened."

Another head shake.

"You should. You need to talk to someone. You sure can't talk to Tori. Liz is probably a good listener, but she's not around." He paused. "You could talk to me, but you've probably figured out I'm not good with stuff like that. I mean, if you wanted to . . ." He trailed off, then came back firmer, shoulders hunching against the morning chill. "It should be Simon. He'd want to know what happened, and he'd want you to be the one to tell him."

I nodded, though I didn't know whether I would. Simon had spent enough time lately on Chloe-comfort duty. I needed to start working stuff out by myself. But there was a related issue I did want help with.

"I've been thinking," I began. "After what happened, I should learn how to defend myself. Some basic self-defense moves."

"That's a good idea."

"Great, so could you——?"

"I'll ask Simon to teach you some," he continued.

"Oh. I thought . . . I guess I thought that would be more your area."

"Our dad taught us both. Simon's good. Unless . . ." He glanced down at me. "I mean, if you want, sure, I can help out. But Simon would be a better teacher. He's got the patience for it."

"Right. I'll talk to Simon then."

He nodded and we lapsed into silence again.

We reached the bus station with twenty minutes to spare. Derek had me hang back, where the agent could see I was a teenager without getting too close a look, in case my photo was circulating. He went up to the counter alone. When he seemed to be having trouble, though, I joined him.

"What's wrong?" I whispered.

"She won't give us the youth fare."

"It's not a youth fare," the woman said. "It's a student fare. If you can't produce ID, you don't get it."

"But we got tickets in Buffalo without any ID." I put my used ticket on the counter.

"That's Buffalo," she said with a sniff. "Here in the state's *capital* we follow the rules. No ID, no student fare."

"Okay, adult tickets, then."

"We don't have enough," Derek murmured.

"What?"

"It's thirty-eight each for adults. We're six bucks short."

I leaned into the wicket. "Please, it's really important. You can see on our ticket there that we already bought fares to New York, but my friend got sick and we had to get off the bus—"

"Doesn't matter."

"How about one adult and one youth? We have enough—"

"Next!" she called, and waved up the man behind us.

The bus station also serviced Greyhound, but their sign clearly stated that their student fares required a special card, which was why we hadn't bought from them in Buffalo. I tried anyway. The woman there was more sympathetic, but she explained that she couldn't issue the reduced fare tickets without entering a student discount card number into the computer. So we were out of luck.

"We'll figure something out," I said as we moved away from the Greyhound counter.

"You go. I'll give you directions to Andrew's house. He can pick me up here—"

"What if he's not there? He could have moved or could be away. Then I'd have to find Simon, use a good chunk of money for us all to come back and get you. . . ."

Derek nodded, conceding my point.

"You lived around here for a while." I raised my hands. "I know, it's not your favorite place to remember, but is there anyone you could borrow ten bucks from?"

"A friend?"

"Well, sure, maybe . . ."

A small laugh. "Yeah, you sound as doubtful about that as you should. You may have guessed I don't go out of my way to make friends. I don't see the point, especially when I'm never in one place long. I've got my dad and Simon. That's enough."

His pack . . .

He continued, "I suppose I could find someone. Simon's bound to have a friend or teammate who owed him money. He's bad for stuff like that—lends it and never asks for it back."

"On second thought, considering you vanished under bad circumstances, reappearing now might not be the wisest idea. The last thing we need is someone calling the cops."

I walked to the stand of brochures and took one listing

fares and schedules. Then I went to the map of New York State and studied the two. Derek read over my shoulder.

"There," he said, pointing to a town on the map. "We can afford the full fare to New York from there."

"As for how we'll get there . . ."

That was the question.

Thirty-one

O UR BEST SHOT OF getting where we wanted to go was by hitchhiking. We weren't stupid enough to thumb a ride, but we might be able to sneak one. So we decided to go back to the truck stop. I dozed for a few minutes while we rode the city bus, then we started the long walk.

We were about halfway there when Derek said, gruffly, "I'm sorry."

"About what?"

"This. You helped me last night after all the crap I put you through. And this is your reward. Stranded in Albany."

"It's an adventure. I can't remember the last time I took a city bus. I'm getting my exercise, too. After a week cooped up in Lyle House and that laboratory, I've never been more in the mood for a long walk."

We walked a while longer.

"I know you're tired," he said. "And hungry. And pissed off."

"Tired, yes. Hungry, a bit. Pissed off? No." I looked up at him. "Seriously. I'm not."

"You've been really quiet."

I laughed. "I'm *normally* really quiet. But these last couple of weeks have *not* been normal."

"I know you don't always say a lot, you've just been . . ." He shrugged. "I thought you were mad." He shoved his hands into his pockets. "About that—being mad. You were right the other night, after what happened in that alley. I was mad at myself. It just took me a while to calm down enough to figure that out."

I nodded.

"What I did, when we lived here, hurting that kid. I didn't think it could ever happen again. I've been through it so many times, thinking of what went wrong and what I'd do if I ever got into that situation again, all the coping strategies Dr. Gill taught me."

"Dr. Gill?"

"Yeah, I know. She creeped me out even before we knew about the Edison Group. But she was a real shrink, and she did try to help. It was in their best interests to teach me to control my temper. So I was sure, if anything like that ever happened again, there was no question that I'd handle it better. And what happened? Almost the exact same scenario . . . and I did the exact same thing."

"You stopped yourself before you threw her into the wall."

"No, *you* stopped me. If you hadn't yelled, I would have done it. All those strategies. All that mental rehearsal. And when it happened, I never considered doing anything different. I couldn't. My brain just shut down."

"But it didn't take much to turn it back on again."

He shrugged.

"That's got to be progress, right?"

"I suppose so," he said, but he didn't sound convinced.

At the truck stop, our plan was to stow away in a transport. We sat in the restaurant, nursing sodas while Derek listened to the conversations around us, and picked out truckers heading our way.

The first truck was parked up front, making it impossible to sneak on without being seen. The second time, the trailer had a huge padlock on it, too big for Derek to break. The third time, as the saying goes, was the charm.

We'd followed the driver to his vehicle, which turned out to be a cube van. After he got into the cab, we snuck in the back.

The guy ran some kind of construction business. The van smelled of wood chips and oil and was full of tools, ropes, ladders, and tarps. When the truck reached the highway and the road noise was loud enough to drown us out, Derek took the tarps and made a bed on the floor.

"You need sleep," he said. "They stink but . . ."

"They're softer than cardboard. Thanks."

He handed me half an energy bar that he must have been saving.

"No, keep it," I said.

"You'll sleep better if your stomach isn't growling. And don't say it isn't. I can hear it."

I accepted the bar.

"And take this." He stripped off his sweatshirt. "Again, it might not smell great, but it's warm."

"You need—"

"I don't. I've still got a touch of fever from last night."

I took the sweatshirt. "It's okay, Derek. I'm not mad."

"I know."

I settled onto the tarp bed and pulled the sweatshirt over me, like a blanket. Then I ate the rest of the energy bar.

When I finished, Derek said, "You can't sleep with your eyes open, Chloe."

"I don't want to drift off, in case anything happens."

"I'm here. Go to sleep."

I closed my eyes.

I woke when the truck slowed. Derek was at the back, opening the door to peek out.

"Is this our stop?" I asked.

"We should be far enough. We aren't in a town, though. It's another truck stop."

"A pee break after that mega-coffee he bought."

"Yeah." He opened the door farther for a better look. "I'd rather be in a town. . . ."

"But he might not stop at one. We should get out while we can."

Derek nodded and closed the door. The truck pulled into a spot and stopped.

"Get under a tarp," Derek whispered, "in case he checks the back."

A minute later, the rear door squealed open. I held my breath. The cube van wasn't that big, and if the driver climbed inside to get something, he'd probably step on us. But he stayed at the tailgate. Tools clattered, like he was getting one from a box. Then the noise stopped. I tensed.

"I did forget the new vise grips," the man muttered. "Great."

The door shut with a bang. When I started pulling off the tarp, Derek whispered, "Wait. He's still walking away."

A minute passed as he listened, then he said, "Okay."

I got up and pushed the tarps back where we'd found them as Derek peeked outside again.

"Trees to our left," he said. "We'll head through there, then circle and grab something to drink from the restaurant before we head out."

"And use the bathroom."

"Yeah. Follow me."

We slipped out of the van and darted to the trees. Running behind Derek was worse than running behind Tori—with his long legs he barely needed to walk fast before the gap between us widened.

When he stopped short and spun to face me, I expected a scowl and an order to keep up, but his lips formed a curse. Running footfalls sounded behind me. I was about to break into a sprint when a hand clamped down on my shoulder.

Derek started to charge. I saw his expression, that telltale curl of his lip, and I wildly gestured for him to stop. He did, skidding to a halt, but his gaze stayed fixed over my head, watching my captor.

"I thought I'd picked up a passenger or two," said a man's voice.

He turned me around. It was the driver of the van. He was middle-aged with a gray ponytail and a craggy face.

"W-we didn't take anything," I said. "I'm sorry. We just needed a ride."

"Jesus," he said, shifting me into the sun for a better look. "How old are you?"

"F-fifteen."

"Just barely, I'll bet." He shook his head. "Running away from home. I'd bet on that, too." His voice softened. "That's not a road you want to take, kids. Speaking from experience, it is not the road at all."

Derek sidled closer, gaze fixed on the man, so intent I don't think he heard a word the guy said. I slid my hand into my pocket, fingertips touching my knife, not taking it out, just reminding myself it was there, that I wasn't as helpless as I felt.

I caught Derek's attention, not sure he'd notice, but he did, nodding absently, letting me know he was still in control.

The man continued, "Whatever is going on at home, it's not as bad as you think."

I lifted my gaze to his. "And if it is?"

A pause, then a slow, sad nod. "All right. Maybe that's so. It happens, more than you think, but there are other ways to deal with it. Places you can go. People who can help."

"We're fine," Derek said, his voice a low rumble.

The man shook his head. "You're not fine, son. You're, what, seventeen? On the run? Catching rides in the back of vans?"

"We're fine." Derek's rumble had gone lower, a growl now. He cleared his throat and eased back. "We appreciate your concern, sir."

"Do you, son? Do you really?" He shook his head. "I'm going to take you both inside and get you a hot meal. Then I'll make some calls. Find you a place to stay."

"We can't—" I began.

"No one's going to send you home. Now come on." His hand tightened on my shoulder.

Derek stepped forward. "Sorry, sir, but we can't do that."

"Yes, you can."

Derek waved for me to come over to him. I took a step. The man's hand tightened more.

"Let her go." The growl had returned to Derek's voice.

"No, son. I won't hurt your friend, but I'm going to take her inside and call someone who can help. I'm hoping you'll come with us, but that's your choice."

"Go," I whispered, low enough that only Derek could hear. "I'll catch up."

I was sure he'd heard, but he pretended not to.

"I'm going to ask you again, sir. Let her go."

"That sounds an awful lot like a threat, son. You're a big boy, but you don't want to take on a guy who's been in construction for twenty years and in more fights than he cares to admit to. I don't want to hurt you—"

Derek sprang, lightning fast. He had his arm around the man's throat before the guy even got his fists up. As he yanked the man down in a headlock, I stumbled out of the way, my hand flying from my pocket, knife sailing to the ground. The man stared at it. I scooped it up and put it back in my pocket.

"We don't want to hurt you either," Derek said. "But you can see"—he tightened his grip until the man's eyes bugged—"that I could. I know you're trying to help us, but you don't understand the situation."

Derek looked at me. "Run back to the van. Grab rope and some rags."

I took off.

Thirty-two

TWENTY MINUTES LATER, WE were a mile from the truck stop, trudging through a field. Ahead was a road that ran alongside the highway.

"You don't think we did the right thing," Derek said.

I shrugged.

"I didn't tie him too tight. He'll get out in an hour, probably less, and I left his cell phone right there, in case there's any problem."

I nodded. We walked another fifty feet.

"What would you have done?" he asked.

"You know my plan. It's the one you pretended not to hear."

We reached the roadside before he answered. "Yeah, okay. I heard. But it didn't look to me like he was going to give you a chance to escape. I knew I could take him down

261 ◆

safely, without hurting him, before things got worse. And if I can do that, then that's the choice I'm going to make. It's how our dad taught us to handle situations like that."

I considered it, then nodded. "You're right."

He looked surprised.

"I don't have experience with this stuff, these kinds of decisions," I said. "With the girl in the alley or the Edison Group, the answer was easy. If someone's trying to hurt us, we have every right to strike back. It's just . . ."

"That guy was trying to help a couple of runaways. He didn't deserve to end up bound and gagged."

I nodded.

"Even someone like that is a threat, Chloe. Whether he means to be or not. We had to get away or his 'help' would have landed us back with the Edison Group."

"I know."

We moved to the side of the road for a passing car, tensing as it went by, making sure the brake lights didn't flash, the car didn't slow. It wouldn't matter if the driver was a psycho trying to abduct us or a grandmother offering us a lift. We had to react the same way. Run. And if we couldn't run, fight.

The car continued, speed unchecked.

"We can't trust anyone now," I murmured, "even the good guys."

"Yeah. Sucks, doesn't it?"

It did.

* * *

We continued down back roads running roughly parallel to the highway. Judging by how long we'd been in the van, Derek figured we had to be close to the next town with a bus stop, but the truth was that we had no idea. However far it was, we had to walk it—we weren't about to hitch another ride.

One problem with our quiet country stroll was the dogs. Those tied up launched into a barking frenzy when they caught a whiff of Derek. No one seemed concerned, though— out here, I guess there were so few passersby that dogs did tend to bark at them, and owners ignored it.

However, being in the country also meant that a lot of those dogs *weren't* chained. More than one came charging down a driveway. Eventually, our reaction became automatic. At the first note of a bark, we'd stop walking. I'd move behind Derek. He'd stand his ground and wait. Once the dog got within eye contact range, it would take one good look at Derek and run, yelping, for safety.

"Do they always back down like that?" I asked as we watched a yellow Lab race back home, tail between its legs.

"Depends on the dog. Big country dogs like these? Yeah. It's the fancy city ones that give me trouble. Overbred, Dad says. Makes them skittish and screws up their wiring. I had a Chihuahua attack me last year." He showed me a faint scar on his hand. "Took a good chunk out."

I sputtered a laugh. "A Chihuahua?"

"Hey, that thing was more vicious than a pit bull. I was at a park with Simon, kicking around a ball. All of a sudden, this little rat dog comes tearing out of nowhere, jumps up, and clamps down on my hand. Wouldn't let go. I'm shaking it, and the owner's yelling at me not to hurt little Tito. I finally get the dog off. I'm bleeding all over the place and the guy never even apologizes."

"He didn't think it was strange? His dog attacking you like that?"

"Nah. He said the soccer ball must have provoked it, and we needed to be more careful. When strange stuff happens, people come up with their own explanations."

I told him about the girl in the alley, accusing Tori of tasering her.

"Yeah," he said. "We have to be careful, but they'll usually explain it away themselves."

We moved aside as a pickup passed, the driver lifting a hand in greeting. I waved back, then watched until I was sure he wasn't going to stop.

"So do all animals react that way to you? I know you said rats steer clear."

"Most do. They see a human, but they smell something else. It confuses them. Canines are the worst, though." He paused. "No, cats are the worst. I really don't like cats."

I laughed. As the shadows lengthened, Derek moved us across the road to the sunny side.

"I went to the zoo once," he continued. "Fifth grade field

trip. Dad said I couldn't because of the werewolf thing. I was pissed. Really pissed. Back then, I didn't freak animals out. I just made them nervous. So I decided Dad was being unfair and went anyway."

"How?"

"Forged his name and saved my allowance."

"So what happened?"

"Pretty much what Dad figured. I made the predators nervous and totally freaked out the prey animals. My classmates thought it was cool, though. They got to see an elephant charge."

"Seriously?"

"Yeah. I felt bad. So I stayed back from the pens after that. They weren't what I wanted to see anyway."

"Which was? Wait. The wolves, right?"

He nodded.

"You wanted to see if they'd recognize you as one of them."

"Nah. Nothing silly like that." He walked in silence for a moment. "Okay. Exactly like that. I had this . . ." He struggled for a word.

"Fantasy?"

A glower said that wasn't the word he'd have chosen. "This *idea* that they'd smell me and . . ." He shrugged. "I don't know what. Just that they'd do something. That something cool would happen."

"Did it?"

"Sure, if you consider it cool to watch a wolf batter itself bloody against the fence."

"Oh."

"It was . . ." His gaze went distant, staring off down the road, expression unreadable. "Bad. I got out of there as fast as I could, but he didn't stop. The next day a kid at school said they put the wolf to sleep."

I looked up at Derek.

He continued, gaze still fixed on the road. "I went home and grabbed the paper. The city section was missing. Dad had gotten to it first. He'd figured out what had happened, but he wasn't going to say anything. He knew I'd been upset about something that night, and I guess he thought that was punishment enough. So I went to the store and bought a paper myself. It was true."

I nodded, not sure what to say.

" 'Sudden, unprovoked aggression toward humans,' " he recited, as if he'd never forgotten the words. "Wolves don't normally act like that. All those stories about the big, bad wolf are crap. Yeah, they're predators, and they're dangerous. But they don't want to have anything to do with humans if they can avoid it. The only time they do is if they're sick, starving, or defending their territory. I was a lone wolf invading a pack's turf. He was the alpha. It was his duty to protect his pack. And he got killed for it."

"You didn't mean for that to happen."

"That's no excuse. Dad taught me about wolves. I knew

how they behaved. I'd seen it with the other boys, the other subjects . . ."

"Do you remember them? Simon wasn't sure you did."

"Yeah. I do." He rubbed the back of his neck as he walked, then looked at me. "You getting tired?"

"A little."

"It shouldn't be far now. So, uh . . ." He seemed to be searching for something to say. I hoped it was more about himself or about the other werewolves, but when he finally spoke, he said, "That special school you go to. You take theater?"

"I'm in the theater arts stream. We still take all the regular classes, like math, English, science. . . ."

And so we shifted to simpler subjects for the rest of the walk.

"A little."

thirty-three

W E REACHED THE NEXT town and found the bus stop—a flower shop, actually, with tickets sold at the till. We tried again for youth prices and, as in Buffalo, got them without question. Figures.

That meant we had extra cash and a little more than two hours before departure. As for what we'd do with that time and money? Our grumbling stomachs answered that question.

It was getting dark now, still early evening though, so no one paid any attention to a couple of teens walking around. We went a few blocks looking for a place that sold hot, cheap food. Derek's nose led us to a fast-food Chinese restaurant. A popular destination, unfortunately, with a huge line. I saved us a table while he went up to the counter.

The line barely seemed to be moving, and the restaurant

was stifling hot. Before long, my eyelids were flagging.

"Tired, dear?"

I straightened to see an elderly woman in a yellow coat standing beside my table. She smiled at me. I returned it.

"Mind if I sit for a moment?" She waved at the empty chair across from me.

My gaze shot to Derek, still five people from the front of the line.

"I'll leave when your young man comes back," she said. "It's terribly busy in here, isn't it?"

I nodded and waved for her to take the seat. She did.

"I have a great-granddaughter your age," she said. "About fourteen, I'm guessing."

"That's right," I said, hoping I didn't sound too nervous. I shouldn't be answering questions, even incorrectly, but I didn't know what else to do. I glanced at Derek, hoping for rescue, but he was studying the menu board.

"Ninth grade?"

"Yes."

"And what's your favorite subject, dear?"

"Drama."

She laughed. "I haven't heard that one. Is it like acting?"

I explained and as we talked, I relaxed. Once we got beyond age and grade, she didn't ask anything too personal— not even my name. She was just an old lady who wanted to talk, which was nice for a change.

We chatted until Derek was second in line. Then laughter erupted at a table behind me. I turned to see two couples, a year or two older than me. The girls were sneering in disgust. One guy was red-faced with stifled laughter. The other wasn't bothering to hold his in, laughing so hard he was doubled over.

All four were looking at me.

The entire restaurant was looking at me.

It was like a nightmare where kids are laughing at you, and you keep walking through the halls, not knowing why until you realize you aren't wearing any pants. I knew I was wearing pants. The only thing I could think of was my black hair. It wasn't *that* bad, was it?

"Oh, dear," whispered the old woman.

"Wh-what's wrong? Wh-what did I do?"

She leaned over, her eyes glistening. Tears? Why would she be—?

"I'm sorry," she said. "I only . . ." She gave a sad twist of a smile. "I only wanted to speak to you. You seemed like such a nice girl."

I caught a glimpse of Derek, out of line now, striding over, glowering at the snickering boys. The woman got to her feet and leaned across the table again.

"It was very nice talking to you, dear." She put her hand on mine . . . and it passed through.

I leaped to my feet.

"I'm sorry," she said again.

The look on her face was so sad that I wanted to say it was okay, it was my fault. But before I could get a word out, she faded away, and then all I could hear was the laughter around me, the mutters of "crazy" and "schizo," and I stood there, rooted to the floor, until Derek took my arm, his grip so soft I could barely feel it.

"Come on," he said.

"Yeah," the laughing guy called. "I think your girlfriend's day pass has expired."

Derek slowly raised his head, lip curling in that too-familiar look. I grabbed his arm. He blinked and nodded. As we turned to go, the other guy at the table chimed in.

"Trolling for chicks at the psych ward?" He shook his head. "Now *that's* desperate."

As we passed the front window, I swore every eye inside followed us. I caught a few looks: sympathy, pity, distaste, disgust. Derek moved between me and the window, blocking my view as we walked.

"They didn't need to do that," he said. "Those kids, sure. They're idiots. But the grown-ups should know better. What if you *were* mentally ill?"

He led me around to the parking lot, then stopped at the back, under the shadow of the building overhang.

"You'll never see them again," he said. "And if they'd treat a real mentally ill person like that, then you shouldn't care what they think. Bunch of morons."

I said nothing, just stared out at the parking lot, shivering.

He shifted in front of me, trying to block the wind.

"W-we should go," I said. "You need to eat. I'm sorry."

"For what? Talking to yourself? So what? People do it all the time. They should have ignored it."

"Would you?"

"Sure. None of my business. I—"

"—wouldn't laugh or stare. I know. But you couldn't ignore it. Maybe you'd pretend not to notice, but you'd still think about it, about the person doing it, what was wrong with her, whether she was going to freak out and pull a gun or . . ." I wrapped my arms around myself. "I'm babbling. But you know what I mean. I was sitting in a restaurant, carrying on a conversation with someone and I never even guessed she was a ghost."

"You'll figure it out."

"How? They *look* like people. They *sound* like people. Unless they walk through the furniture, there's no clue. Do I have to stop talking to strangers? Ignore every person who walks up to me? *That'll* look normal." I gave my head a sharp shake. "Babbling again. I'm sorry. And I'm sorry you got caught up in that."

"You think I care?" He put one hand on the wall and leaned down to me. "You'll work it out. Other necromancers do. You just need to figure out the tricks of the trade."

"Before I get locked up?"

"Much more of this on-the-run stuff, and you might be going into restaurants, talking to yourself on purpose, trying to get locked up someplace with a bed and a hot shower."

I managed a smile. "Right now, I'd settle for hot food."

"How about hot chocolate?"

"What?"

"On the way here I saw one of those fancy coffee places, some Starbucks knockoff. Big armchairs, a fireplace . . . Didn't look too busy. This isn't exactly a five-dollar-coffee town."

I pictured curling up in a chair, in front of a fire, sipping a huge, steaming hot chocolate. I smiled.

"It's settled then," he said. "We'll get brownies or cookies to eat. A real nutritious dinner. Now I think it was this way . . ."

We set out.

The coffee shop had been on the street with the bus stop. We tried to get there—and out of the freezing cold—as quickly as possible. After cutting through a couple of parking lots, we saw our next potential shortcut: a playground. When I started to cross the street, Derek stopped me.

"That's not always the kind of place you want to be at night."

He was right, of course. It looked innocent enough—a narrow strip of park with a line of swings and slides, a big plastic play center at the end—but between the equipment and the trees were a lot of shadows. After dark, when the kiddies had gone home, it made the perfect place for bigger, more dangerous kids to hang out.

Derek scanned the park as he sampled the breeze.

"Empty," he said finally. "Let's go."

We jogged across the road. Out in the open now, the wind got even worse, swirling around us, bitter cold. The swings twisted and creaked. As we passed, a sudden gust sent one slamming into my shoulder. I stumbled back with a yelp and caught a mouthful of sand, whirling up from the ground. As I sputtered, Derek's head shot up. I spit out the sand and turned to him. He'd gone still, face lifted.

"What do you smell?" I asked.

"I'm not sure . . . I thought I—" The wind changed and his nostrils flared. His eyes went wide. "Run!"

He gave me a shove and I broke into a sprint. In the last few days, I'd done this "running from danger" stuff often enough that my brain kicked my legs into high gear automatically, my aching feet forgotten.

Derek stayed behind me, footsteps pounding.

"Chloe!" he yelled as a figure stepped into my path.

Derek grabbed me by my shoulders, my feet flying off the ground before I'd even stopped running. He backed us up against the plastic play set. A man was sauntering our way. Another walked from the other direction. Two escape routes, both blocked. Derek glanced up at the play set, but we were against a solid wall of plastic, a crow's nest ten feet overhead. There was a fireman's pole ten feet away, but that wouldn't take us anywhere useful.

The men looked like they were in their twenties. One was tall and lean with blond hair to his collar. He wore a plaid jacket and boots, and looked like he hadn't bothered with a razor in days. His companion was shorter and beefier, swarthy with dark hair. He wore a leather jacket and sneakers.

Neither looked like the kind of guy you'd expect to hang out in a park, hassling kids for cigarettes and pocket money. Hanging out at the monster truck races, maybe, hassling girls for their names and phone numbers.

They didn't seem drunk either. They were walking straight and their eyes looked clear, glittering in the dark like . . .

I shrank back.

Derek's hands tightened on my shoulders and he leaned down, whispering, "Werewolves."

thirty-four

THE TWO WEREWOLVES STOPPED a few yards away from us.

"We're just passing through," Derek said, voice steady. "If this is your territory—"

The blond one cut him off with a laugh. "Our territory? Did you hear that, Ramon? He's asking if this is our territory."

"I know you're werewolves and I know—"

"Werewolves?" Ramon drawled. "Did he say werewolves?"

The blond lifted a finger to his lips in an exaggerated "shhh!" and jerked his head at me.

"She knows," Derek said.

"Tsk-tsk. That's against the rules, pup. You don't go telling your girlfriends what you are, even the cute ones. Didn't your daddy teach you better than that? Who is your daddy, by the way?"

Derek said nothing.

"He's a Cain," Ramon said.

"Think so?" The blond squinted, his head tilting. "Guess he could be."

"If you'd met more than one, Liam, you wouldn't be questioning. That"—he pointed at Derek—"is a Cain. Three things every Cain has in common. Big as a house. Ugly as a mud fence. Dumb as a brick."

"Then he's not—" I began before Derek shushed me.

Liam stepped closer. "Did you say something, cutie?"

"We're just passing through," Derek said. "If this is your territory, then I apologize—"

"Hear that, Ramon? He *apologizes*." Liam took another step closer. "You have no idea whose territory you're on, do you?"

"No, I don't know you. If I should, then—"

"This is *Pack* territory."

Derek shook his head. "No, the Pack is in Syracuse—"

"You think they claim one *city*?" Ramon said. "Their territory is New York *state*."

"You do know what the Pack does to trespassers, don't you, pup?" Liam said. "Your daddy must have shown you the pictures."

Derek said nothing.

"The pictures?" Liam pressed. "Of the last guy who trespassed on Pack territory?"

Still Derek said nothing.

"Your daddy didn't like you much, did he? 'Cause if he did, he would have shown you those pictures, so you didn't make the mistake you're making right now. The last time a mutt got too close to Pack turf, they carved him up with a chain saw. Then they took photos, and they passed them out as a warning to the rest of us."

My stomach lurched. I squeezed my eyes shut until the image passed. They were just making this up to scare us . . . and it was working——at least on me. My heart pounded so loudly I was sure they could hear it. Derek squeezed my shoulder, his thumb rubbing, telling me to stay calm.

"No, I haven't seen them. But thanks for the warning. I'll——"

"Who *is* your daddy?" Ramon asked. "Zachary Cain? You're darker, but you've got his look. You're about the right age, too. And that might explain why he didn't raise you right."

"Him being dead and all," Liam said. "But if it was Zack, then you should *know* to keep off Pack territory."

"Should I?" Derek said, his voice emotionless.

"Don't you know how your daddy died? Dumb ass decided to join an uprising against the Pack, got himself caught. Tortured to death, right up there in Syracuse." He looked at

Ramon. "Think they used the chain saw?"

Derek cut in, "If the Pack's so bad, why are *you* on their territory?"

"Maybe we're Pack."

"Then you wouldn't be talking like you were, saying 'their' territory, what 'they' do."

Liam laughed. "Check this out. A Cain with brains. Must come from your momma."

"Do you want to know why we're here?" Ramon said. "A mission of mercy, and we're the ones praying for mercy. See, we hooked up with this kid from down under last year. We quickly found out why he'd left home."

"Man-eater," Liam said.

"M-man-eater?" I didn't mean to say it aloud, but it slipped out.

"It's a disgusting habit. Now hunting humans? Killing them?" He smiled. "That's always good sport. But eating? Not my style. Well, unless you count that time in Mexico—"

Derek cut him off. "So if *you're* allowed on Pack territory, I'm sure they won't bother me. I'm not causing trouble."

"Can I finish my story?" Ramon said. "So this Aussie, he's not very discreet about his bad habit. The Pack catches wind of it. Next thing you know, all three of us are on their hit list."

"The Aussie dude goes to ground," Liam said, "leaving me and Ramon holding the bag. The Pack doesn't care if we're man-eaters or not. We've had some run-ins with them before so, as far as they're concerned, we've used up our free swings. Batter out. They already caught up with Ramon once. Luckily, he got away. Or most of him."

Ramon pulled up his shirt. His side was pitted and puckered with healing scar tissue, the kind of thing I'd only seen in SFX demonstrations.

"So now you're heading up to Syracuse to talk to the Pack," I said. "Set them straight."

"That's right. Or that was the plan. But it's Russian roulette, see? We throw ourselves at their mercy, and we might never stand up again. Then we caught an amazing break."

He looked at Ramon, who nodded. For a moment, neither said a word. Liam stood there, a smirk playing on his lips, as he dragged it out.

"The break?" I asked finally, knowing Derek wouldn't.

"I had to take a piss. About two miles north of here. Pulled off the highway, got out of the car, and guess what I smelled."

"Me," Derek said.

"The answer to our prayers. A Cain?" Liam shook his head. "What did we do to get so lucky? The Pack hates Cains. Bunch of Neanderthals too stupid to keep out of trouble. If we hand them you, tell them *you* were the one snacking on humans . . ."

I felt Derek shift behind me.

"Thinking of leaving, pup? That would be rude. You bolt, we'll have to grab your girl, hold on to her until you decide to come back and hear me out."

Derek went still, but I could feel his heart thumping against my back, hear his shallow breaths as he struggled to stay calm. My hand slid into my pocket, grasping my knife. Derek squeezed my shoulder, rubbing it again.

"It's okay," he whispered. "It's okay." But his heart kept pounding, telling me it wasn't.

"Sure," Liam said. "It'll be just fine. The Pack aren't complete monsters. This poor orphaned kid just screwed up. He'll never do it again. They'll understand. He's probably got a—" He glanced at Ramon. "Fifty-fifty?"

Ramon considered it, then nodded.

Liam turned back to us. "Fifty-fifty chance of surviving. And even if he doesn't, they'll make it quick. No chain saws for you."

"Why are you telling us this?" I asked. It was like the classic James Bond scene, where the villain explains what he'll do to Bond, giving him time to think up an escape plan. Which I really hoped Derek was doing. I might not be much help—not when it came to plotting against werewolves—but I was really good at stalling.

"Good question, cutie. Why not just grab him, tie him up, toss him in our truck, and deliver him to the wolves up in Syracuse? Because the Alpha isn't stupid. If we throw him a kid who's screaming he didn't do it, he might listen. See, there's only one way this can work. If your boyfriend comes along voluntarily and confesses."

Derek snorted. "Yeah."

"You don't like that plan?"

Derek shot him a look.

Liam sighed. "All right then. Option two it is. We kill you and have some fun with your girl."

"I'll do the killing," Ramon said. "You can take the girl. She's a little young for me."

Liam grinned. "I like them young."

His gaze traveled up and down me, his look making every hair on my body rise. Derek's hands vise gripped my shoulders.

"Leave her out of this," Derek rumbled.

"Never." Liam bared his teeth. "I was almost hoping you'd say no. Sure, I'd love a scapegoat to feed the Pack. But a little cutie like that, who already knows what I am? That's . . ." He smiled. "Sweet."

He gave me a look that made me shrink back into Derek, my hand gripping the knife so hard it hurt. When Liam stepped forward again, Derek's arm shot around me, a growl vibrating up from his stomach.

Liam put his hand out toward me. When Derek tensed, he pulled back, then did it again, testing his reaction, laughing when he got one, until even Ramon started to laugh.

"Check this out," Liam said. "I think the pup's got himself a mate. Isn't that the cutest thing?" He leaned toward Derek, voice lowering. "It won't work out. It never does. Why don't you just give her to me now, let me help you get over it.

Painful, but quick. It's the best way."

Derek moved me behind him. The werewolves let out a howl of laughter.

"I think he's saying no," Ramon said.

"Leave her out of this," Derek said.

Liam shook his head. "How can I do that? Look at her. So tiny and cute, big blue eyes all wide and scared." He leaned around Derek to look at me. "That hair doesn't do anything for her. I can still smell the dye. What color is it really? Blond, I bet. She looks like a blond."

His look made my insides twist.

"If I go with you, she walks away," Derek said. "Right?"

"No," I whispered.

"Course she does," Liam said.

"Derek," I whispered.

He put his hand behind him, gesturing for me to be quiet. It was a trick. He had a plan. He must have a plan.

"Here's the deal," Derek said.

"Deal?" Liam laughed. "This isn't up for negotiation, pup."

"It is if you want my cooperation. I'll go with you, but the first thing we do is get her on a bus. After I've seen her leave safely, I'm all yours."

"Uh-huh." Liam rolled back on his heels. "Is your intelligence feeling a mite insulted, Ramon?"

"Sure is." Ramon strolled up beside his friend.

"You said you'd release her—"

"And we will. Once you've done your part. Until then, she's our collateral to make sure you do. And don't worry; we'll take good care—"

Derek shot forward so fast it caught them both off guard. He grabbed Liam by the front of his shirt and whipped him into Ramon. The men went down.

"Run," Derek said.

I pulled out my knife.

"Run!"

He gave me a shove that sent me flying. I started running, but slowly, my hand on the knife as I watched over my shoulder, getting far enough so Derek would think I was safe without abandoning him.

Derek caught Ramon and whipped him against the steel fireman's pole, his head hitting with a twang.

Liam lunged for Derek. He feinted out of the way. As Ramon lay motionless on the ground, Derek and Liam faced off, circling. Liam lunged again, and Derek twisted, but Liam caught the back of his sweatshirt, yanked him off his feet, and threw him.

Derek hit the ground in a slide. Liam bore down on him, taking his time as Derek struggled to get up, wheezing and coughing, crawling along the ground. I veered to race back. Then Derek shot to his feet and broke into a run.

thirty-five

W E ZIGZAGGED THROUGH A dark commercial district, with Liam at our heels the whole way. When we reached a town house complex, he fell back, like he didn't want to be seen chasing a couple of kids. He kept about fifty feet behind us, clearly planning to close the gap when we got to a more secluded place.

On the far side of the complex was a strip mall. When we reached it, we looked back, and he was gone. We kept going, though, until we were another two blocks away, behind a closed bakery.

I leaned against the cool brick wall, gasping for air.

"You wanted tips on self-defense?" Derek said, breathing hard.

I nodded.

"The first lesson our dad taught us? If you're up against

a better fighter, the first chance you get, surprise him with your secret move . . ." He leaned down to my ear. "Run like hell."

A laugh bubbled up and my teeth stopped chattering. I took a deep breath and let myself relax against the wall.

"So he was as strong as you are?" I asked.

"Whatever those scientists tweaked, it wasn't my strength. He might have been smaller than me, but he was just as strong, and he's got a lot more fighting experience. I was seriously outclassed." He wiped off gravel embedded in his chin. "You aren't the only one who's going to need training. My dad taught me to use my strength to my advantage. Only that doesn't work fighting other werewolves."

He rolled his shoulders, then pushed sweat-sodden hair out of his eyes. "We'll catch our breath, but then we need to move. Once he figures out he lost us, he'll go back and pick up our trail."

"I'm good," I said, straightening. "Any time you want to go——"

Something moved above our heads. I looked up as Liam leaped from the rooftop. He landed on his feet right behind Derek.

"Your boy's not quite ready to leave, cutie. He has some business to finish first."

Liam hit Derek with an uppercut that sent him reeling, blood spraying from his mouth. I fumbled for my knife, but it caught in the folds of my pocket. By the time I had it out,

Derek had hit Liam back and now they were both on the ground, rolling, each trying to get a grip on the other.

How many movie fight scenes had I seen? I'd even written a few. But being there, watching it, with someone I knew in serious danger, made those movie fights seem like they'd been filmed in slow motion. This was a whirlwind of fists and feet and grunts and gasps and blood. Mostly what I saw was the blood, flying, spattering, dripping, as I darted back and forth, knife in my hand.

I thought of all the times I'd been in an audience, snarking about the stupid, useless girl hovering on the sidelines of a fight, holding a weapon but doing nothing, watching the guy get pummeled. I knew I had to help Derek. I knew he was in trouble, that most of that blood and those gasps and grunts were his. I wasn't afraid to use the knife. I *wanted* to use it. But there wasn't a chance. The fists flew and the bodies flew and the kicks flew, and every time I thought I had an opening, I'd dash forward only to find Derek in my path, not Liam, and I'd pull up fast before stabbing *him*.

Then Liam got Derek on his knees, in a headlock, his free hand in Derek's hair. He yanked Derek's head back, and I saw the girl at the truck stop, her throat slashed, and I didn't stop to think whether I could do it, I ran at Liam and I drove the knife into the back of his thigh, ramming it in to the hilt.

Liam let out a howl and backhanded me. I sailed into the air, knife still clutched in my hand. I heard Derek shout my name as I hit the wall. My head cracked back against the brick. The floodlights overhead exploded into shards of light.

Derek grabbed me before I hit the ground.

"I-I'm fine," I said, pushing him away.

I got my footing, wobbled, and found it again.

"I'm fine," I said, stronger now.

I looked around. My knife had fallen beside me. I scooped it up.

Liam lay behind Derek, writhing on the ground, snarling as he tried to stanch the blood. We took off.

This time no one was chasing us, but it didn't matter. We kept running, knowing Liam would come after us the moment he was able.

"We need to get you to a bathroom," Derek said as we rounded a building.

"Me? I'm—"

"We *need* to get you to a bathroom."

I closed my mouth. Derek was obviously in shock and *he* did need a bathroom, to clean up and check the damage.

"He's going to follow our trail," I said. "We have to trick him."

"I know. I'm thinking."

I was, too, recalling every fugitive movie I'd ever seen where someone evaded tracking dogs. I slowed when I saw a huge puddle from the rain and a trash-clogged gutter. The water stretched at least ten feet across. Then, I had a better idea.

"Climb on the curb and walk along the edge," I said.

"What?"

"Just do it."

We jogged along the curb until I saw a door to a small apartment building. I led Derek over and pulled on the knob. It was locked.

"Can you break it?" I asked.

He wiped off his bloody hands, then grabbed the knob. I tried to get a better look at him to see how badly he'd been beaten, but it was too dark, and I could see only smears of blood everywhere—on his face, his hands, his sweatshirt.

He yanked the door open. We went inside, circled around a bit, then came back out.

"Now we'll follow the path we came on," I said. "Along the top of the curb. Backtrack."

When we reached the puddle, I stopped. "We're going to cut through."

Derek nodded. "So he'll reach this, keep following our trail and think we're somewhere in that apartment, not realizing we doubled back on our tracks. Smart."

Wading ankle deep through frigid water seemed to knock away the last of Derek's shock. Once we reached the other side, he took over and got us downwind so Liam couldn't smell us. Then he hustled me into a coffee shop. There were only a handful of people inside, all clustered at the counter, chatting with the server. No one even looked up as we made a beeline for the bathroom.

Derek scooted me into the men's room and locked the door. He hoisted me onto the counter before I could protest, then scrubbed his hands well, sleeves pushed to his elbows, like he was preparing for surgery.

"Uh, Derek . . . ?"

He wet a paper towel, and took my chin, lifting and wiping my face.

"Derek? I'm not hurt."

"You're covered in blood."

"But it's not mine. Honest. It's from—"

"The werewolf. I know." He picked up my hand and started cleaning it. "That's why I have to get it off."

"Derek?" I leaned down, trying to see his face. "Are you okay?"

He kept scrubbing. "There are two ways to become a werewolf. Either you're born one or you get bitten by one. If you get the saliva in your bloodstream, it's like a virus."

"Blood, too?"

"Dad says no, it's just saliva. But he could be wrong, and you've got cuts and scrapes and blood all over."

I had a *few* cuts and scrapes, and I was only flecked with blood, but I kept my mouth shut and let him clean.

As he did, I tried to check out how badly *he* was hurt. His scraped cheeks were pitted with gravel. His nose was bloodied. Broken? One eye was already darkening. Was that blood in the corner? His lip was cut and swollen. Were any teeth loose? Missing?

"Stop fidgeting, Chloe."

I couldn't help it. His injuries obviously needed more attention than mine, but there was no sense saying anything until he was done.

Finally, when he seemed to have scrubbed off every fleck of blood—and a few layers of skin—I said, "Okay, now on to you."

"Take off your jacket and sweatshirt."

"Derek, I'm *clean*. Trust me, I've never been this clean."

"You've got blood on your cuffs."

As I took off the jacket, the zipper snagged my necklace.

"It's caught—" I began.

Derek gave the jacket a tug . . . and the chain snapped, the pendant dropping. He swore and grabbed it before it hit the floor.

"—on my necklace."

He swore some more, then said, "I'm sorry."

"The girl in the alley grabbed it," I lied. "The clasp was probably weak. No biggie."

He looked down at the pendant in his hand. "Wasn't this red before?"

I hadn't taken a good look at it for a couple of days—no mirrors and the pendant had been under my shirt. I'd thought the color seemed different before, but it had changed even more now, almost blue.

"I—I think it's some kind of talisman," I said. "My mom

gave it to me, to ward off bogeymen—ghosts, I guess."

"Huh." He stared at it, then shook his head and handed it back. "Better keep it on you then."

I stuffed it into my pocket, down at the bottom where it would be safe. Then I took off my sweatshirt and pushed up my sleeves. No blood had seeped through, but he still made me wash my forearms.

"Okay, *now* can we take care of the guy who was actually *in* the fight? There's a lot of blood. It seems to be mostly from your nose."

"It is."

"You got hit in the chest a few times. How are your ribs?"

"Maybe bruised. Nothing critical."

"Shirt off."

He sighed, like now *I* was the one fussing too much.

"If you want me to leave, so you can look after it yourself . . ."

"Nah."

He pulled off his sweatshirt and folded it on the counter. There wasn't any blood below his collar, where it had dripped from his nose and lip. I guess that's to be expected when you're fighting with fists, not weapons. He said his ribs on the right were sore to the touch but, to be honest, I wouldn't know bruised from broken. He was breathing fine, and that was the main thing.

"Okay, your nose. Is it broken? Does it hurt?"

"Even if it was broken, there's nothing you can do."

"Let me check your eyes."

He grumbled, but didn't resist. The bloodshot corner was already clearing, and I couldn't see any cuts. He'd have a shiner, though. When I told him that, he just grunted. I wet a fresh paper towel.

"You have dirt in your cheek. Let me—"

"No."

He caught my hand before I could touch his face. He took the cloth and leaned over the counter to wipe the dirt out himself. I tried not to wince as I watched. The gravel had gouged his cheek badly.

"You're going to need to get that checked out."

"Yeah." He looked at himself in the mirror, his expression unreadable, until he noticed me watching, then turned away and stepped back from the mirror. I handed him another wet paper towel and he cleaned his neck and collar, freckled with dried blood.

"Still got that deodorant?" he asked.

I retrieved it from my jacket pocket and set it on the counter. He kept washing.

"In the playground," I said, "when you were negotiating, you weren't serious, right? About going with them? It was a trick."

Silence stretched for way too long.

"Derek?"

He didn't look up, just reached over and got a fresh

towel, his gaze averted.

"Did you hear *anything* they said?" I asked.

"About what?" His gaze still on the towel, he folded it carefully before throwing it into the trash. "Hunting humans for sport? Eating them?" The bitterness in his voice cut through me. "Yeah, I caught that part."

"That doesn't have anything to do with you."

He lifted his eyes, gaze shuttered. "No?"

"Not unless being a werewolf transforms you into a wolf *and* a redneck moron."

He shrugged and ripped off more paper towels.

"Do you want to hunt humans, Derek?"

"No."

"Do you think about it?"

"No."

"How about eating them? Do you think about that?"

He shot me a look of disgust. "Of course not."

"Do you even dream about killing people?"

He shook his head. "Just deer, rabbits." When I frowned, he went on. "For the last few years I've been dreaming of being a wolf. Running in the forest. Hunting deer and rabbits."

"Right. Like a *wolf*, not a man-eating monster."

He wet the paper towel.

"So why would you ever let these guys take you to—" I stopped. "The Pack. Is that what you wanted? Tell them you'll go, and after they release me, tell the Pack the truth and use that as a . . . an introduction? Meet them? Be with your own kind?"

"No. That doesn't matter to me. Dad says it does to other werewolves. It mattered to the other boys—they hated anyone who wasn't one of us. Me? I don't care. The only reason I'd want to meet a werewolf would be the same reason you'd want to meet a necromancer. To talk, get tips, training, whatever. Preferably from one who doesn't think hunting humans makes good sport."

"Like this Pack. They kill man-eaters and they don't seem that thrilled about man hunters. Is that what you thought? You could go to them and they'd help you? When I asked if you were listening to those two goons, that's the part I meant—about the Pack. What they'd do to you. Killing werewolves with chain saws and stuff."

Derek snorted.

"You don't believe it, then." I relaxed, nodding. "No one would do that. Cut someone up with a chain saw and pass around photos? Those guys were just trying to scare you."

"No, I'm sure there are photos. And I'm sure those guys *believe* the Pack carved up someone. But the photos must be fakes. You can do that kind of stuff with special effects and makeup, can't you?"

"Sure, but why?"

"For the same reason you just said. To scare people. Liam and Ramon think the Pack really did it, so they steer clear of its territory. Doesn't seem like a bad idea to me."

"But would you ever think of it yourself?"

That look of disgust returned. "Of course not."

"But you considered entrusting your life to people who would? Werewolves who play judge and jury for their own kind? Torture and kill other werewolves? Knowing that, you'd go to them, pretend you killed humans, and hope they'd go easy on you because you're a kid? Or were those odds okay with you? If they decided you didn't deserve to live, maybe they'd be right?"

I meant it as sarcasm. But when his answer was slow coming—much too slow—my heart hammered.

"Derek!"

He trashed the wet paper towel. "No, I don't have a death wish, okay?"

"You'd better not."

"I don't, Chloe," he said softly. "I mean it. I don't."

Our eyes locked and the panic buzzing in my head turned to something else, my heart still hammering, my throat going dry. . . .

I looked away and mumbled, "Good."

He backed up. "We gotta go."

I nodded and slid off the counter.

Thirty-six

I GAVE DEREK MY jacket and he wore it without argument—it covered the blood spatter on his sweatshirt. As we left the bathroom, the people in the coffee shop finally noticed us, but only to call out that the bathroom was for paying customers only.

The coffee shop had a post-winter clearance on promotional thermoses, emblazoned with their name, so Derek got one filled with hot chocolate, plus two paper cups. Add a half-dozen donuts and we had dinner to go.

We couldn't just waltz back to the bus station, though. Liam would still be hunting for us, maybe joined by Ramon. If they'd been following us earlier, they might know we'd gone to the bus stop and would wait for us there.

So we stayed downwind or behind buildings, then waited a half block away until we saw the bus coming. There was no sign of the werewolves. I'm sure it helped that it was just a bus stop, not a terminal—if they'd followed our trail to the flower shop, they probably hadn't figured out that we'd been there to buy bus tickets.

Yet it was only after we were on and the bus pulled away that I finally relaxed. I was on my second cup of chocolate when my eyelids started to droop.

"You should get some sleep," Derek said.

I stifled a yawn. "It won't be that long, will it? An hour and a half?"

"Close to double that. We're on the milk run."

"What?"

"The route that hits all the little towns," he said.

He took my empty cup. I shifted, trying to get comfortable. He balled up my discarded sweatshirt and put it against his shoulder.

"Go on," he said. "I don't bite."

"And from what I hear, that's a good thing."

He gave a rumbling chuckle. "Yeah, it is."

I leaned against his shoulder.

"In a few hours, you'll be in a bed," he said. "Bet *that's* a good thing, huh?"

Had anything so simple *ever* sounded so amazing? But as I thought of it, my smile faded and I lifted my head.

"What if—?"

"Andrew isn't there? Or he didn't take them in? Then we'll find Simon and we'll splurge on a cheap motel. We are getting a bed tonight. Guaranteed."

"And a bathroom."

He chuckled again. "Yeah, and a bathroom."

"Thank God." I laid my head on the sweatshirt pillow again. "What are you looking forward to?"

"Food."

I laughed. "I bet. *Hot* food. That's what I want."

"And a shower. I really want a shower."

"Well, you'll have to fight me for it. If that guy could smell my hair color, I didn't do a very good job of rinsing it out. Which may explain why it feels so gross."

"About that. The color. I didn't mean—"

"I know. You just picked something that would make me look different. And it did."

"Yeah, but it looks fake. Even those guys could tell. Wash it out, and we'll get some of that red stuff you like."

I closed my eyes. As I drifted off, Derek started humming, so softly I could barely hear it. I lifted my head.

"Sorry," he said. "I've got this stupid tune stuck in my head. No idea what it is."

I sang a few bars of "Daydream Believer."

"Uh, yeah," he said. "How'd . . . ?"

"My fault. My mom used to sing it to me when I couldn't sleep, so I was singing it last night. It's the Monkees—the world's first boy band." I glanced up at him. "And I've just lost any scrap of cool I ever possessed, haven't I?"

"At least you're not the one still singing it."

I smiled, rested my head against his shoulder, and fell asleep to his soft off-tune humming.

We got off at one of those small "milk run" stops. When Simon said Andrew lived outside New York City, I figured he meant in the Hudson Valley or Long Island, but the bus dropped us in a town whose name I didn't recognize. Derek said it was about thirty miles from the city and about a mile from Andrew's place.

Maybe it was because we knew the house was close, but that mile seemed to pass in minutes. We talked and joked and goofed around. A week ago, if someone had told me Derek *could* joke or goof around, I wouldn't have believed it. But he was at ease now, stoked even, with our destination so near.

"It's just up there," he said.

We were on a narrow road lined with trees. It wasn't really farm country. More like a rural community, with houses set way back from the road, hidden behind fences and walls and evergreens. As I squinted, Derek pointed.

"See the old-fashioned gas lamps at the end of that drive? They're on, too, which is a good sign."

We turned into the driveway—as winding and treed as the road, and seemingly just as long. Eventually we rounded a corner and the house came into sight. It was a cute little cottage, like something you'd see in an old English town, with stone walls and ivy and gardens that I'm sure would be beautiful in a month or two. Right now the most beautiful part was the light blazing from a front window.

"They're here," I said.

"*Someone's* here," Derek corrected.

When I hurried forward, he caught my arm. I looked back to see him scanning the house, his nostrils flaring. He tilted his head and frowned.

"What do you hear?" I asked.

"Nothing." He turned to survey the dark woods surrounding the house. "It's too quiet."

"Simon and Tori are probably asleep," I said, but I lowered my voice and glanced about, his anxiety contagious.

When we reached the cobblestoned walk, Derek dropped into a crouch. He lowered his head a foot from the ground. I wanted to tell him to come on, just knock on the door and we'd know whether they were here, stop being so paranoid. But I'd learned that what I would have once considered paranoia was, in this new life, sensible caution.

After a moment, he nodded and some of the tension went out of the set of his shoulders as he pushed to his feet.

"Simon's here?" I asked.

"And Tori."

He took one last slow look around, almost reluctantly, like he wanted to race to the front door as much as I did. Then we continued along the walk, the stones squeaking beneath our wet sneakers.

Derek was so busy looking out at the forest that I was the one who had to grab his arm this time. I pulled him short and directed his attention to our path.

The front door was ajar.

Derek swore. Then he took a deep breath, as if fighting off the first twitches of panic. He motioned for me to get behind him, then seemed to think better of it and waved for me to stand beside the door, against the wall.

When I was out of the way, he prodded the door open an inch. Then another. A third tap and he caught a smell, nostrils flaring. His eyebrows gathered in confusion.

After a moment, I smelled it, too. A strong bitter smell, familiar . . . "Coffee." I mouthed. He nodded. That's what it was—burned coffee.

He eased the door open wider. I pressed my back against the wall, resisting the urge to sneak a peek. I watched him instead as his gaze scanned the room beyond, his expression telling me nothing immediately caught his attention.

He motioned for me to stay put and stepped inside. Now I really fidgeted, tapping my thighs, scrunching my toes in my shoes, heart tripping. I wished I was the kind of girl who always carried a compact mirror. I could use it like they do in spy movies, to see what was happening around the corner.

When I leaned a little too close to the doorway, my inner voice piped up, telling me not to be stupid. The guy with bionic senses was better equipped for this.

Finally Derek backed out. He started to pantomime that he'd go in and look around while I stayed out here. Then, after a glance at the surrounding darkness, he seemed to think better of his first instinct. He pointed to my pocket and mimicked opening a switchblade. I took it out. He gestured for me to stay behind him, his emphatic jabs and accompanying scowl saying better than any words, *I mean it, Chloe.* I nodded.

We went inside. The front door led into a small foyer with a closet, then opened into the living room. A few pieces of mail were scattered in front of the closet door. I thought maybe it had been shoved through a mail slot, but there wasn't one, and I remembered seeing a mailbox at the end of the long drive. A small table leaned precariously against the corner, and a piece of ad mail rested on top of it.

Derek was moving into the living room. I hurried to catch up before I got "the look."

It was small and cozy, like you'd expect in a country cottage. The chairs and sofa were piled with mismatched pillows. Hand-knitted blankets were neatly folded over each back. The tops of the end tables were clear, but the shelves underneath bulged with magazines, and the two bookshelves were overflowing. One blazing lamp was the only electrical appliance—there was no TV, computer, or other techno gadget to be seen. An old-fashioned sitting room, for lighting the fire and curling up with a book.

Derek headed for the next doorway. When the floorboards creaked, he stopped short and I nearly plowed into him. He cocked his head. The house was silent. Eerily still and silent. Even if everyone had gone to bed, it shouldn't be so quiet, considering both Simon and Tori snored.

We stepped into the kitchen. The stink of burned coffee was gag-inducing. I could see the coffeemaker on the counter, the red light still on, a half-inch of sludge in the bottom, like a full pot of coffee had been simmering for at least a day. Derek walked over and turned it off.

There was a plate on the counter. On it was a piece of toast with one bite gone. An open jam jar rested beside it, the knife still inside. A coffee mug sat on the table, on top of an opened newspaper. I looked in the cup. It was two-thirds full, the cream congealing in an oily white film.

Derek waved for me to fall behind him again and he headed for the back of the house.

thirty-seven

T HE HOUSE WAS BIGGER than it looked, with four doors off the rear hall.

The first led to a guest room, the bed covers pulled tight, towels folded on top of the dresser, no sign that anyone had used it recently. The next was an office with a futon couch—more room for guests, but again, no sign that any had been here in a while. Across the hall was a bathroom. It, too, looked unused, with wrapped soap and unopened shampoo on the counter, ready for guests.

At the end of the hall was the master bedroom. It was as tidy as the rest of the house, but the bed was unmade. A bathrobe lay crumpled on a chair. On one nightstand sat a half-filled glass of water and a paperback novel. There was an attached bathroom, with a rumpled bath mat and a towel draped over the shower stall. I squeezed the towel. Dry.

Back in the hall, Derek dropped again to sniff.

"They were here," he said.

"Simon and Tori?"

He nodded.

"They didn't sleep here last night, though," I said. "No one's used this room in a while.

He nodded again.

"Can you smell anyone else?" I asked.

"Just Andrew. I'll check the front again."

He walked off, apparently having decided that the house was empty, so it was safe to leave me behind. I met up with him back in the kitchen as I examined the toast. He bent to sniff it.

"Andrew?" I asked.

He nodded.

I walked to the table and looked at the newspaper. "It's like he was reading this, drinking his coffee, and waiting for the toast to pop. He puts jam on it, takes a bite and then . . ."

And then *what*? That was the question.

I picked up the coffeepot. "It's been on since at least this morning."

He walked over and eyed the pot. "Rings show it was almost full. To evaporate that much, it's been on since yesterday."

"Before Simon and Tori arrived."

Derek didn't answer. He was staring out the window over the sink, his gaze blank.

"Is this . . . like your dad?" I asked. "When he disappeared?"

He nodded.

"Were there any other scents at the door?"

He turned slowly then, his attention shifting back to me. "Yeah, but there are lots of reasons why someone would come to the door. None seem to go past it. No recent trails, at least."

"The table in the front hall looks like someone bumped into it and the mail fell off. From the looks of this place, Andrew doesn't seem the type to leave a mess like that."

"No, he's not."

"Something happened at the door, then. Someone came or someone called and Andrew left in a hurry."

Like their dad. I didn't say it again—I already knew he was thinking it.

I circled the kitchen, looking for more clues. Everything was so neat that any disruption would stick out, and I couldn't see any.

"It's definitely breakfast for one," I said. "And there's no sign that Simon or Tori used the spare bedrooms or guest bath. That would suggest that whatever happened here, it happened before they arrived."

Derek nodded, like he'd already come to this conclusion.

I opened cupboards, all perfectly ordered inside. "It seems like Simon did exactly what we did—came in, walked around, realized something had happened and then . . ."

And then what? That question again.

"If they left, there'll be a second trail outside," Derek said as he strode to the kitchen door. "I'll see if they went back to the road or—"

"Or maybe this will help." I snatched a drawing hung among the bills and notes on the fridge. "This is Simon's work, isn't it?"

It wasn't as obvious as the message he'd left in the warehouse—a comic-book character would stand out too much on Andrew's fridge. Simon trusted Derek to recognize his work even when it was a simple sketch.

"Yeah, it's his."

"It's someone swimming. I have no idea what it means but—"

"Pool house," Derek called back, already striding toward the rear of the house.

I scrambled after him, but by the time I reached the door, it was already shutting. I stepped out into the pitch-black yard, huge trees closing in on all sides, blocking the moonlight. Derek popped from the shadows, making me yelp. He waved me back inside and shut the door.

"He's not there?" I said.

"Running outside might not be such a smart idea."

He took the picture again and studied it, like he was looking for any clue that Simon hadn't drawn it willingly.

"Front door," he said. "We'll go the long way. Sneak up."

With an impatient wave for me to stay close, he started

off. I took out my switchblade again and followed. It was a slow trip to the pool house. Derek stopped every few feet to look, listen, and sniff. It was too dark for me to do anything except stay as close as I could. With his dark clothing and quiet walk, that wasn't easy; and every so often I had to reach out and brush the back of his jacket to reassure myself he was still in front of me.

Finally we could see a clearing ahead and, in it, a pale building. Then came a shrill whistle.

"Simon," Derek said.

He broke into a jog, leaving me scrambling after him. Before he reached the door, it clicked open.

"Hey, bro," Simon whispered. He thumped Derek's back, the nylon jacket crinkling. "Where's Chloe?"

"Right behind——" Derek turned and saw me stumbling along. "Sorry."

"Forgot not everyone has your night vision?" Simon thumped him again and strode past, greeting me with a one-armed hug and a whispered, "Good to see you."

He squeezed my upper arm, then started to say something before Derek cut him off with a hissed, "Inside."

We stepped through the door into the glow of a lantern. Noticing that, Derek looked around sharply.

"Relax," Simon said. "No windows. You didn't notice the light, did you?"

Derek grunted and walked farther in. As he'd said, it was a pool house, filled with neatly stacked and organized pool and yard supplies. Simon and Tori had set up two lawn chairs. Wrappers and Diet Coke cans covered a nearby table-top. I glanced around for Tori and found her asleep on an inflated raft.

"The longer she sleeps, the better," Simon said. "It's a good thing you two showed up because another day alone with her?" He pantomimed throttling.

"I saw that," said a sleepy voice. Tori lifted her head. "Believe me, the feeling is mutual."

She sat up and raked her hair back, stifling a yawn. "There's nothing like spending a whole day alone with a guy to make a girl say, 'What was I *thinking*?'"

"At least one good thing came of it," Simon murmured.

Tori looked at me. "He *left* me here. Alone. Unarmed. At the mercy of whoever took his dad's friend—"

"First, from what I hear of your spells, you're a helluva lot better armed than I am," Simon said. "Second. Left you? Excuse me? You refused to come along."

"Because I didn't see the point. Why go racing off look-ing for the bad guys? I'm sure if we stick around here, they'll find us soon enough. The smart thing to do would have been to get as far from this place as possible. But no, poor Derek and Chloe might not find us. Hello?" She waved at Derek. "Human bloodhound. He'll find us."

Simon leaned down to me and whispered, "It was fun."

"And then—" Tori continued.

I cut in, "And then we remembered that we called a

moratorium on bickering and if we have any issues to discuss, we should wait until we're someplace safe."

"We need to discuss a game plan, too," Derek said, "in case this happens again. Right now, the important thing is Andrew." He turned to Simon. "What did you find when you got here?"

Exactly what we had, as Simon explained. The front door had been ajar, and they'd left it that way to warn us to enter with caution. They'd walked through the house, and when Simon realized it looked like when his dad had vanished, they got out of there quickly. Simon left the note, and found the keys, and they retreated to the pool house.

"Do you have the keys?" Derek asked.

Simon handed them to him.

Derek flipped through. "Looks like a full set. Is the car still in the garage?"

Simon swore under his breath. "Totally forgot to check."

"We'll look, but I'll bet it is."

"Car?" Tori walked over. "We have a car?"

"No, we do not—" Derek began.

"You're sixteen, right?" Tori said.

"I turned sixteen two months ago, locked up in Lyle House, meaning I don't have a license and even if I did—"

"But you can drive, right?" she said. "You look old enough that no cop would pull you over as long as you keep to the speed limit, don't run a yellow—"

"I'm not stealing a car from a guy who has disappeared

and may be reported missing at any moment. My only point about the car was that if it's still here, Andrew didn't drive off. Someone took him. We just don't know whether it was with his permission."

"So what are we going to do?"

"Presume he was kidnapped and get as far from here as we can, in case they come back."

Tori turned to Simon. "See? We can get some sleep, then we're taking *my* advice——"

"I mean right now," Derek said.

He was right—the sooner we left, the better—but I couldn't help feeling my shoulders slump at the thought of hitting the road again. Walking again. Eating energy bars and sleeping in alleys again. I tried not to picture the house, warm and cozy, with beds, food, showers . . .

Feeling Derek's gaze on me, I straightened. "I'm good."

"Of course she is," Tori said. "Our perky little——" This time, she cut herself off. "Okay, sorry, but you know what I mean, guys. As long as Chloe can walk, she's not going to admit she needs to rest."

"I slept on the bus."

"For about an hour," Derek said. "And none last night."

"What happened last——?" Simon stopped. "Later, I know. But Tori has a point. Chloe needs to rest and she's not the only one. We're beat. It's already late. If we can rest here safely, we should all recharge our batteries. Otherwise they're going to quit when we need them most."

I could tell Derek wanted us to move out, but after a moment's consideration, he waved us to the door. "We're up at dawn, gone a half-hour later. If you aren't ready, you stay behind. Any light that isn't on, leave it off. Stay away from all the windows. . . ."

thirty-eight

W E ALL SHOWERED. HAVING two bathrooms made that quick. While I was waiting, I tried to tie a knot in my necklace chain—I didn't like keeping the pendant in my pocket. When that didn't work, I looked for string and instead found a piece of ribbon and tied it on that.

After the showers, we ate. Andrew had a lot of convenience food—his housekeeping skills didn't seem to extend to cooking. We found decent frozen meals, cooked them in the microwave, and they tasted so good—better than any gourmet dinner.

Simon organized our watch shifts as we ate. Derek insisted on taking the first, and the rest of us headed to bed, with Tori and me sharing the spare room and Simon on the office futon. No one felt right sleeping in Andrew's bed.

I made a bathroom stop first. When I came out, I saw the photos along the hall, and stopped at a shot of Simon and Derek. Maybe twelve, they were roasting marshmallows over a campfire. Simon looked like Simon, with his spiked dark-blond hair and big grin as he showed off his flaming marshmallow for the camera.

Derek looked different. The picture had been taken before puberty hit. His skin was clear and he had a shock of black hair, still falling into his eyes. He was taller than Simon, but not as much, and he was thinner—he hadn't started filling out yet. He still wasn't magazine cover material, but he was the kind of guy that, at that age myself, I might have stolen a glance at across the classroom and thought he was kind of cute, with really nice eyes.

"That was taken out back here."

I jumped. Simon laughed and shook his head.

"Yes," I said. "I'm still jumpy. So this was here?" I pointed at the picture.

He nodded. "The summer before Dad and Andrew had their fight, I think. There's a clearing where Derek and I camped out." He paused, thinking. "I wonder if Andrew kept all that gear. I'm sure Tori isn't the backpacking type, but . . ."

"If it means no more sleeping in rat-infested buildings, she'll go for it."

"I'll talk Derek into giving us time to look for the camping gear tomorrow. I know you're exhausted, so I won't keep you up chatting, but you will tell me about the adventures I missed this time?"

I managed a tired smile. "Sure." I started to turn away, then stopped. "You've got your watch alarm set, right? You'll get me up after your shift?"

"I doubt either of us will be taking a turn. Derek only let me organize shifts because he wasn't in the mood to argue. I'll go out at three, but he won't give up his post."

"He needs sleep, too."

"Agreed, and I *will* hassle him. But he doesn't like us being here and there's no way he'll let someone without super-hero strength and senses stand guard. The best thing we can do is find those tents and sleeping bags in the morning, get him to the nearest campsite, and let him sleep then."

I got a few steps away before he said, "Chloe?"

I turned. The hall was dark, lit only by the living room light behind him, throwing his face into shadow.

"Was Derek . . . okay with you today? I know he was getting up in your face before we left Buffalo and I was worried. You guys seem fine now. . . ."

"We are."

When he said nothing, I said, "Really. We got along great, actually. A nice change."

I couldn't see his expression, but could feel his gaze on me; then he said softly, "Good." A pause and a more emphatic, "That's good. I'll see you tomorrow then. We'll talk."

We headed for the bedrooms.

*   *   *

Once again, sleep and I weren't on speaking terms. My brain was too busy playing in the land of nightmares.

I kept thinking of the woods surrounding the house. I'd hear a branch scrape the window and leap up, certain it was a bat and, of course, then start thinking of zombie bats, trapped in their crushed bodies. . . .

After a Disneyfied dream of prancing through the forest, leading a singing trail of undead critters, I bolted awake, sweating, and decided it was time to give up the ghost . . . so to speak. I got out of bed and checked the clock. It was almost five, meaning Simon had been right about Derek not letting us take a turn. I got up, grabbed a coat from the front closet, and headed for the kitchen.

"Chloe," Derek's growl vibrated from the forest long before I could see him. "I told Simon I want you guys to sleep—"

He stopped as the smell of sausages drifted his way. I could imagine him sniffing the air, stomach rumbling, and I tried not to laugh.

I found him sitting on the grass in a clearing. I held out a lawn chair and a plate of sausages in buns.

"I know you won't come in, so you might as well be comfortable. Unless you aren't hungry . . ."

He took the sausages. I pulled a bottle of Coke from my pocket, then shucked the coat and passed them over.

"You should be sleeping," he said.

"I can't."

"Sure you can. Just close your eyes and . . ." He studied me, then grunted, "What's up?"

I looked out over the forest. The air smelled very faintly of woodsmoke, reminding me of the photo.

"I saw a picture of you and Simon. He said you guys had a camping spot out here. Is this it?"

"So we're changing the subject?" He shook his head, set up the chair, sat, and looked at me expectantly for a moment, "Yeah. This is the spot."

"It smells like someone else had a campfire going earlier tonight. Someone burning leaves? Or kids getting a jumpstart on summer?"

"So we're definitely changing the subject?"

I paused, then lowered myself to the grass. "It's just . . . this." I waved at the forest. "I'm worried that I'm going to, you know, in my sleep . . ."

"Raise another corpse?"

I nodded.

"That's why you couldn't sleep last night, isn't it? I thought about that later, on the bus. You were afraid she was buried out there—the girl you saw get killed."

I nodded. "I was worried that if I drifted off, I'd keep thinking about her, about summoning her, like with the homeless guy. I can't control my dreams. And I figured there was a good chance she *was* buried out there, never found."

"So if you did raise her, and we left her body there to be

found, that wouldn't be such a bad thing, would it?"

"Maybe . . . if I knew I could safely raise her and release her quickly. But what if I . . . What if she didn't dig her way out and I never realized I'd raised her and . . ."

I turned to look into the forest again.

"I'll get you a chair, too," he said.

I protested that I wasn't staying, but he just kept going. When he returned, he came around the other way.

"I circled the house," he said. "If there was a body on the property, I would have smelled it. The wind's good tonight. You're safe."

"It's not . . . it's not just people I'm worried about."

I finally told him about raising the bats in the warehouse.

"I didn't summon them," I said. "I didn't even know I could do that with animals, that they had a soul, ghost, spirit, whatever. If I go to sleep and dream of any kind of summoning, there's got to be a dead animal somewhere nearby. I could raise it and never know. I'd just walk away and leave it trapped in its corpse for—" I took a deep breath. "Okay, I'm freaking out, I know."

"You've got a reason to."

"It's not like I'd do it intentionally, and maybe that should make a difference but . . ."

"It's still not something you want to do."

I nodded.

He took a gulp of the Coke, then capped it, stuck it into

his pocket, and stood. "Let's go."

"Where?"

"I'll hear anyone who comes near the property. So there's no need to sit here doing nothing. We might as well hunt up some dead animals for you."

I scowled. "That's not funny."

"I'm not being funny, Chloe. You're worried because you don't understand why it's happening and how it works and how to stop it. We can experiment and get some answers. It's not like either of us has anything better to do for the next couple of hours."

thirty-nine

D EREK CROUCHED BESIDE A flat, matted creature that had once scampered through the forest and now looked like it had been run over with a steamroller.

I tapped it with my toe. "I was thinking of something with more . . ."

"Remaining body parts?" he said.

"With more recognizable features, so I'll know what I'm summoning. But, yes, more remaining body parts would help, too."

"That was a mole. I think there's a rabbit over there somewhere."

"You can smell everything, can't you? That's cool."

He looked at me, brows lifted. "Being able to find decomposing animals is cool?"

"Well, it's a . . . unique talent."

"One that will get me far in life."

"Hey, someone has to find and clear away the road kill. I bet it pays well."

"Not well enough."

He stood and inhaled, then walked a few more feet, stooped, and prodded a chunk of rabbit fur.

"I'm definitely thinking something with more body parts," I said. "Like a head."

He gave a snort of a laugh. "It's probably around here somewhere, but I suppose you want the parts *attached*, too." He paused. "I wonder what would happen if—"

"Keep wondering, because that's one experiment I'm not conducting."

"We'll find something."

He walked a few more feet, then stopped again, shoulders going rigid as he surveyed the forest.

I moved closer and whispered, "Derek?"

Another slow scan of the woods, then he shook his head and resumed walking.

"What was it?" I asked.

"Voices, but they're far off. Probably whoever had that campfire."

Despite the dismissal, he slowed every few steps to listen.

"Are you sure it's okay?" I asked.

"Yeah."

"Should I be quiet?"

"We're fine."

After another few strides, I cleared my throat. "About the other night. When I said I didn't know that having a dead body around was a problem. Well, obviously, it happened after the bat thing so . . ."

I waited for him to fill in the blank, but he kept walking.

"I knew it was a problem," I went on. "I knew I should say so. I just didn't want to . . . overreact, I guess. When I raised that man, I wanted to admit it, about the bats, but . . ."

"You didn't need me telling you you'd done something stupid when you already knew it." He pulled back a low branch for us. "Yeah, you need to be more careful. We all do. But you don't need me making it worse by getting on your case. I know that."

He looked at me for a moment, then his nostrils flared and his face lifted to catch the breeze. He waved for us to turn left. "And about me not figuring out I was ready to start Changing? I lied. With the itching and the fever and the muscle spasms, I knew that's what it had to mean. I just . . . Same as you, I didn't want to overreact and freak out Simon. I figured I could handle it."

"We all need to be careful. Especially now, knowing what they did, the . . ."

I trailed off, feeling the now familiar bubble of rising panic, that part of me that couldn't stop reading those words. *Genetic modification. Uncontrollable powers.* How bad it would get, how far it would go, how—?

"Chloe?"

I bumped into his arm and saw that he'd stopped, and was looking down at me.

"We'll figure it out," he said, his voice soft. "We'll handle it."

I glanced away. I was shaking so hard my teeth chattered. Derek put his fingers on my chin and turned me to face him again.

"It's okay," he said.

He looked down at me, fingers still on my chin, face over mine. Then he let his hand fall and turned away with a gruff, "There's something over here."

It took me a moment to follow. When I did, I found him crouched beside a dead bird.

"Is this better?" he asked.

I bent. The corpse looked so normal that it seemed to be only sleeping. My conscience could live with temporarily returning the spirit to this body. I started to kneel, then leaped up.

"It's not dead."

"Sure it is." He nudged it with his toe.

"No, it's mov—" A maggot crawled from under the bird's wing and I stumbled back. "Could we get one without hitchhikers?"

Derek shook his head. "Either it's going to be like this, with maggots, or too decomposed for maggots." He bent to peer at it. "They're first stage blowfly larvae, meaning the bird hasn't been dead more than—" His cheeks flushed and his voice lowered another octave. "And that's more than you need to know, isn't it?"

"Right, you did a science fair project on this, didn't you?" When he looked up sharply, I said, "Simon told me about it when I was checking out that corpse in the abandoned building. He said not to mention it to you, though, because you only came in second."

He grunted. "Yeah. I'm not saying mine was the best, but it was better than the winner's, some eco-fuel crap." He paused. "That's not what I meant. There's nothing wrong with stuff like that, but the kid used junk science. Got the environmental vote. I won the people's choice award, though."

"Because, apparently, people are more interested in checking out maggoty dead things than saving the environment."

A short laugh. "Guess so."

"Back to this particular maggoty dead thing . . . I guess I should get to work, trying to make it *un*dead."

I knelt beside it.

"We'll start with—" Derek began.

He stopped when I opened my eyes.

"Shut up, right?" he said. "I was going to make some suggestions for a, uh, testing regimen, but I guess you can do that."

"Having only the faintest clue what a testing regimen is, I'll save myself the embarrassment and graciously turn that part over to you. When it comes to the summoning, though . . ."

"Shut up and let you work." He sat cross-legged. "You said with the bats, you were summoning a ghost you couldn't see. So it was kind of a general summoning. You should start by doing a specific one. That'll tell us whether you still raise a nearby animal if you're trying to raise a specific person."

"Got it. I'll try Liz."

I figured if we were being all scientific about this, I should use some kind of control measures. I'd start with the lowest "power setting"—just mentally saying "Hey, Liz, are you there?" I did that, then checked the bird. No response.

I pictured Liz and called again. Nothing. I imagined pulling Liz through. Nothing. I tried harder, still clearly focusing on her image. I kept checking the bird and kept looking—hoping—for any sign of Liz herself.

"How hard should I try?" I asked.

"As hard as you can."

I thought of what the demi-demon had said about raising zombies in a cemetery two miles away. I was sure she'd been exaggerating. And yet . . .

"Try as hard as you're comfortable with," Derek said when I hesitated. "We can always do more another time."

I ramped it up a little. Then a little more. I was closing my eyes after checking the bird again when Derek said, "Stop."

My eyes flew open. The bird's wing was twitching. I stood and moved toward it.

"It could just be the maggots," he said. "Hold on."

He got up, took a branch and was reaching it toward the bird when his chin shot up. His eyes narrowed, and his nostrils flared.

"Der—?"

A distant crack cut me off. He lunged and hit me in a football tackle. I toppled over. Something stung my upper arm right above the bandages, then whizzed past as we dropped. It hit the ground behind us with a *thwack* and a geyser of dirt. Derek quickly lifted off me, but stayed over me, like a shield . . . or more likely making sure I didn't jump up. He glanced over his shoulder.

"You okay?" he asked. As he turned to me, his nostrils flared again. "You're hurt."

He plucked my sleeve. There was a hole clear through a fold in it.

"I think they shot a dart," I said. "It grazed me. It landed over—"

He'd already found the spot. What he dug out, though, wasn't a tranquilizer dart.

FORTY

AS DEREK HELD UP the bullet, my heart slammed against my chest. I took a deep breath and pushed aside thoughts of the Edison Group.

"Are we on Andrew's property?" I asked.

He nodded.

"But it could still be hunters."

Another nod. He shifted off me and surveyed the forest. All was quiet.

"Crawl that way," he whispered, "into the thicker bushes. I'll get closer and take a look—"

The long grass at our feet erupted. Derek threw himself over me again with a whispered "Stay down!" like I had a choice, with a two-hundred-pound guy over me.

A horrible squawking echoed through the forest, and we looked down to see the dead bird on its feet, wings drumming the ground. I'll point out, with some satisfaction, that I wasn't the only one who jumped.

Derek scrambled off me. "Release—"

"I know."

I crawled to the other side of the clearing, far enough that I didn't need to worry about the bird trying to jump on me.

"Hear that?" a voice called between the bird's cries.

As the bird screamed, I concentrated on releasing its spirit, but all I could think was *Shut it up. Shut it up!* Another crack. We both hit the ground. A bullet zoomed over our heads, hitting a tree trunk in a rain of bark.

Still lying on my stomach, I closed my eyes. Derek grabbed my arm.

"I'm trying," I said. "Just give me—"

"Forget it. Come on."

He propelled me forward, hunched over, moving fast. Behind us, the bird continued to scream, covering the sound of our retreat. When it stopped, we did. I could hear something thrashing in the undergrowth—the bird or our pursuers, I couldn't tell. After a moment, the bird started again, its cries taking on an edge of panic that made my skin crawl.

I closed my eyes to release it.

"Not yet," Derek said.

He led me farther, until we found a cluster of bushes. We managed to get into the middle of them and hunkered down. The bird's cries subsided, but I could hear it moving.

"What the—?"

It was a man's voice, cut off by a *pfft* that anyone who watches crime movies recognizes as the sound of a silenced gun. I was pretty sure they didn't make silencers for hunting rifles . . . and that hunters didn't carry sidearms.

The bird's cries got louder. And the man's curses got louder still. A couple more silenced shots, then a crack, like he'd tried the rifle, too. The bird's screams turned to an awful gurgling.

"Jesus, what is that thing? I practically blew its head off and it's still alive."

Another man answered with a harsh laugh. "Well, I guess that answers our question, doesn't it? The Saunders girl found those boys."

I glanced at Derek, but his gaze was fixed straight ahead, in the direction of the voice. I closed my eyes and focused on the bird. After a moment, those pathetic sounds finally stopped.

When another squawk came, I squeezed my eyes shut, certain it meant I hadn't released the bird's spirit after all. But it was only a radio. Derek strained to listen. I couldn't catch most of what was said, just enough to confirm that these men were indeed an Edison Group security team.

They'd found us. And they weren't bothering with tranquilizer darts anymore. Why would they? We were dangerous experimental subjects who'd escaped twice. Now they didn't need an excuse to do what they'd have been happy to do all along: abandon rehabilitation and "remove" us from their study. The only one who might have fought to keep me alive was Aunt Lauren, a traitor. Easier to kill us here and bury the bodies, far from Buffalo.

"Simon!" I hissed. "We need to warn him and—"

"I know. The house is through there. We'll circle."

"But we can't go back to the house. That's the first place they'll go, if they aren't there already."

His eyes dipped away, his jaw setting.

"I—I guess we have to try, don't we?" I said. "Okay, if we're careful—"

"No, you're right," he said. "I'll go. You wait here."

I grabbed the back of his coat as he crawled forward. "You can't—"

"I need to warn Simon."

"I'll come—"

"No, you stay here." He started turning, then stopped. "Better yet, get farther away. There's a road about a half mile north." He pointed. "You can't miss it. It's an easy walk— Simon and I used to do it all the time. When I give the signal, take off. Get to the road and hide. I'll find you there."

He started walking away. I wanted to argue, but knew there was no use—nothing would stop him from going back for Simon. And he was right not to want me along. I'd only be one more person to protect. Best to wait for his signal and—

Derek's earsplitting whistle cut through the night. Then he whistled again, and a third time and I knew that's what he'd meant by "signal," not just for me, but for Simon, trying to wake him up.

It was loud enough to wake *everyone* up—and to tell the whole security team exactly where—

The thought stuttered in my head. Then I started cursing him, mentally calling him every name I could think of, including a few I didn't realize I knew.

He knew his whistles would draw the attention of the entire Edison Group team. That's why he'd done it, rather than something subtle like throwing stones at Simon's window. He was drawing their attention to himself, giving Simon and me a chance to get away.

I wanted to scream at him. Those men had guns. Real *guns*. And they weren't afraid to use them. If they did take his bait—

He'll be fine. He gave you a chance to escape. Now use it. Move!

I forced myself out of the bushes and set out at a slow, crouching jog, picking my way over open area and avoiding the noisy undergrowth. When I heard footsteps, I glanced around for cover and, seeing none, hit the ground.

Two figures passed just ten feet away. Both were dressed head to foot in camouflage, like army snipers. Even their hats had net screens covering their faces.

A radio squealed, and a man's voice came over it. "Bravo team?"

One of the two—a woman by her voice—responded.

The man continued. "He's over here. Head in from the east and we'll surround—"

A rifle shot knocked my heart into my throat. The crash of undergrowth sounded over the radio.

"Did you get him?" the woman asked.

"Not sure. That was Charlie team. Signing off. Get over here."

Another shot. More distant crashing. I was sure my heart was pounding loud enough for the two to hear, but they kept going, heading for that distant racket. Heading for Derek.

Bravo, Charlie . . . I'd seen enough war movies to know that meant there were at least three pairs out here. Six armed security agents. Enough to surround Derek and then—

Just keep going. He'll find a way out. He's got super-powers, remember?

None of which would help him against six trained professionals. None of which would stop a bullet.

I waited until the two were gone, then I scanned the tree-tops. The last few summers at drama camp, we'd had Survivor days. In most athletic challenges, I'd been a washout, but there'd been one where being small seemed to be an advantage . . . that and having a few old gymnastics trophies on my shelf.

I raced to the nearest tree with low branches, grabbed one, and tested it. If Derek swung onto it, he'd crash back to the ground, but I was able to get up and onto the next, sturdier one with the branch giving no more than a faint groan of complaint.

I kept climbing until I was confident that the canopy of new leaves hid me. Then I got into a secure position and whistled—a thin, reedy screech that would have Derek rolling his eyes.

What makes you think they're even going to hear that?

I whistled again.

And even if they do, why bother with you? They know where Derek is. They'll stick with him.

The distant tramp of boots from the departing pair stopped. A murmur of voices. Then the footsteps returned my way.

Now what are you going to do? You'd better have a plan or—

I shushed the inner voice and gave another, softer whistle, just to be sure they heard me.

The radio crackled.

"Alpha? This is Bravo. We think we heard the Saunders girl. She's trying to contact Souza. Do you have him yet?"

I strained to hear the reply but couldn't make it out.

"We'll swing by and help as soon as we have her."

Meaning they didn't have Derek.

Or they have him; they just need help controlling him.

The radio sounded again, another transmission I couldn't make out. The woman signed off, then said to her partner,

"They want you to go back and help with the boy. I can handle the Saunders girl."

Well, that didn't work out so well, did it?

The man took off. I held still as the woman began searching for me. She passed my tree by at least a dozen feet and kept going. I waited until I was sure she wasn't going to return on her own, then knocked my foot against the tree trunk.

She turned. For a moment, she just stood there, shining her flashlight beam in a full circle. I prepared to knock again, if she walked away, but she headed toward me, moving slowly, beam skimming the ground, pausing at every bush or clump of tall grass.

When she walked under my tree, I tightened my hold and flattened myself against the branch. As I moved the foot I'd kicked with, it brushed the tree trunk. A chunk of bark fell at the woman's feet.

She shone the beam down at it.

Please, don't. Please, please—

The flashlight beam swung up into the branches.

I dropped. I didn't think about the stupidity of dropping onto an armed woman probably twice my size. I just let go and rolled off the branch, that inner voice screaming *What are you doing?!* . . . in far less polite language.

I hit the woman. We both went down, her cushioning my fall. I leaped up, ignoring the squeaks of protest from my jolted body. I yanked out my knife and—

The woman lay at the foot of the tree, her head a few

inches from it. She had a net veil hanging from her hat but through it I could see that her eyes were closed, and her mouth lolled open. She must have hit the trunk and been knocked out. I resisted the urge to check, grabbed her radio, and spun, searching for the gun. It wasn't there. No rifle and no pistol . . . or not one I could see. I took a good look around to see if she'd dropped it. Nothing.

Either her partner had it or she had one hidden under her jacket. I paused, wanting to check, but was afraid of rousing her. One last look, then I snatched up the fallen flashlight and ran.

forty-one

I WAS SURE I was heading in the direction Derek told me,
so all the security teams should be behind me. But after
less than a minute, I heard the tramp of boots again. I
dropped and covered my radio. I turned the volume all the
way down, even though it had been silent since I'd taken it.

I crawled into the nearest patch of brush and lay on my
stomach. The footsteps seemed to be going parallel to me,
neither approaching nor retreating.

"Tell me how a full squad of us can lose four teenagers in
less than twenty acres of woods," a man's voice said. "Davidoff is not going to be happy."

Another man answered, "With any luck, he'll never find
out. We've still got an hour before daylight. Plenty of time.
How far can they get?"

They continued walking and talking, their voices and

steps receding. When they were gone, I started creeping out, then stopped. If all four of us were out here, should I be heading for safety? Or trying to find the others?

Um, if you go to that safe spot, where Derek expects you to be, you won't have to worry about finding them. They'll come to you.

What if they need my help?

You accidentally knocked out one woman and suddenly you're Rambo?

It felt cowardly getting myself to safety, but my inner voice had a point—if that's where Derek expected me to be, then I'd better head there and meet him.

But I *did* feel a bit like Rambo—switchblade in one hand, radio in the other, flashlight jammed in my waistband—as I stealthily crept through the thick woods.

Yeah, as long as you don't trip and impale yourself on your own knife.

I closed the blade.

"Chloe?" a female voice whispered.

I whirled so fast my foot slid on the soft ground. "Tori?"

I squinted into the night. The woods here were so dark I could only make out shapes that could as easily be trees and bushes as people. My fingers touched the flashlight, but I pulled back and kept looking.

"Tori?"

"Shhh. This way, hon."

The endearment made the hair on my neck rise.

"Aunt Lauren?"

"Shhh. Follow me."

I caught a glimpse of a figure. It was as faint as the voice, and all I could see was a pale shirt glowing ahead. I didn't move. It sounded like Aunt Lauren and the figure was her size, but I couldn't be sure and I wasn't running after her like a little kid, so desperate to believe that I raced into a trap.

I took out my flashlight and clicked it on, but she was darting between trees, and it was impossible to make out more than her shape and shirt. Then she glanced back and I got just a glimpse of a profile, a swing of blond hair—an imperfect view, but enough for my gut to say *that's her.*

She waved for me to hurry, then veered left into deeper forest. I followed, still cautious, no matter what my gut said. I was jogging past a patch of bushes when a figure lunged out. Before I could spin, it grabbed me, a hand clamping over my mouth, cutting short my yelp.

"It's me," Derek whispered.

He tried pulling me into the bushes, but I resisted.

"Aunt Lauren," I said. "I saw Aunt Lauren."

He gave me a look like he must have heard me wrong.

"My aunt. She's here. She's—" I pointed in the direction she'd gone. "I was following her."

"I didn't see anyone."

"She was wearing a light shirt. She ran past—"

"Chloe, I've been right here. I saw you coming. No one else ran—" He stopped short, realizing what he was saying.

339 ◆

If I'd seen her and he hadn't . . .

My chest seized. "No . . ."

"It was an illusion," he said quickly. "A spell to trap you. My dad's done stuff like that and . . ." He rubbed his hand over his mouth, then said, firmer, "That's what it was."

I'd wondered the same thing, but now, hearing it from his mouth, when it should have supported my own doubts, all I could think was: a ghost. I saw Aunt Lauren's ghost. The forest blurred, and his hand on my arm seemed the only thing holding me up.

"Chloe? It was a spell. It's dark. You didn't get a good look."

All true. Totally true. And yet . . . I shook it off and straightened, pulling from his grasp. When he hesitated, hand out, ready to grab me if I collapsed, I stepped away.

"I'm fine. So what's the plan?"

"We'll wait here—"

Footsteps sounded. We pushed into the bushes and crouched. A flashlight beam skimmed the trees like a searchlight.

"I know you kids are back here," a man said. "I heard voices."

Derek and I stayed still. His shallow breathing hissed at my ear. My back was against him and I could feel the thump of his heart. The flashlight beam kept coming, cutting through the darkness. It passed over our bushes. Then it stopped, came back, and shone full in our faces.

"Okay, you two. Come out of there."

I could only see a veiled figure silhouetted behind the flashlight's glare.

"Come out," he said again.

Derek's breath warmed my ear. "When I say run, run." Then, louder, "Put the gun down and we'll come out."

"It is down."

With the light shining in our eyes and the man hidden behind it, there was no way to know if he was telling the truth.

He lifted his free hand and waved it. "See, no gun. Now come—"

The man dropped forward, like he'd been hit from behind. The flashlight tumbled to the ground, beam arcing through the air. Derek shot past me and tackled the man as he started to rise. Simon stepped from the darkness behind the man, hands raised for another knock-back spell.

"Run," Derek said, holding the struggling man. When Simon and I hesitated, he snarled, "Run!"

We took off but kept checking behind. We could hear the sounds of a fight, but it was a short one; and before we'd gone far, Derek was behind us. When we slowed, he thumped us both in the back, telling us to keep moving. The moon through the trees gave us enough light to see where we were going.

"Tori?" I whispered to Simon.

"We split up. She—"

Derek motioned us to silence. We ran until we saw the glittering light of houses through the trees and knew we must be approaching the back road. We took another few strides. Then Derek thumped us again, this one a hard whack between the shoulder blades that knocked us off our feet. He landed between us. When we tried to rise, he pushed us back down.

Simon lifted his dirt-streaked face and rubbed his jaw. "I kinda like my teeth. All of them."

Derek shushed him and twisted around to lie on his stomach, facing the other way. We did the same. I followed his gaze as it traveled over the forest, until it stopped and I heard footsteps.

Derek tensed, ready to leap up, but they were still a good distance away when they stopped, footsteps replaced by the murmur of voices. The radio in my pocket chirped. I took it out and checked the volume.

Simon looked past Derek and mouthed. "Radio?" then pointed toward the voices, asking if it was one of theirs.

I nodded.

"Sweet," he mouthed, then shot me a thumbs-up that made me blush. Derek glanced over with a nod and a grunt that I interpreted to mean, *Good job . . . as long as you didn't do anything stupid to get it.*

"I found Alpha one," a man's voice said, so low I had to strain to hear him.

Simon motioned for Derek to turn up the volume, but

Derek shook his head. He could hear fine so there was no need to risk it.

"Where is he?" a woman's voice answered over the radio.

"Knocked out. Looks like he went a couple of rounds with our young werewolf."

"Get him to safety. Delta team still has the Enright girl, right?"

I shot a look at Derek, but his expression didn't change as he concentrated on listening.

"Delta two does. I'm not sure how well she'll work as bait, so I sent Delta one to get Carson from the truck."

That got Derek's attention. Simon mouthed "Andrew" to me. The voices retreated, but a moment later, the woman's came again over the radio, calling Delta two. A man answered.

"Have you got Carson?" she asked.

"I'm almost there."

"Good. Your job is to persuade him to call those kids. He's going to lure them in."

"He won't."

"I don't expect him to volunteer," the woman snapped, "but considering he's in our custody, he'll do what we say. If he refuses, shoot him."

Simon's head shot up, his eyes dark with worry. Derek motioned for him to be quiet as we listened.

Delta two came back on. "Um, did someone move the truck?"

"What?"

"The truck. With Carson. It's . . . not here."

The argument that followed was loud enough that Derek put his hands over the radio speaker, muffling it more. They spent the next few minutes making sure Delta two had the right spot and that no one else had moved Andrew and the truck. But there was no such simple explanation—their hostage was gone . . . with their truck.

"So Andrew's safe. What about Tori?" I asked when the radio went silent.

For a moment Derek said nothing, which was better than what I expected—a snapped *What about her?* As quick as he'd been the other day to say that he didn't care if Tori walked in front of a speeding car, it wasn't so easy to actually stand by, knowing she was in mortal danger.

"I'll do a sweep," he said. "If I find her, great."

He didn't say the rest, but I understood. *If I don't find her, we have to leave her behind.* As bad as that sounded, it was the right thing to do. I didn't want Derek putting himself in a bullet's path for Tori. That was an awful thing to admit. I didn't hate Tori—I didn't even really dislike her anymore. But when it came down to the cold, hard choice of putting a life on the line to save hers, I couldn't do it. Not Derek's, not Simon's, not mine. And that choice was going to haunt me for a very long time.

"Be careful and . . ." The other words that rose to my lips were "be quick," but I couldn't be that callous—even to think it shocked me. So I swallowed and repeated, "Be careful."

Derek wasn't leaving, though. We were. He made us set out first, so he could stand watch. When we were safely on our way to the back road, he'd go after Tori.

We made it about twenty paces before a figure appeared in our path. Simon's fingers flew up.

"Simon, it's—" the man said, ending in an *oomph* as the spell hit and he fell backward to the ground.

"Andrew!" Simon rushed forward.

The man rose, giving a wry smile as he brushed himself off. "I see your knock-back spell has improved."

Andrew wasn't much taller than Simon, but he was squarely built, sturdy, with a broad face and crooked nose. His crew-cut hair was gray, though he wouldn't be any older than my dad, and looked like a retired prizefighter. Not what I expected from that cozy, tidy little house.

When he looked at me, his smile faltered, the wrinkle between his brows deepening, like I looked familiar, but he was having trouble placing my face. He started to say something. Then he glanced up sharply.

"Someone's coming," Andrew said.

Simon glanced at the approaching shadow, big but moving silently. "It's Derek."

"No, that's not—" Andrew began.

Derek stepped into the light of the clearing. Andrew looked up at him and blinked. He stared at Derek, like he was trying—and failing—to find the boy he knew.

Behind the surprise in his eyes, there was something sharper, a note of worry, maybe even fear, like in that moment, he saw not his friend's son, but a big, powerful young were-wolf. He blinked the fear back, but not before Derek saw it, his gaze shunting to the side, shoulders and jaw tensing, as if to say that was okay, he didn't care. But I knew he did.

"You've . . . grown."

Andrew tried for a smile but couldn't quite find it, and that, for Derek, seemed worse than the fear. He looked away completely, muttering, "Yeah."

Simon waved at me. "This is—"

"Let me guess. Diane Enright's girl."

I shook my head. "Chloe Saunders."

"It's the hair," Simon said. "She's blond, but we had to dye it because—"

"Later," Derek said, then looked at Andrew. "They have the Enright girl. Victoria."

Andrew frowned. "Are you sure?"

Simon took the radio from me and waved it. "Chloe got this from them. We heard about you escaping and them catching Tori."

"I'll go get her then. You three, get to the truck." He told us where to find it, then started to leave.

"I'm coming with you," Derek said. "I can find her faster than you can."

Andrew seemed ready to argue, but one look at Derek told him it was useless, so he took the radio from me and sent us to safety.

forty-two

W E FOUND THE TRUCK—an old SUV—hidden behind a neighboring barn. The door was open. A piece of metal had been jammed into the ignition to hotwire it. Simon was checking that out, trying to see if he could start it up, when three people ran from the woods: Derek, Andrew, and Tori.

Simon and I flung open the front doors and climbed into the back. Derek took the passenger seat. Tori sat on my other side in the rear.

"That was a quick rescue," Simon said as Andrew started the truck.

"No rescue required," Tori said. "I can take care of myself."

Derek muttered something about remembering that the next time he risked his life to help her.

As Andrew got the truck moving, I asked Tori what happened. She'd been taken captive and held under guard as the others searched. At first, she'd had two guards, but when things started going wrong they'd left her with only a single guard.

"One handy binding spell later? They lost their only remaining prisoner."

"You think they'd have taken your spells into account," Derek said.

"Well, they underestimated me," she said.

Derek grunted. Simon started asking something, but Andrew shushed us while he drove the truck over a rough field. He kept the lights off and rolled along slowly.

Simon shifted beside me, getting comfortable in the cramped backseat. His hand brushed my leg, then found my hand and took it. When he smiled over at me, I smiled back.

I expected him to give his usual reassuring squeeze and let go. Instead he seemed to take my smile as a sign of encouragement and entwined his fingers with mine and rested them on my thigh. As tired as I was—my brain reeling with questions, adrenaline still pumping—a little buzz passed through me. Silly, I guess. Making a big deal out of holding hands? So fifth grade.

I was sure, for Simon, it *was* no big deal. While he wasn't the first guy to hold my hand, let's just say my experience with boys didn't go further than that.

The buzz passed quickly, though, as we reached the road

and Andrew turned on the headlights. He asked if we were all okay, and the first thing out of my mouth was, "Was my Aunt Lauren with you?"

His eyes met mine in the rearview mirror as he frowned. "Lauren Fellows. She works for—"

"I know your aunt, Chloe, but, no, she wasn't there."

"Chloe thought she saw her," Derek said.

Simon twisted to face me. "What?"

"I—I saw someone. It sounded like her and it kind of looked like her, from what I could see in the dark. . . ."

"Did *you* see her?" Simon asked Derek.

"He didn't," I said. "And he should have, because she ran right past him."

"You saw a ghost," Tori said. "And you think it was your aunt."

"More likely a spell," Derek said. "They have stuff like that, right, Andrew?"

"Absolutely. Glamour spells and other illusions. If you didn't get a good look, that's probably intentional—whoever cast it didn't want you studying the illusion too closely."

That made sense, but I still couldn't shake the gut feeling that I *had* seen her. Not Aunt Lauren but her ghost.

Simon leaned into my ear and murmured reassurances, saying they wouldn't kill Aunt Lauren—she was too valuable.

"How's your arm?" Derek asked when I stayed quiet too long, lost in my worries.

"Did you pull your stitches?" Simon asked.

"No," Derek said. "A bullet grazed it."

"A *bullet*?"

Andrew steered to the curb and hit the brakes. "You were shot?"

"No, no. It's just a scratch."

Andrew hesitated, but I assured him—and Simon—that I was fine, and Derek confirmed that the bullet had only just passed through my shirt, grazing me.

Andrew turned back onto the road. "We'll get it cleaned up when we stop. I can't believe they . . ." He shook his head.

"Hey, I skinned my palm," Tori said. "Ground it up pretty bad."

"You need to check Chloe's stitches, too," Derek said. "She got cut with glass a few days ago. They fixed her up, but it should be looked at."

Tori waved her injured palm. "Anyone? Anyone?" She rolled her eyes. "Guess not."

"It looks sore," I said. "We should get some iodine on it."

She gave a wan smile. "I can always count on you, can't I? Guess I know who sent the cavalry back to rescue me."

"But you said you didn't need rescue, remember?" Simon said.

"It's the thought that counts."

"We wouldn't have left you there, Victoria." Andrew glanced back at her. "Tori, is it?"

She nodded.

He smiled at her. "It's good to see you and Simon together."

"Whoa, no," Simon said. "We're *not* together."

Tori agreed, just as emphatically.

"No, I meant—" Through the mirror, Andrew's gaze went from Simon to Tori. "I, uh, meant all four of you. I'm glad to see you together. That's one thing Kit and I agreed on, that the group was wrong to keep the subjects separated."

"So you worked for them, too?" I asked. "The Edison Group?"

Simon nodded. "He got out just before our dad." He looked at Andrew. "That's how they knew where to find you, isn't it? When we escaped, they figured we'd come here, so they grabbed you to use as bait."

"That seems to have been their plan. And, anyway, it was a good excuse for picking me up, something they've wanted to do for years."

"How come?" Tori asked.

"We'll talk about that later. First, let's find something to eat while you guys tell me what's been going on."

The only place we found open was a fast-food drive-thru in the next town. I wasn't hungry, but Simon insisted on getting me a milkshake and I sipped it as he explained to Andrew what had happened with us—Lyle House, our escape, the compound, the experiment, the deaths of Liz and Brady and Amber. . . .

"Rachelle is still there," Simon said as he finished. "Chloe's aunt, too, who's obviously their hostage now, like you were."

"Unless she's—" Tori began.

Simon's glare shut her up. "She's fine. But we need to get them and our dad out. Chloe's aunt doesn't think he was taken by them, but he must have been."

"I'd have to agree," Andrew said. "Nothing in my own searches has suggested any other explanation."

Derek looked over sharply. "You've been looking for him?"

"For all of you."

We drove for almost an hour and passed through only one big town. We were getting farther and farther from New York City. Finally, Andrew turned into a private drive even longer and more winding than his own.

"Where are we? A safe house for supernaturals?" Simon nudged me. "Like something out of a movie, huh?"

"Well, it certainly has played that role before, for supernaturals on the run from Cabals," Andrew said.

"Cabals?" Tori said.

"A whole other situation. But this place really serves more as a hostel for visiting members of our group. It was owned by one of our first members—an ancestral estate that he willed to us for the cause."

"What cause?" Tori asked.

"Monitoring and ultimately disbanding the Edison Group."

He slowed as the dirt lane turned rough. "Or that was our original goal. We started as a band of former Edison Group employees, defectors like me who were concerned about their actions. Not just the Genesis Two project—that *is* one of our main concerns, but the Edison Group goes far beyond that. Eventually, we were joined by others, who took issue not only with the Edison Group's activities but with those of the Cabals and other supernatural organizations. Still, the Edison Group has remained our primary focus—monitoring their activities, conducting small acts of sabotage."

"Sabotage?" Simon said. "Cool."

"*Small* acts. Our main goal has been on monitoring, to the growing disgust of some of our members, myself included."

"Was Dad involved?" Simon asked.

Andrew shook his head. "I suppose you know your dad and I had—"

"A falling-out."

"Yes. And it was over this group. Your dad always stayed out of it. Too political for him. He'd been willing to help, but otherwise he didn't participate. He thought it would call undue attention to you boys. But I was pressured by the others to bring him in. As the father of two subjects from the Edison Group's most ambitious—and potentially dangerous—project, he'd be the perfect person to help attract powerful new members from the supernatural community. He was furious. All his work to keep you hidden, and now I wanted this. I'll admit, I supported the idea. But I underestimated the danger you faced from the Edison Group. I see that now."

He turned another corner, slowing more as the ruts in the road got deeper. "After your dad and you two disappeared, and we heard rumors the Edison Group had you boys, some of us began arguing for a more active stance. We were convinced you—and the other subjects—were in danger. Others with more influence insisted that the group wouldn't hurt you."

"Well, they were wrong," Tori said.

"Yes, and with your story, we'll have the proof we need to take action."

We turned yet another corner and the house appeared. For a moment, all we could do was stare. It was like something out of a gothic novel—a huge rambling Victorian, three stories tall, surrounded by forest. If there were gargoyles up there, shrouded by darkness, I wouldn't be surprised.

"Cool," Simon said. "Now this is where supernaturals should live."

Andrew chuckled. "And, for the next few days, it's where *you're* going to live. You can settle in here and rest while we make plans." He glanced back at us as he parked. "But don't get too comfortable. I'm about to ask the group to conduct a jailbreak at Edison Group headquarters, and it's been a lot of years since any of us have been there. We're going to need your help."

forty-three

I WENT TO BED and I slept. I wasn't sure I would, with the lingering excitement of the night, my fear over Aunt Lauren, my worries about the surrounding forest, filled with animal corpses waiting to be raised. But for the first time in weeks, we were safe, and that was all the encouragement my exhausted brain and body needed to shut down and bless me with deep, dreamless sleep.

I knew this wasn't the end. Not by a long shot. Even the first step—persuading the rest of this group to go back—wouldn't be as easy as Andrew hoped. And even when it was over, it wouldn't truly be over. Not for me.

I was changed. Not just the genetic modification, but me—I was different. The very thought of going home to Dad and our condo and my school and friends made my brain reel. That life was gone now. Maybe I'd go back to it someday, but it would be like replacing an actor with someone who looked, sounded, and even behaved differently. I wouldn't be the same person. I wasn't even sure I could play the role.

My old life felt like a dream—a mostly pleasant, uneventful dream. Now I'd awakened from it and realized who I was and what I was, for better or worse. There was no closing my eyes and sliding back into that blissful dream of normal. This was my normal now.

acknowledgments

I MISSED THIS WITH the last book, so I have a bunch of folks to thank. First, to Sarah Heller, my agent and fairy godmother for this series, who took my wish of wanting to write for young adults and made it happen. To Rosemary Brosnan of HarperCollins, who worked with me for the first time on *The Summoning*. Working with a new editor can take some adjusting, but she made it a breeze from day one. Also a huge thanks to Maria Gomez of HarperCollins for introducing Rosemary to my books. Thanks, too, to editors Anne Collins of Random House Canada and Antonia Hodgson of Little, Brown UK, who have been with me from the start and are always willing to let me try something new. And thanks to Kristin Cochrane at Doubleday Canada for her support and hard work behind the scenes.

On this particular book, I had my first batch of Darkest

Powers beta readers. Thanks to Sharon B, Terri Giesbrecht, Stephanie Scranton-Drum, Matt Sievers, and Nicole Tom, who read an early copy and helped me find errors that slipped past everyone else (apparently the shark in *Deep Blue Sea* was a Mako, not a Great White—whoops!).

about the author

Kelley Armstrong lives in rural Ontario, Canada, with her husband, three children and far too many pets. She is the author of the bestselling Women of the Otherworld series, the highly acclaimed Darkest Powers young adult series and two adventure novels about a hit woman, *Exit Strategy* and *Made to be Broken*. For further information visit www.kelleyarmstrong.com and www.darkestpowers.com